C000192884

OF ALL FLESH

A Detective Loxley Nottinghamshire Crime Thriller

By
A L Fraine

Book List

www.alfraineauthor.co.uk/books

Acknowledgements

Thank you to Crystal Wren for your amazing editing and support.
Thanks to Kath Middleton for her incredible work.
A big thank you to the Admins and members of the
UK Crime Book Club for their support, both to me and the wider author community. They're awesome.

A big thank you to Meg Jolly and Tom Reid for allowing me to use their names in these novels. I really appreciate it.
Thank you also to the Authors I've been lucky enough to call friends. You know who you are, and you're all wonderful people.

Thank you to my family, especially my parents, children, and lovely wife Louise, for their unending love and support.

Table of Contents

Book List 2

Acknowledgements 2

Table of Contents 3

1...5

2...18

3...31

4...35

5...42

6...47

7...54

8...60

9...68

10...76

11...90

12...96

13...109

14...119

15...124

16...130

17...139

18...148

19...160

20...169

21...178

22...182

23...194

24...201

25...207

26...213

27...221

28...230

29...239

30...242

31...248

32...256

33...262
34...268
35...276
36...286
37...290
38...297
39...305
40...312
41...331
42...334
43...338
44...345
45...352
46...358
47...369
48...384
49...396
50...402
51...407
52...413
53...422
54...431
55...436
Author Note 446
Book List 447

1

The churning, roiling waters of the River Trent, several metres below, were the perfect metaphor for what was going on inside Malcom's head. His thoughts were chaotic, troubled, and crashing through his mind like a tidal wave of pain and regret.

He'd had an absolute nightmare of a day, and now he was here, a couple of miles away from home in the middle of the night, with no idea what to do or where to go.

Leaning on the railing of the Trent Bridge, with the occasional car driving by behind him, Malcom buried his head in his hands and sobbed, letting out the emotions that had been building up inside.

"Oh, God," he muttered, sniffing and wiping his eyes. Was it too much to ask for, to have a mum who cared and friends who didn't hate him? He didn't feel like that was asking for a lot, but he had neither of them right now.

Malcom stared out over the river. On his right, the Nottingham Forest football ground stood proudly on the banks of the Trent, but right now, in the depths of the night, it was as quiet as a tomb.

Gripping the railing, he closed his eyes and took a long breath. He'd stormed out of the house maybe two hours ago, leaving his mum to deal with her boyfriend, Ernie, alone. He'd

5

had it with their arguments, his violence, and her complete dereliction of duty as a mother. Rather than run after him or come looking for him, she'd probably just opened another bottle or, worse, gone straight to the crack pipe.

She didn't care about him and hadn't for years now. All she cared about was that next high. It just seemed to be how she dealt with everything in life.

When another past-due bill came in, she had a drink. When the food ran out, she sparked up the crack pipe. And when Ernie hurt her again, her chosen coping method was to get as drunk and as high as she could and forget about her life.

But that meant she forgot about him too.

She wouldn't be out looking for him, she wouldn't call the police, she just didn't care enough. He'd stayed out before, at a friend's house or whatever, and she'd never batted an eyelid.

A small part of him hoped that today would be different. When they started fighting tonight, and Ernie started hurting her, he'd jumped in to help. Ernie punched him in the face for his trouble.

That had been Malcom's breaking point, and he'd stormed out, fed up with his mum, his friends, and his life. He wanted out. Out of that house, out of the Hyson Green estate, and out of this city.

6

But he was fifteen, and it simply wasn't that easy.

He'd seen what some of the other kids his age and younger were doing to make money. There was no way he was getting involved in the gangs. It was far too dangerous, and no matter how much he wanted to earn more money to buy the things he wanted, there was no way he was going to do that.

On the one hand, it looked glamorous and alluring with the stacks of cash, the new trainers and new phones. But these trinkets hid a life of danger and violence that Malcom had no interest in at all.

He knew friends that had disappeared for days and then turned up beaten and bruised or worse, all because they'd been seduced by the 'Trap Life' as they referred to it.

No, that wasn't for him. He wanted out of the life he was in, but drug dealing was not the way.

The right way was to work hard at school and stay away from those idiots, but that was easier said than done.

Turning away from the water, Malcom continued south over the Trent Bridge, recalling the day he'd had with his mates in the park. Jordan was nice enough, as usual, although he was too easily led by Zeke.

Malcom sighed. He never quite knew where he stood with Zeke. One moment he was his best mate, laughing and joking, and the next moment he was being an abusive, racist bigot and getting Jordan and Angel to side with him.

Things had got a little out of hand today, with Zeke turning on him for some perceived slight that was just stupid. But when he decided he wasn't taking Zeke's shit and stood up for himself, Zeke threw a punch.

They roughed each other up until Angel managed to separate them and march Zeke off with Jordan helping, leaving Malcom to make his way home alone.

The argument continued over WhatsApp for the next few hours, with insults being traded until Zeke's older brother joined in and threatened to kill him. That was when Malcom turned off his phone. He'd had enough and didn't want to be subjected to that abuse any longer.

He should have stopped hanging out with Zeke years ago. He'd always been volatile, snapping at the slightest thing, but that was easier said than done, and it wasn't as if he could talk to his mum about it.

She was always drunk or high when he got home from school, so he just shut himself in his room and hid from it all.

Malcom turned left off the bridge and walked around to the water's edge, feeling drawn to its rushing flow as it meandered through the city. The water's hissing white noise soothed his nerves and calmed his senses, allowing him to take a breath and let some of the day's stresses fade away.

8

He was looking north, past the recently built apartment blocks, to the city beyond. A couple of miles that way was Hyson Green, the deprived estate that was ruled over by the HGK Posse, a violent, drug dealing gang that ruled the streets near him with an iron fist. The residents were cowed into submission by their shocking violence, and the local kids were being sucked into the gang lifestyle on a daily basis, lured in by the promise of earning more than their parents did in a week for a single day's work.

He saw the effect that environment had on his mum and her boyfriend all the time. Hell, he was a direct product of it. His mum didn't talk about it, but Ernie seemed to make it his mission to remind him that he was the child of an affair his mum had with a dealer fifteen years ago. It also seemed to be why Ernie hated him so much, because he was a walking, talking reminder of his mother's infidelity.

Was it any wonder that he ran away, desperate for a new, better life anywhere else?

Maybe leaving his house tonight was the first step to leaving his life behind? Maybe he'd try to find a new life on the streets somewhere or even in a new city. He wasn't sure, and the only thing he knew was that he didn't want to go back home.

The wind picked up, and the cool air chilled him to the bone in the dead of night. Feeling a little cold, Malcom turned towards the Trent Bridge. He spotted the pair of tunnels beneath and decided to seek shelter. Maybe they'd provide a little protection against the elements while he pondered what to do with his life.

The pavement went through the right-hand tunnel. On his left, another threaded through the base of the bridge, but there was no marked path leading through it.

Preferring to be away from prying eyes, Malcom mounted the verge and walked into the darkness of the left-hand tunnel. He saw discarded boxes and rubbish on the floor and, sitting amongst it all, a man and a woman, talking quietly. They wore warm but threadbare clothing in layers, with fingerless gloves, and used some cardboard as a makeshift blanket.

For a moment, he judged them as somehow lesser, as if he was better than them. But that feeling of superiority soon faded. Right now, with all he was considering, he was as homeless as they were, except he was new to all this and didn't know what to do.

Spotting a dry patch of cardboard, Malcom walked over, sat on it, and hugged his knees tight. It might be spring, but the nights were still cold. Even with his coat on, he could feel the chill in the air. Sitting still only seemed to make it worse.

Burying his head in his arms, Malcom wondered what the hell he was doing. He was miles from home, sitting in a tunnel, freezing his arse off, and didn't know if he would ever return home. He squeezed his eyes shut, feeling the prick of tears.

With a sniff, he stifled a sob, trying to get a grip on himself. What on earth would his friends think of him if they could see him now? Malcom shook his head in frustration, annoyed that he was still referring to those idiots as friends. Friends didn't treat each other like that. They stuck up for and helped each other, they didn't set their big brothers on them.

"Hey, you okay?"

Malcom glanced up to see the homeless woman standing close by. She looked like she was in her thirties, with dry, knotted hair and poor skin. But her eyes were bright, keen, and so very alive. She tilted her head to one side and offered him a smile.

"Hi," she said. "Are you alright?"

"Leave him, Viv," said the man. "You don't know who he is."

"Ignore him," Viv said, waving her friend off. She pointed to the cardboard beside him. "Can I?"

Malcom sighed. "Yeah, sure. Why not?"

"What's your name?" she asked, sitting next to him. "I'm Vivian."

"Viv!" her friend exclaimed, but she ignored him.

11

"That's Aaron. He doesn't like me talking to other people. But just ignore him. He's harmless."

"Oh, okay. Sure."

"What's your name?"

"Malcom. But, call me Mal."

"Mal. Nice name. What are you doing here?"

Malcom frowned. "What do you mean?"

"Forgive me for saying so, but you don't look like you've been sleeping on the streets."

"Oh. Well, no. I guess not... Or, well, I wasn't. Now, I'm not sure. Maybe I will."

"Aaah," she said, and nodded in understanding. "I see. You just ran away, right?"

"Is it that obvious?"

"Kinda. Where are you from?"

"Hyson Green," Malcom answered, noticing the flicker of recognition that briefly appeared on her face. "Yeah, it's rough up there."

"It is."

"Is that why you ran away?" She seemed genuinely curious.

"Maybe. It's part of it. It's my friends and mum, they don't care about me. They couldn't care less."

Viv fixed him with a look. "Are you sure about that? She might care very much."

12

"Not while she's high, she won't. She won't care."

"Well, she might surprise you, but maybe I can help in the meantime?"

Further up the tunnel, Viv's friend, Aaron, stood up and walked over. He didn't look too happy. "Viv. What are you doing? Come away. You don't know him."

"I know," she said, unconcerned. "I just wanted to…"

"Screw that. No. Come away."

"Chill out, he's just a kid, look…"

"I don't care," Aaron said. "You don't know him from Adam. He could be anyone. For all you know, he could be one of those brats that comes round here causing trouble."

"Aaron, no, he's not."

"I'm not," Malcom added, feeling perplexed.

"Yeah, well, excuse me if I don't believe you," Aaron spat. He reached for Viv and grabbed her by the wrist. "Come on."

"Get off me," Viv protested and pulled her hand away.

Aaron raised his hands in surrender. "Fine, be like that. I don't care." He turned and stormed up the tunnel. "But I won't sit here and watch you get into more trouble. I'm off."

"Aaron," she pleaded. "Don't be like that."

"Forget it," Aaron said. He grabbed a bag from where he'd been sitting and continued up the tunnel. "Do what you like."

"Damn it," Viv hissed and went to get up. She turned and put her hand on Malcom's knee. "Stay here. I'll be back."

13

"Okay," Malcom replied with a nod, her touch like a bolt of electricity through his body.

Viv got up and jogged after Aaron, who was exiting the other end of the tunnel. "Aaron. Aaron, wait," she called and followed him out.

They disappeared from view, leaving Malcom alone. Aaron was suspicious of him, which was only natural. But he was struck by how kind Viv had been. She seemed friendly and acted like she honestly wanted to help him. It was amazing, and he found himself wishing his mother could be more like this. It would make all the difference if she showed that she cared, just a little bit.

Maybe then, he could make a go of things.

After a few moments of sitting, waiting in the cold and dark with no one around, he heard movement to his right and the sound of an engine. Looking out to where he'd entered the tunnel, he saw a van backing up along the verge between the path and the river. The slope made the van lean precariously until it turned between the low bollards along the path's edge and backed onto the tarmac. It stopped a short distance away from the tunnel, with the engine still running.

Malcom frowned at it and the three words on the back door.

"Food and Snacks."

His stomach rumbled. Was this a good Samaritan coming to feed the local homeless? No one seemed to be getting out of the vehicle.

Malcom turned and looked the other way, in the direction that Viv had gone, but she wasn't there. No one was there. The area was deadly quiet, apart from the soft rumble of the van's engine.

Malcom got to his feet. Maybe Viv would appreciate some food when she got back. It was the least he could offer for her friendship. Malcom approached the van, looking down one side to the driver's door, but saw no one. He walked up to the rear doors and re-read the words a few more times. The decals were faded and torn but still legible. Wondering if maybe the owner was inside the back of the van, getting ready to serve them, Malcom knocked and waited. But there was no answer.

He frowned again, thinking it was odd. He turned and stepped away from the van, looking around the quiet nook beside the bridge but couldn't see anyone. There wasn't anyone up on the bridge, either. It felt odd and a little eerie.

He caught a brief sound of shifting clothing before something wrapped around him. There was a flash of metal as it caught the light before disappearing beneath his chin.

Pain, hot and intense, exploded across his neck. Something cold and sharp cut deep into his throat. Warm lifeblood gushed and spurted, soaking his chest. He briefly fought against the attack, flinging blood everywhere, but it was too late.

The attacker let go, and any strength in his legs vanished instantly as raw, primal panic set in. He fell to the floor with one hand on his neck, trying to stem the bleeding. He couldn't breathe, and there was this wet, bubbly sound as he tried to suck in air. Blood covered his hands and splashed on the ground. The crimson glow from the van's brake lights bathed everything in a wash of deep red. A harsh, warm metallic taste filled his mouth as he sensed movement behind him. He heard the van doors open.

He tried to speak, to say something or call out for help, but no sounds came as he gasped for breath. Feeling utterly helpless and fearing that this was the end for him, tears streaked down his face.

Whoever had attacked him suddenly grabbed him again. Malcom panicked, but his flailing and desperate attempts to fight back were useless. Within moments, he was dumped into the back of the van, which was curiously lined in plastic.

Looking up, he saw the dark figure stare at him for a moment.

Darkness crowded in from the edges of his vision, making it hard to focus. Behind the figure, at the far end of the tunnel, Malcom saw Viv step out and stop. She froze for a moment before ducking back and leaning out to watch.

In a last, desperate attempt to get help, Malcom raised a hand and reached for the doors, the ragged remains of his neck bubbling and spurting as he tried to call out.

Then the van doors were slammed shut.

2

Walking into the office of the East Midlands Special Operations Unit, or EMSOU as it was affectionately known, Rob dropped his bag off at his desk and nodded to Nick at the next desk over.

"Mornin'," he said in greeting.

"Hey, Rob," Nick replied. "How's things?"

"Yeah, alright," Rob answered. "Looking forward to another day of ticking boxes and all that bollocks."

Nick smirked. "I hear yeh." He clicked his mouse. "Tick."

Rob smiled and wandered over to the kitchenette, passing Scarlett's empty desk. She'd been off on compassionate leave for two weeks since the death of her friend, Ninette. All the evidence for her death pointed towards Karl Rothman, whom they'd arrested for the murder of Detective Superintendent Lee Garrett earlier the same day. But despite the gun matching up to the wounds they found on the victims, including Ninette, and the gun sporting Karl's fingerprints, he insisted he didn't kill her.

According to Karl, he'd been set-up by the Mason gang.

Rob believed him, but others didn't, including the superintendent. So it looked like he would be charged for the murders of Lee, Ninette, and the gang member turned informant, Ambrose Gordon, better known as 'Rice'.

Just a few days ago, Rob had been to see Scarlett to update her on the progress of the investigation and what would be presented to the CPS. He'd left that visit feeling a little concerned, mainly because it seemed that Scarlett wanted to return to work as quickly as possible. He wasn't sure that was a great idea, but he admired her dedication.

Ultimately though, it wasn't his decision.

Finally, with a mug of hot tea in hand, Rob crossed the room again. As he returned to his desk, he spotted a familiar shape striding into the office. Wearing a fitted suit with her blonde hair tied up in a bun, Scarlett's fierce eyes scanned the room, meeting the shocked gazes of those within.

She met Rob's eyes and nodded as she approached her desk.

"Scarlett," Rob said as he walked over. "Hi. You're back?"

"Hey. Yep, I am."

"Are you sure that's a good idea?" he asked, concerned.

"It's a great idea," she said, placing a takeaway paper cup on her desk. "I'm going stir-crazy at home. I can't do it anymore. I've taken what time I need."

"Are you sure about that?" Rob asked. "You don't have to do this."

Her intense, piercing blue eyes met his, revealing a steely expression that contained the raging fire of a woman on a mission. "I do. It's best for all of us if I do. I'm driving Chris around the bend at home. He'll probably call off the wedding if I'm forced to stay home any longer… and I wouldn't blame him."

"Really?" That didn't sound good.

She sighed. "Well, no, probably not. Chris has been great, and he's doing what he thinks is best, but I can't just sit at home watching bloody Loose Women. Christ, that programme does my head in. It's inane. I don't know how anyone watches it."

Rob smiled, pleased to hear her familiar good humour again. "I wouldn't know. Not my cup of tea."

"I like it," Ellen piped up from her desk without her eyes leaving her monitor. "It's not exactly award-winning journalism, but it can kill some time on my days off."

"Sorry about her," Tucker said and turned to Ellen. "That's ten 'Hail Marys' and five 'Our Fathers' young lady. You've clearly been possessed."

"Nah, I don't think so. I've just got taste," Ellen shot back, one eyebrow raised.

"It's worse than I thought," Tucker said. "She's lost all sense of reality."

"Piss off," Ellen said, shaking her head.

Scarlett rolled her eyes and took a seat at her desk. Rob crouched beside her and lowered his voice. "How's Chris? Is he okay with you coming back?"

"Yeah. He's good. And it's best for us if I return to work. I'm not doing anything productive at home, and I'm just going over the same thoughts again and again. It's not healthy. I need the distraction. I need to work."

He wasn't sure she'd fully answered his question. "So, Chris is happy for you to return?"

She pulled a face at his question. "I don't need his approval."

Rob cringed. "I know. I'm just concerned."

She let out a long breath and seemed to accept his explanation. "I'm not sure happy is the right word, but Chris knows I need to work. I guess we'll see. We're supposed to be going to a neighbour's meal tomorrow night."

"I'm sure that will be nice. I'm sure you'll have fun."

"Chris doesn't think it's a good idea. But I can't let him go alone. Besides, I want to meet our neighbours."

"Well, I kind of sympathise with him. Coming to work is one thing. You can keep your mind off things, but socialising is a different kettle of fish. I think you need to be careful."

"Piss off," she snapped. "I've told you, I'll be fine. I'm done hiding away at home." She leaned in closer and lowered her voice. "And I'll tell you another thing. They might be your

21

family, Rob, but I will take down the Mason gang if it's the last thing I do. They will pay for what they've done."

Rob suppressed the grimace that threatened to break out on his face. He hated his family as much as she did and would relish the day they were locked up, but he didn't like the idea of revenge being Scarlett's motivation for returning to work.

It was something that could get out of hand and easily consume her if she wasn't careful.

Rob's long estrangement from his family gave him some perspective on things, but he didn't have to think too hard to remember his own hot-headedness in those early months following his escape from them. He'd harboured the same feelings of hate and vengeance, but time had mellowed them. So maybe that was all she needed. Time. Because two weeks was no time at all, and those wounds would still be raw.

He went to reply, but his DCI beat him to it.

"Loxley," Nailer called out from his office door. "Have you got a minute?"

"Duty calls," Scarlett said with a smile and turned to her PC.

The moment had passed, and he didn't feel he could delve back into the subject of revenge right now, not with his boss waiting for him.

"It certainly does." He walked into Nailer's office to find another detective he didn't recognise in the room.

"Shut the door behind you," Nailer said.

He did as the DCI asked and approached the desk. The third man got up and offered his hand.

"Detective Loxley, it's a pleasure," he said. He wore a suit with short dark hair and looked to be in his early thirties. "I'm DS Burton White." Rob shook the offered hand and nodded in greeting.

"Nice to meet you, Burton. How can I help?"

"I'm here in my capacity as a PSU officer." Rob tensed and felt his blood run cold. Burton smiled. "Don't worry, it's not as bad as you might fear. I'm sure you've heard about what happened to Bill Rainault?"

"Yeah," Rob answered. "He's been disciplined and warned to keep away, hasn't he?"

"He has," Burton confirmed.

"He pissed his DCI off once too often," Nailer added. "If he comes after you again, Paige has assured me she'll take it seriously, and he could lose his job."

"DCI Nailer is correct," Burton confirmed. "He's not to harass you anymore. If he does, the repercussions will be grave."

Rob grimaced. "I wish I could say that I think this will keep him away, but…"

"Yeah," Nailer agreed and looked at Burton. "He's had it in for Rob, for years now."

"All this because he found out about my family back when we were partners." Rob shook his head in disbelief.

"He felt betrayed," Nailer added.

"Well," Burton said, "hopefully, this will draw a line under it. In the meantime, DCI Paige Clements has asked me to look into your position and your current relationship with the Mason family. So, in the interest of being fair and open, I wanted to come and talk to you directly. I want this to be as quick and painless as you probably do."

"Sounds good," Rob said.

"Excellent. So, I've been speaking to DCI Nailer about this, and he has assured me that you have not initiated any contact with your family since you left them, twenty-one years ago, is that correct?"

"It is," Rob answered, wondering what else Nailer had told Burton.

"But is it also correct, as DCI Nailer had told me, that your brothers have recently initiated contact?"

"Unfortunately, yes. Twice now in recent weeks."

Burton nodded. "The first time was in Clipstone with your brother, and more recently several members of your family, including your father, broke into your apartment. Correct?"

"That's right."

Nailer had been honest, it seemed. Rob watched as Burton jotted down a note on his pad.

"Has there been anything else?"

"No," Rob confirmed. "But I will report back to Nailer if it happens again. Did you want to know about the recent cases we've handled involving the Masons?"

"No, Nailer has given me all I need. I just wanted to speak to you directly. Is there anything more you wish to say about your relationship with your family?"

"I don't think so, other than to say, I don't have a relationship with my so-called 'family'. I cut them out of my life twenty-one years ago, and I have never wanted anything more to do with them. I'd be happy never to see them again. And by the way, Nailer has been more of a father to me than my biological father has ever been."

Burton nodded. "Okay, thank you. I think that should do. Thank you for your time, gentlemen, I won't keep you any longer." With that, Burton shook hands with them both and walked out of the office, closing the door behind him.

"Well, that was interesting," Rob commented, as he retook his seat opposite Nailer.

"It's a positive move by the PSU. Your history will be a constant weight around your neck, and there'll always be prejudice, but maybe this will help us all move past it, somewhat."

25

"Mmm. I'll wait and see, if it's all the same to you."

"Very wise," Nailer agreed. "So, I got off the phone with Phil Pittman a little while ago, before the PSU darkened my doorstep."

He was the cover officer, or handler, for the un-named undercover officer embedded within the Mason gang, and they'd briefly worked with him on a sting up in Worksop recently.

"Oh, right? Everything okay?"

"Everything's fine," Nailer confirmed. "He was just asking for feedback on the Worksop sting operation and on the information he got you at the conclusion of the Rothman case. He wanted to know if it was useful so he could report back. I said it was, but I wondered if you had anything to add?"

"Not really, no. I agree with you. The tip about a corrupt officer close to EMSOU was very timely."

"So, nothing to add?"

"Nope. His UCO is doing a great job."

"Aye. They are. Okay, that's it, really," Nailer said.

"Great," Rob replied and got up. He turned and noticed Scarlett at her desk through the window and paused. "Did you know she was coming back?"

"Hmm?"

"Scarlett."

"Oh. Yeah, I did. We had a long chat yesterday on the phone. She assured me she was fit to work, so I said okay." Nailer leaned back into his seat. "It *has* been two weeks, Rob, and the victim was a friend, not a family member. She should be okay."

"I hope so. I just don't want her getting obsessed with the Masons and ruining her career." He gave Nailer a meaningful look. "We both know another obsessed officer who's taken things a little too far, don't we?"

Nailer nodded in understanding. "And Bill is paying the price for that now."

"I hope so."

"I guess what you're asking me is, am I happy for her to come back to the team, right?"

"Right," Rob agreed. "This isn't a warehouse job or stacking shelves. Our work carries certain responsibilities, and our team needs to work to the best of their ability."

"You're right, of course. But from talking to her, I believe she's ready, and I'm happy for her to come back to work," Nailer said.

Looking away, Rob briefly analysed why he was asking these questions. Scarlett was clearly a capable person with a strong will, and he agreed that two weeks was probably enough time to mourn the death of a friend and return to work. But this was a brutal murder, and Scarlett's choices had

27

probably led to Ninette's death. In addition, she was a police officer and would be required to do her job to the best of her ability. So this wasn't a typical bereavement or return to work.

Ultimately, Rob was torn and wasn't sure which was the right choice, coming back or staying off.

One thing he did know for sure was that he missed working with her, but his personal feelings about their friendship were a secondary concern. He needed to focus on her welfare and make sure she wasn't making a mistake.

"And I would have thought that you'd be happy for her to return, too."

"I am," Rob confirmed.

"Then your heart's in the right place, and you're just being a good friend. I say, carry on."

"And Chris was cool with all this, too, right?" Rob asked.

"He was. Remember, he has his upcoming marriage to consider, and this is his bride-to-be."

"Yeah. Poor sod." Rob chuckled as he thought about Chris's situation. "If this was your wife? Would you want her throwing herself back into work so soon?"

Nailer smiled. "Well, I'm not sure I'm the best person to answer that with a failed marriage to my name and no current partner."

"That was twenty years ago," Rob protested.

"Twenty-one years, but who's counting." The DCI sighed and paused for a moment. "You've never been married, have you?"

Rob shook his head. "Nope. I've never come close, either. I'm not sure this job really suits married life. Besides, who'd want to marry into my family?"

"Someone would, I'm sure." Nailer's eyes narrowed. "I hear on the grapevine that you've been seen with a certain duty solicitor."

Rob's breath caught in his throat before he smiled and sighed. "Matilda Greenwood. Yeah, we've had a drink, but that's it."

"That's good. I'm pleased for you, Rob. You should start seeing people, and Matilda is a lovely woman."

"Except, I told her I'm not in the market for a girlfriend right now."

"And why the hell did you do that...? Wait, let me guess. The Masons?"

Rob nodded. "I can't put her through that."

Nailer shrugged. "Look, it's your life, and you do what you feel is best, but maybe, just maybe, you should let her make that choice. It's taking on a lot, and it's a risky proposition, I understand that probably better than most, but it's her life. Also, you don't want to end up alone like me."

Nailer's dark eyes fixed him with a knowing look, and for a moment, he seemed older than Rob usually thought of him.

"You're not alone," Rob replied brightly, "you've got us!"

Nailer grimaced. "Yeah, riiiight. I think you made my point for me."

3

Vivian stared at the dark red stain at the entrance of the tunnel. There were splatters across the ground, on the nearby cardboard and up the wall, although some had been washed away by an earlier shower.

When she closed her eyes, all she could see was the van at the end of the tunnel and that poor kid bleeding to death in the back. He'd seen her, and his haunted, terrified eyes had followed her around the rest of the night.

That and the blood.

My god, there'd been so much blood. She'd not got a good look at the wound, but it looked like Malcom's throat had been cut. Those images in her head and the thought of it happening to her, it made her gag.

She closed her eyes and took a long breath in an attempt to still her troubled thoughts, but the images remained burned into her retinas.

Seeing those van doors being slammed shut by the silhouetted figure brought back hideous memories.

As her mind replayed the scene from the previous night, images from months ago bubbled up, mixing in with those from last night. She'd seen a similar thing happen months ago up in Bobber's Mill, when a gang kidnapped two people right in front her. She'd learned after the fact that they were being taken up to Sherwood to be hunted by some psycho with a bow and arrow.

Not very 'Robin Hood' of him, was it?

She remembered the two detectives she'd met, Rob and Scarlett, and bit her lip in frustration.

"I need to report this in," she said, not for the first time. She looked up the tunnel towards the man sitting halfway along.

"No, you don't," Aaron replied, sounding annoyed. He shook his head as he spoke. "You do not need to go talking to the police. They probably know about it by now, anyway. All the police do is cause problems. I don't want to talk to the pigs about this."

"But, we saw him being kidnapped."

"*You* saw it," he snapped. "I didn't. I didn't see shit." He set his jaw and stared at the ground by his feet.

Vivian frowned, annoyed as she remembered what had happened. After storming off, she'd convinced Aaron to come back and talk to Malcom, and he'd reluctantly followed her back to the bridge. When she'd seen the first tunnel empty, she'd moved to the second and looked down it, which was when she saw the van. "You were there. You saw it. I remember."

"I was behind you," Aaron protested. "I didn't see anything."

"Oh, whatever..."

"I didn't." He sighed, annoyed. "You're mad, wanting to report it in and go talking to the cops again."

"No I'm not. It's the right thing to do."

"Is it? Are you sure? You told me what happened the last time, remember? You said a police officer tried to kill you."

"That was different."

"Is it? I don't think it is. Have you got a death wish? Do you want that to happen again? What if they succeed this time?"

"That officer was arrested," she explained, but she was doubting herself now.

"And? So what? Are you saying there's only one bad apple in the police? You've seen the news. They're all corrupt these days."

"When have you watched the news?" she scoffed, disbelieving.

"At the shelters, at the soup kitchens. It's always on."

"Oh, yeah," Vivian grunted, agreeing. He was right. They put it on to keep the homeless up to date with current events, but she rarely paid much attention to it. It was too depressing.

Aaron pressed on with his argument. "They won't take you seriously and just throw you in the slammer. We're not people to them; you know it as well as I do. No one listens to people like us."

"They... wouldn't do that..." she answered hesitantly, but she wasn't sure how much she believed her own words.

"Are you certain? Because I'll tell you this for nothing. If you go to the pigs, I'm gone. I don't want any part of that. They're nothing but trouble, and I've got enough shit to deal with."

4

Pulling into his driveway, Nailer gathered his things from the passenger seat and climbed out of his Land Rover Defender. He took a moment to check his surroundings before walking to the rear of the 4x4. Satisfied he was not being watched, he removed the suitcase from the boot.

Again he checked the street, looking each way for anything suspicious, and when he saw nothing untoward, he turned to his townhouse on Derby Road, on the north edge of the Park Estate, close to where Scarlett lived.

The evening was closing in after another long day in the office. They were dealing with a few minor cases, which were mostly paperwork by now, and handing them off to the CPS.

As always, they did their best to gather the evidence and clean up the shit these model citizens left behind. They recorded this evidence, put it in boxes, and filed them away in the hope they might be useful in some court case one day.

It was all too easy to get downhearted about the job when things went poorly, and all their hard work was for nothing. But then, the opposite was also true. When things went well, and the prosecution succeeded, there really wasn't a feeling quite like it.

Nailer made his way into the house, pausing to pick up the mail that had built up as he closed the front door behind him.

With the noisy street shut off, the silence of an empty house was a welcome sensation. He dumped his coat by the door, carried the stack of mail into the kitchen, and deposited it on the side. There were several days' worth here, so he took a moment to scan through the pile in case anything was urgent.

No, nothing.

With a sigh, he grabbed a glass and poured himself some water, which he drank greedily.

Feeling refreshed, he returned to the hall, grabbed his suitcase and carried it upstairs to his forlorn and unused bedroom. He wasted no time dumping his used clothes onto the bed and grimaced at the pile of washing he had before him.

He spent the next half an hour sorting the clothes out, getting a load into the wash and then packing another suitcase of clothes he'd cleaned the last time he'd done this.

It was a routine he knew well, had honed into a finely tuned machine, and he resisted changing it, even though she'd offered to do all this for him. He'd refused her help, though, preferring to do it himself and continue the façade that he lived here alone.

Maybe one day he could sell this place and move into hers, or she into his, but right now, that just wasn't possible. Things seemed to be in a delicate place, and with recent developments, they needed to remain vigilant and careful. If they got sloppy, people could get hurt.

All in all, he spent about forty minutes in his house before he was back out into his Defender and on the road.

He headed southeast through the city, avoiding the routes that took him too close to the main police stations while keeping well within the speed limit. There was no need to draw attention to himself.

About halfway through the journey, he finally left the urban sprawl of the city behind and cut into the countryside, making his way along lanes lined by emerald hedges, surrounded by fields of crops or livestock. Out here in the failing light, he kept one eye on the rearview mirror, looking for patterns or a single car sticking to his tail for a little too long. But there was nothing unusual or anything that might cause him concern.

He passed through Plumtree, Cotgrave and Colston Bassett, along a route that he knew all too well by now.

As he approached the tiny village of Harby, Nailer slowed and turned right, off the road onto a dirt track. He passed an old wooden post box by the junction and a makeshift painted sign that read 'Hill Farm House' in peeling black paint, now partially obscured by the rapidly growing foliage.

The Defender navigated the track easily, bumping along at a rate of knots between two tall hedges until a small oasis of trees surrounding a house appeared, hemmed in by fields on all sides.

The gate forced him to stop and get out, and as he opened the barrier, he glanced at the CCTV camera that had been trained on the entrance. It wasn't much protection, but at least it would provide an early warning should the wrong people turn up.

He drove in and parked up, closing the gate behind him before plucking the case from the boot and approaching the front door. He unlocked it and walked inside.

"Hello?" Nailer called out. "Anna? Something smells good."

"Hi John," a female voice answered. Moments later, as he locked the door behind him, a middle-aged woman with fair skin and greying hair appeared from around the corner. She was slim, and seeing her smile always melted Nailer's heart. "How was work?"

He leaned in for a kiss, and she obliged, hugging him briefly. "Work wasn't too bad," he answered. "Mainly paperwork and meetings."

"Fancy a drink?"

"On a Monday night?"

"Why not?" she asked. "Dinner's almost ready."

"Lovely," he answered, the thought of food filling him with happiness. Leaving his suitcase for later, he followed her to the kitchen, where Annabelle was already pouring a glass of white wine on the kitchen table. He took a seat. "Thank you."

She smiled and sat beside him. "My pleasure."

He rubbed at his temples, trying to work out the day's frustrations, which were threatening to turn into a full-blown headache. Wiping his face with his hand, he sighed and picked up his drink. This would probably help.

"You look tired. Everything okay?"

Nailer grimaced as several thoughts sprang to mind, but one poked its head above the others at this particular moment.

"I lied to him again today."

Annabelle met his gaze and stiffened for a moment. "Are we talking about Rob?"

"Yeah. We were talking, and he asked what I'd do if my ex-wife wanted to return to work after a bereavement."

"Was this about Scarlett?"

"It was."

"I see."

39

"Anyway, I mentioned that I was single and not a good person to ask."

"Aaah."

Nailer sighed. "I know. It's silly, but I do not like lying to him, not over this," he waved his hand between Annabelle and himself, "even though I know I have to."

"That's right, you do. You have to. You know that."

"I know. It just… It doesn't sit right. That's all, and it's been troubling me for a while. I don't know. I think it's been worse lately because of all this with his family. There's been almost nothing for years, and then now, all of a sudden, they're taking an interest in him again."

"Which is why we need to be even more careful, John. You know that, and…" She sighed. "Do we need to think about Erika, too? I can't say I'm very happy about her living next door to him."

"I know. Me neither, but she made that choice without us, and I can't see her agreeing to move out now."

"I know, and that's what worries me. I mean, I get it. She was curious and wanted to be close to him, but…"

"I don't blame her for that," Nailer said. "Do you?"

"Of course not. It's only natural. But, we need to keep an eye on her, and if things turn dicey…"

"I know," Nailer confirmed. "I know."

5

After finally making it back to the modern Trent Bridge Quays development he called home, Rob walked up the stairwell in the westernmost block, to the first floor. After hours on his feet, attending CPS meetings and dealing with disclosures for older cases going to court, the steps were not a welcome end to his day. He had to drag himself up them, silently promising himself a drink when he got in.

Was it too early in the week to have a beer?

Reaching his floor, he glanced at the first door on his right as he exited the stairwell. He wondered if Erika was in and how her day had gone. He'd not seen her for a few days, but that wasn't anything unusual.

The door to Rob's apartment was the third of four around from the stairs, and as he approached it, he heard footsteps behind on the stairs but couldn't see anyone as he opened his door and stepped into his apartment.

He was greeted by a loud meow from Muffin, his black cat, who padded into the short L-shaped hall leading into his apartment.

"Hello, you," he muttered and crouched to give the tom cat a scratch behind his ears. Muffin purred appreciatively before meowing again and turning back into the apartment. He probably wanted food. "I know, I know, I'm coming."

Muffin stiffened suddenly and hissed back at him.

Rob pulled a face. "Hey, we've all had a long day. Just hold your horses." He turned to shut the door and was confronted by a broad-shouldered man in a dark suit.

Rob jumped as the man slammed the door open and stepped in.

"Owen!" Rob exclaimed, recognising his thug of a brother. He backed off around the corner and into his open-plan apartment to give himself space while clenching his fists and gritting his teeth. He fully expected Owen to attack.

Owen followed, but to Rob's surprise, he raised his hands. "I'm not here to cause any trouble."

An incredulous expression spread across Rob's face. "What?"

"I'm here on behalf of Dad. He just wanted to let you know that he doesn't hold any bad feelings towards you and is happy to live and let live. He understands your position and respects it."

Rob watched Owen closely as he spoke, amazed by what he was saying, while searching for any hint of deception but finding none. Instead, all he saw was disgust towards the words he'd been compelled to say and a restrained but bubbling rage that simmered beneath the surface.

Owen had always been the most volatile of his three older brothers, but he seemed to be keeping his temper at bay for the time being.

"He respects me?"

"That's what he said." Owen groaned, his distaste for this message growing with every moment. "You're an officer of the law now, and he's happy you've found your calling."

"I don't believe a word you've just said," Rob said with a sigh

Owen shrugged. "Believe what you want, but that's what he told me to tell you."

"And you've told me, so bye." His brother's presence in his apartment filled Rob with anxiety. He wanted nothing to do with him and needed him to leave.

Owen nodded and went to turn away before seeming to remember something. "Oh, and he wanted me to give you this." Owen held out a small package wrapped in brown paper.

"What's that?" Rob asked suspiciously.

"A peace offering."

He couldn't quite believe his ears. "You're kidding."

"No."

"What's inside?"

"How should I know?"

Rob's eyes flicked between the package and Owen's face as he briefly contemplated taking it and then quickly dismissed the idea. He had no idea what was inside, but he didn't trust Owen or his dad, in any way, shape or form. "Well, you can take it back to Isaac, and tell him I'm not interested in anything he has to offer."

Owen pouted. "Are you sure?"

Rob crossed his arms. "Are you done? Because I'd quite like you to bugger off."

Owen narrowed his eyes in obvious contempt. "Yeah, we're done." He turned and left, stalking out of his apartment and across the landing before disappearing into the stairwell. Rob watched him go from his front door until he heard the main entrance to the building close.

Satisfied that his brother was gone, Rob stepped out of his apartment and approached the building's rear window. From his vantage point, he watched Owen climb into a car parked on the side of the street and then drive away.

What the hell was all that about? It was a bizarre interaction and couldn't have been more different to their previous meeting. But he had a feeling that there was method behind the madness. He just needed to know what it was.

"That was him again, wasn't it."

Rob turned to see Erika standing at the entrance to her apartment. She leaned against the door frame, her dark brown hair framing her pretty face. She fixed him with a concerned look, her brown eyes sparkling.

"Yeah," Rob confirmed. She no doubt remembered her brief confrontation with Owen a few weeks ago.

He'd returned home to find his apartment apparently broken into, so he'd investigated with Erika in tow, only to find his dad and brothers inside waiting for him. Owen had been his usual charming self, threatening to hurt Erika before she was allowed to leave. It had been a heart-stopping moment he did not want to repeat it.

"He gives me the creeps," Erika said.

"Understandable," Rob sympathised.

"What did he want?"

Rob sighed and glanced out the window again, still perplexed by the curious interaction. "I honestly have no idea."

6

Engrossed in filling out a report, Bill failed to see his DCI, Paige Clements, approach until she was standing right beside him.

"Hey," she said, making him jump.

Bill took a moment to catch his breath. "Christ, don't do that."

"Sorry," she replied before grabbing a seat from a nearby empty desk and scooting it over. She dropped into it, bringing her down to his eye level. "I just wanted to come over and have a little chat." She spoke quietly.

"Oh," Bill replied and glanced around the room, noting a couple of his PSU colleagues sneaking looks their way. Amongst them was DS Burton White, who was apparently looking into Rob Loxley's past as a way to put all this to bed, once and for all. But it didn't matter to Bill. Rob's family connections were a clear problem that needed to be addressed, and until he was ejected from the force, that issue would not go away.

Seeing all the eyes of his fellow PSU officers glancing up at him made him feel like he was in some kind of fishbowl, and he hated every moment of it. They shouldn't be throwing dirty looks his way, not when a bent copper like Loxley was walking their corridors.

Feeling his chest tighten, he coughed and adjusted his sitting position. "What did you want to chat about?"

"It's been a week since we gave you our feedback from the internal investigation regarding your conduct on the Lee Garrett murder case."

Bill let out the breath he'd been holding. So, it was about this again… great! "Yeah, I know." Every day had been like torture, but what choice did he have?

"Just so you know, everything's fine," she reassured him. "I just wanted to say, well done. I've seen a marked improvement in your attitude, and to your credit, you've not mentioned a certain detective in all that time, which is great. Keep it up. I don't want to lose you as an officer, as I feel that you have a lot to offer, and I'm pleased to see that you have taken this warning seriously."

"Well, I didn't have much choice, did I? It was that or lose my job."

"I don't know about that, but there would have been consequences. However, you have respected that Loxley is out of bounds for now, which is great."

Bill clenched his jaw at her condescending tone. She was treating him like a naughty schoolboy, which made him bristle with disgust. Part of him wanted to tell her where to shove her so-called restrictions, but he knew what the end result of that would be. Instead, he kept his jaw clamped shut and offered her a brief but utterly fake smile.

It was a shame, because he'd always liked Paige and respected the office of the PSU. But recent events had tainted it, and he was starting to wonder if the department was fit for purpose.

Why were they not investigating this clear conflict of interest? Why were they not taking this obviously compromised officer more seriously? What hold did Loxley and the Mason gang have over the police and the Professional Standards Unit?

But despite his misgivings, there was nothing he could do right now. He needed to play the game and sink beneath his DCI's radar.

"Thank you," he said, doing his best to accept his DCI's compliment and not throw it back in her face. "It's not been easy."

"I understand, but you have done the right thing by accepting our findings and moving on. I can tell you that I personally appreciate that, and I will be reporting back accordingly. This will look good for you, Bill."

"Thank you," he answered in clipped tones.

She stood up. "Carry on."

As she walked away, Bill spotted several of his colleagues shooting him nervous or accusatory glances. He'd had run-ins with several of them over the last couple of weeks. Some believed he was bringing the office into disrepute, while others seemed to be on the verge of violence over his so-called misogynistic behaviour. It was all utter bullshit as far as he was concerned, and he had no qualms about letting them know it when they confronted him.

Bill looked away from the room and focused on his screen, doing his best to shut out the pregnant stares that were coming his way.

He wasn't about to give up on his mission to bring Rob down, though, not by a long shot. This was little more than a delay.

Still feeling on edge, Bill relaxed back into his chair and closed his eyes for a moment. He needed to calm down, so he focused on his breathing.

In through the nose, hold, and out through the mouth.

He'd barely begun when his phone vibrated, alerting him to the presence of a new message or email.

With a sigh, Bill pulled the device from his trouser pocket and checked the screen. Sure enough, there was an email to his personal address with the subject line, 'I believe you'.

Through narrowed, sceptical eyes, Bill unlocked the phone, opened the email, and started reading.

'To DI William Rainault.

I'm a serving detective within the Nottinghamshire Police, and I wanted you to know that I believe you about Rob Loxley. He's a compromised man who does not deserve his place within the force during this current climate of distrust. How he's managed to attain the rank of DI, I do not know, but someone isn't doing their job.

I have heard about what's happened to you, and it's just not right.

I know you have had certain restrictions put upon you, so if you would prefer not to agree to the following request, I completely understand.

But, I wanted to reach out because I think I might be able to help you. I've come into the possession of something that might finally help you bring Loxley to justice.

So, if you're interested, I'd like to meet.

Thank you.

A sympathetic Officer.'

With his heart thumping in his chest, Bill read the email through a couple more times. Could it be, he wondered breathlessly, before a concerning thought occurred to him. It might be a trap.

Lowering his phone, Bill scanned around the room, looking for anyone still taking an interest in him, but none were.

He frowned and looked at the email again as a kaleidoscope of thoughts ran through his head. Was this real, or was it a trap of some kind? Were his superiors testing him to see if he would fall for their trap, or was this a genuine message from someone who shared his views on Rob?

There was no way to be sure of anything; the only way to find out would be to meet them, whoever they were.

But he didn't like the idea of outright agreeing to a meeting because if it was a trap, that could be seen as breaking the restrictions placed upon him.

However, maybe there was a middle ground which would hopefully mitigate any blame against him should this turn out to be a trap while still opening up the possibility for a meeting.

Taking a moment to think about his reply, Bill started typing.

'Thanks for your email. I appreciate your sentiment, but recent events mean that I can't really talk about this. I have unfortunately been warned about engaging in any more investigations against DI Loxley, and I would not want to be in breach of those guidelines.

51

If you want to pursue this, by all means, do so, and I will raise a glass to you tomorrow night when I'm at the Arrow Pub in Arnold.

All the best.'

After checking through his email several times to make sure it was suitably vague, he hit send. Again he focused on the room, watching to see if anyone picked up the email, but saw nothing incriminating.

Bill stuffed his phone away with a shrug.

Tomorrow night might be an interesting one.

7

Pulling into the car park of the Longbow Pub in north Arnold, DS Phil Pittman parked and took a moment to check his surroundings. Satisfied that everything seemed normal, he stuffed his police ID badge into his bag and straightened his suit before climbing out of his car.

Again he scanned the car park, but he didn't see anyone he recognised or anything that might cause him concern. Satisfied he wasn't being followed or watched, he approached the building, looking like any other businessman stopping for a drink after a long day at work.

Walking inside and up to the bar, a grinning waitress approached. "Hi, what can I get you?"

Phil smiled back. "Actually, I've booked one of your rooms for a meeting. The name's Ralph Oakley." The lie came easily. Having told it many times over the years, he'd built up Ralph's legend—his history and persona—to a point where it all came very naturally to him.

"Oh, hold on." The girl checked a large logbook on the counter. "Aaah yes, Oakley Holdings, isn't it?"

"That's right," Phil lied, smiling serenely.

"You wanted the small room?"

"I did. It's just a short business meeting. We shouldn't be here long. Someone will be joining me shortly."

"Of course, we'll show them through. It's this way." She walked Phil through the bar and along a corridor before turning into a modest-sized room with a long table and chairs. "Would you like any drinks brought through? Tea, coffee?"

"A large pot of tea and a few cups would be perfect," he replied, checking the time. He still had half an hour to spare, but it was always better to be early and not arrive at the same time as the UCO. You never did know who was watching.

Once the pot of tea had arrived, Phil settled into the room and poured himself a drink while he waited.

To kill time, Phil scrolled through social media on his phone, marvelling at the idiotic crap that people were posting.

It wasn't long before the door opened again, revealing the same waitress.

"Here you go," she said, showing a sophisticated professional-looking woman into the room.

"Thank you," the woman said as she stepped inside. Phil smiled at his charge and rose from his seat to greet her.

"Would you like anything…?" the waitress asked the woman.

"No, thanks," the woman answered succinctly before closing the door and turning to Phil. "Hey," she said, her persona changing instantly. Suddenly she was relaxed and calm, rather than uptight and poised.

"Hi, Maddy. How've you been?"

Undercover officer Madeleine Osbourne shrugged at her cover officer. She wore a business suit with a skirt, had her hair tied up in a neat bun, and looked every part the professional businesswoman.

"Alright, Phil," she answered. "Surviving."

"Well, that's the main thing. This is just a quick debrief now that the Rothman case has been handed off. I think it went well."

"Looks like it," she agreed. As she spoke, he noticed a hint of tension in her voice, and wondered what was causing it. "I've got a question for you too, but I'll save it for the end."

"No problem." Concern briefly filled him, but he quickly dismissed it. "There's not much to say, really. Only that the EMSOU DCI, John Nailer, and his team were very impressed with your work on the sting operation up in Worksop and with the info you handed off to them that helped convict DI Karl Rothwell of the murder of Superintendent Lee Garrett."

Madeleine's brow knitted together. "You mean the tip about the corrupt officer working close to the EMSOU?"

"Yeah, that's right," he confirmed. "It was just one more piece of evidence against Rothwell. They probably didn't need it, but every little bit helps, I guess."

"Aah, well, that's what I wanted to talk to you about actually, because you got it wrong."

"Got what wrong?" He raised an eyebrow in confusion. "What do you mean?"

"Whoever it is, it wasn't Karl Rothwell."

His stomach dropped. "Are you sure? How do you know?"

"Oh, I'm sure. From what I hear, the Mason brothers and Isaac laughed about us pinning that on Karl. Whoever this corrupt officer is that's working for the Masons, they're still embedded in the force, working for the gang."

"Shit," Phil hissed. He'd never even considered this as an option. "And, you're certain of this?"

"Positive."

With his mind racing, Phil's thoughts flailed about, desperately snatching at ideas as he tried to make sense of what Madeleine was telling him. "Do you have anything else we can use? Any clues as to who it might be?"

"No. I don't. I'm not in a position to find out, either. This is high-level stuff, Phil. Whoever it is, they report directly to either the Mason brothers or maybe even Isaac himself. So I can't go around asking too many questions and acting suspiciously. My position is already precarious, and this leak about the corrupt officer has the brothers spooked. They know they have a leak, and they're trying to figure out who it is. I'm putting myself at risk just coming here."

"Shit." She was right about her life being in danger. If the Mason firm found out who she really was, there was a good chance they would kill her. She was literally putting her life on the line for them, and he needed to treat this with the care it deserved. His first thought was to bring in someone at a higher level, who could authorise more. "Right then, I'll need to speak to Nailer and…"

"No. Don't. What if he's the bent copper? We don't know who it is. Don't tell anyone."

"Then, what do we do?"

Madeleine sighed and looked away in thought before answering, "Damn it. Well, we don't have any other option but to look into this ourselves, do we? We need to know who that bent copper is yesterday."

"Do you have the time to do that? Are they watching you?"

"Probably, but I can do this. I've not got much going on with the firm right now, so I have some time. Also, I can spin this investigation into the police easily enough. That kind of info is always useful to the firm. Besides, they've just lost two key informants within the police, so I can say I'm looking for replacements."

Phil wasn't happy about this. "Isn't that a bit flimsy?"

She shrugged. "What choice do we have? We need to know who the bent officer is before more people die. Look, leave it with me. I know what I'm doing. I know how the firm operates. I'll be fine."

"Okay, if you're sure." Phil didn't feel as confident as Madeleine seemed to, but he also knew she was right, and they didn't have many other options. Budgets and personnel were stretched enough without adding another internal investigation into the mix that might spook the corrupt officer and cause them to go to ground.

Besides, he trusted Madeleine, and she was clearly a gifted UCO. If anyone could root out this cancer, it was her.

"Alright," he said. "Tell me what you need."

8

"Aaah, she's back," Rob said with satisfaction as he gazed out through the windscreen towards where his pride and joy sat. His 1985, 2.8 injection, black Ford Capri was waiting for him in its parking space. He took a moment to admire her beautiful lines and polished paintwork.

"She?" Guy asked from the driver's seat. "Who's she?"

"Belle," Rob replied and pointed. "My car."

Guy peered at the car for a moment. "You've named it?"

"*Her*," Rob corrected him. "I've named *her*."

Guy turned back to him. "Why?"

Rob bit the inside of his cheek. He knew why he'd named the car Belle, but it wasn't something he liked to talk about. That was personal. "Just because," he answered.

"Is she named after someone?"

Rob shrugged and decided to change the subject. "Thanks for the lift home." He'd been about to call a taxi when Guy had offered to drive him back instead because Belle had been in for a tune-up. Rob knew the mechanic well. He specialised in older cars and was always more than happy to drop the car back at Rob's when he was done.

"That's okay. Happy to help. At least I'll get back home at a reasonable hour tonight, so I can watch Netflix or something."

"Aye," Rob agreed, thinking about the empty evening ahead of him, alone in his apartment with little to do. On a whim, he turned to Guy. "How about a beer before you head off?"

The DC raised an eyebrow at him but then shrugged. "Yeah, alright. Sounds good."

Guy moved the car into one of the visitor spaces before Rob climbed out and waited for Guy to join him. Rob scanned around the roads, looking for anything untoward. He'd been caught out with surprise visits from his family several times in recent weeks and had taken to checking the area each time he returned home, looking for any hint of trouble.

"It's a nice development," Guy remarked as he walked around his vehicle, looking up at the squat block of apartments. "Very modern."

"Yeah. It does the job," Rob agreed, leading him to the main entrance. They walked inside, and as they climbed the stairs to the first floor, Erika appeared, walking into the stairwell wearing fitted running gear, complete with a cap, earbuds, and her phone strapped to her arm.

"Oh, hi," she said on seeing him.

"Hey," Rob replied. "Going for a run?"

She put her hands on her hips. "Yeah. Just trying to keep fit."

"What are you on about? There's nothing of yeh."

"You charmer." Erika glanced at Guy. She smiled and nodded. "Hey."

"Hi. I'm Guy. I work with Rob." He offered his hand.

"Erika. Rob's neighbour," she said, taking his offered hand and returning the smile. Rob noticed a hint of hesitancy in her voice and posture. She was on her guard around this unknown man. "So, you're a detective too?"

"If by that, you mean overworked, underpaid, and not appreciated, then yes, I am."

Erika smirked and seemed to relax a little. "But you're not complaining."

"I would never."

"I bet. What are you boys up to on a Tuesday night, then?"

"Rob invited me in for a drink. I think he's trying to get lucky, but he's barking up the wrong tree." He leaned in and stage whispered, "I don't swing that way." He winked at her before shooting a mischievous grin at Rob.

Rob rolled his eyes but smiled. "Piss off."

"I think you hit a nerve," Erika replied and gave Rob a cheeky look.

"And you can do one, too," Rob retorted good-naturedly before slipping by Erika, onto the landing. "Do you want that beer, or would you two prefer to keep flirting?"

"I wouldn't want to get in your way, Rob," Erika said. "I'll see you boys later."

Guy followed Rob onto the landing but watched Erika disappear down the stairwell before turning back once she was out of sight.

Rob knew that look all too well. "She's single, as far as I know," he said, moving towards his door.

Guy smiled and nodded. "Good to know. She's a stunner."

Rob shot Guy a look before shaking his head. "She's pretty, sure. A little on the young side, for me, though."

"So, you're not interested in her?"

"I take it you are?" Rob asked, opening the door to his apartment and walking in.

"Maybe," Guy answered coyly.

"Well, you might want to get in line because Nick was asking after her a few weeks back. Besides, I thought you fancied Scarlett?"

Guy shrugged. "Nah. She's well and truly spoken for, so I don't think I'd have much luck there. But you said Erika was single, right?"

"I know she's dating. She's told me about some of her unsuccessful dates. I've not spoken to her about it much recently, though, so I have no idea if she's met someone or not."

"Okay," Guy replied. "What's her full name? Erika what?"

"Macey. Erika Macey. I can talk to her if you like."

"Yeah, maybe. That might be good. Thanks. You can be my matchmaker."

"Just call me Cilla Black," Rob remarked with a smile, but Guy frowned at the reference.

"Who?"

"Oh jeez, my age is showing," Rob said as he led the way through the short L-shaped corridor into the main open-plan room with its view over the River Trent.

"Oh, wow. This is nice," Guy exclaimed as he walked through the living room to the window. "Really nice. I like it."

"Thanks," Rob said. "Yeah, I'm pretty happy with it, and that view is amazing."

"It certainly is," Guy agreed.

Rob opened his fridge and pulled out two bottles. "Stella okay with you?"

"Yeah, that's great." Guy walked back to the kitchenette.

Opening the bottles, he handed one to Guy, who took a swig. Rob did the same and savoured the cool, fizzy beverage. It was just what he needed at the end of a long day.

"Aww, that's lovely," Guy remarked. "Thanks."

"My pleasure."

"So, you're single, right? No girlfriend or anything?"

"Not right now, no," Rob confessed. "I'm not really looking for anything, either. I'm just… I've got enough going on."

"Hmm," Guy grumbled. "Yeah, this job sucks for relationships. Long, unsociable hours filled with traumatic events; it's not a good recipe for a healthy relationship. Some make it work, though."

"Yeah, they do. I mean, Scarlett's getting married, so…" Rob said. "And if anyone can make it work, she can."

Guy nodded in agreement. "I'm inclined to agree with you. Ellen's also in a relationship, isn't she?"

"She is," Rob agreed. "She's a tough one too."

"So it's just us guys letting the side down."

He pulled a face but couldn't disagree. Nick, Tucker, Guy and himself were all single, although that wasn't for lack of trying to make something work.

"What about Nailer?" Guy asked.

"Single, too," Rob answered. "He was married and divorced years ago, but he's a confirmed bachelor as far as I know. He lives alone on the north edge of the Park Estate."

"Christ, we're a bunch of sad sacks, aren't we. We need to follow the girls' examples and find ourselves partners."

"Yeah." Rob pulled a face. "You're probably right."

Guy sighed and turned to the room as he took another mouthful of beer. With a sniff, he turned back to Rob with a curious expression on his face. "You know what we should do?"

"What?"

"We should hold a get-together. We should get the whole team and partners and have some food and drink, you know? I think it would be a great bonding experience."

Rob nodded slowly in agreement. He'd been meaning to organise something like this as a way to build on the foundation they'd created as a team over the last few weeks, and this sounded like a great way to go about that. "Yeah, that's a good idea. I like it."

"We should do it here," Guy added.

That brought Rob up short. "What? Here?"

"Yeah. You've got the space and the view. It's perfect. We could all bring something to make it easier on you, too. A bit like what Scarlett's doing with her meal out tonight with her neighbours."

"She told you about that, did she?"

"Yeah. Sounds like a nightmare to me, though," Guy remarked.

Rob agreed. Getting the team together was easy, as they all knew one another, but this idea of meeting his neighbours, many of which he might not like, sounded like torture. "Yeah,

I've got no interest in doing that. To each their own, I guess. She seemed keen when she told me about it, though."

"Me too," Guy agreed and shrugged. "Right then, so you just need to pick a night when you think you could have us all around."

"Aye. I'll have a look in the diary, but I think Saturday might be good."

"Saturday works for me," Guy confirmed.

"Perfect. I'll tell the team."

9

Curt swaggered along Retford Road in Worksop, imbued with a feeling of power and strength. He eyed the dark pavement ahead like a king would survey his kingdom, looking to his subjects for reverence and respect. Flanked by three of his mates, his guard of honour, no one dared go near any of them.

In the shadows of the early evening, any local that saw the foursome coming found ways to avoid them. As well they should, he thought. No one challenged them on their home turf, no one. Especially not today.

Today, any idiot who came at him with an attitude was gonna get a face full of trouble, that's for sure. Ahead, an approaching woman spotted them and quickly crossed the street. Curt smiled. It made him feel powerful. Did the woman recognise they were not people to mess with, or maybe she knew who he was? She might know his name and be aware of his family and their fearsome reputation.

As far as he was concerned, he ruled these streets. They were his, and he wasn't afraid to let people know it.

"What you gonna do with it, Curt?" Jake asked as they walked.

"Don't know," Curt answered before Rick could reply with a smart comment. "I've just got it in case, ain't I. In case anyone comes at me with shit, bruv. I ain't taking no one's crap today. Not when I'm packin'." He relished the feel of the cold steel tucked into his belt, ready for action at a moment's notice. Having that kind of power close to hand changed everything. He could do whatever he liked.

"Damn straight, fam," Jake hooted, nodding with approval.

As they pressed on towards the collection of shops on the north side of the road, a man approached, walking the other way. He saw them but didn't cross over. Curt's blood boiled as he glanced at his mates, especially Rick. He couldn't afford to appear weak. As the man came close, he veered left to skirt around them, but Curt swerved too and planted himself in the man's path.

"I'm walkin' here," he grunted, staring at the man's downcast eyes.

"Sorry," the man said and moved to dodge around him.

Curt got in his way again. "You will be. These streets are mine. All this is mine."

The man met his gaze for the first time, and to Curt's satisfaction, he saw fear, raw and primal, there. "Yeah, sure. Whatever," he said, still trying to walk by.

Curt let him go, watching the man hustle off down the street. "Fuckin' idiot."

"You told him," Jake crooned.

"Feel better?" Rick asked in a disapproving tone. Curt eyed him but wasn't sure of the deeper meaning. He chose to take it literally.

"A bit." He watched Rick snort and smile to himself and wondered what his mate was thinking. Rick's older brother was a trusted part of the firm, and that carried a lot of weight. But Curt's uncle was one of Sean Mason's right-hand men. One of his captains. You couldn't get much higher than that within the firm without being a Mason, and that brought him kudos. No one messed with the Gates family, not unless you wanted a late-night visit from someone with a baseball bat.

The town's streetlights were already burning bright in the night air, cutting through the gloom and shadows. As cars passed, their headlights rushed over the surrounding houses, bathing them in a bright glow.

He didn't like Rick's attitude, but he also didn't fancy facing off against his older brother, so he let the little comments slide most of the time.

"You wanna hear what I heard?" Curt said, keen to assert his position as leader of his little group again.

"No," Rick replied in a mocking tone.

69

"Rick, don't be an idiot," Melody snapped, defusing the situation.

"I heard from my uncle there's a major deal going down. A big one. There's gonna be a whole load of gear coming in. Loads of it. And you know what that means, right? It means green for us. Lots of green. We're gonna be rich once we sell it."

"Mad love, bruv," Jake said in approval. "I'm gonna get so much drip."

"Are you sure about that?" Melody asked, questioning Curt's information.

"Where'd you hear that shit?" Rick added.

"I just heard it," Curt answered, feeling momentarily superior. "You know who my uncle is."

"Of course," Rick moaned. "You never fuckin' shut up about him."

"So, there you go then."

Rick raised an eyebrow of incredulity. "And you're saying that he just tells you these secrets?"

Curt shrugged. He didn't like where this was going. "Nah, I just listen, bruv. I've got ears like a bloody bat, don't I."

"Fuck off," Rick scoffed. "You're full of crap."

"No, mate. You listen to me," Curt barked, furious and pissed off that Rick would challenge him on this. He raised a pointed finger to emphasize his fury. "I know what I heard, yeah. Something big is goin' down. You watch."

"Oh, I'll watch, alright. You just be sure to tell me when something happens, yeah?" He laughed, clearly not impressed.

"He's got a point," Melody said, looking unsure.

"I believe yeh," Jake added.

"Look, mate," Curt said, getting in Rick's face. "I can do whatever I like. I'm a Gates, yeah? No one says no to me, not while I've got this." He reached into the back of his belt and pulled the heavy, solid object out from under his coat. Holding the gun up between them, pointing it at the sky, Curt jiggled it about to make his point. "This is what makes someone powerful, Rick, not smart comments. No one fucks with you when you've got one of these."

But Rick didn't look too impressed. "Prove it."

"Sure, I'll prove it. Name it, and I'll do it."

"Rob the shop, up there, and use the gun," Rick challenged him with a cruel smile.

Curt stared at Rick for a long moment, weighing up what he might be thinking and wondering why he was demanding this of him? He didn't really come to any conclusions, apart from being acutely aware that this was a challenge to his authority, and he couldn't let it slide. He glanced up the street towards the shop and eyed it apprehensively. Having visited it many times over the years, he wondered if the owner would recognise him. The worry made him hesitate.

"What's wrong?" Rick asked. "Chicken?"

Curt snapped his eyes back to Rick. "Fuck off." If he covered as much of his face as possible, he reasoned the owner would be unlikely to recognise him in the heat of the moment.

Besides, it might be fun to rob the shop. It would certainly brighten up their otherwise utterly dull evening.

"Easy." Curt sniffed and pulled his scarf over his nose and mouth before lifting his hood. "Watch and learn."

"I'm watching," Rick said, smiling serenely, before pulling up his own hood. "Lead the way."

The other two followed suit behind Rick and strode up the quiet street towards the small general store. Curt led the way, gripping the gun with a death grip as he approached the door. Seeing how bright it was inside, he had a moment of doubt as he wondered if the cameras might pierce the shadows of his hood, revealing who he was. But there was no turning back now.

Bursting in through the front door, Curt marched towards the brightly lit counter where a middle-aged man was waiting. He wasted no time in pointing the gun at the stunned shopkeeper, enjoying the shocked look on the man's face.

"Open the till, put the money in a bag," Curt snapped. "Do it now before I come round there and fuck you up."

He glanced into the shop to check that no one would attempt to be a hero, but he saw no one. They were alone.

Curt focused on the shopkeeper. He seemed lost for words and glanced around for help.

"Oi! Shit for brains. Focus! You have one job. Put the money in a bag, now."

"Please, you don't have to do this," the man begged. "We don't have much money. Take whatever you want from the shelves..."

"Money, now," Curt yelled. This was taking too long, which meant he might need some encouragement.

"Please!"

"Fuckin'..." Curt grumbled and scrambled over the counter. The man cowered before him, shaking with terror. Curt grabbed him and got right into his face. "Till! Now!"

"Okay, okay." Reaching over, the man fumbled with the till as tears fell over his cheeks.

"Come on, man, we gotta go." Rick urged while he, Jake and Melody grabbed whatever they could from the shelves and stuffed their pockets.

"Do you want me to do this or not?" Curt snapped back at Rick.

"Whatever," Rick answered.

73

Seconds later, the man opened the till, revealing money inside. "I'll get you a bag," the man said with a whimper while reaching for one.

Curt laughed, finding the comment amusing. The idiot was still in shopkeeper mode. "Fuck the bag," he answered and swung the butt of the gun down onto the man's face.

Blood flew, and the man grunted in pain as the strength vanished from his legs. "Please, Curt…"

For a moment, Curt frowned. Had the man said his name, or was he imagining it? He'd not quite caught the man's slurred words.

"Curt!" Rick shouted.

Curt dismissed the worry and hit him again and then a third time before the man hit the floor. Satisfied that he wasn't getting back up, Curt scooped the notes out of the tray, stuffed them into his pocket, and vaulted the counter.

Within moments they were out the door. Curt whooped at the top of his lungs. The adrenaline spike was huge. He'd be riding that feeling for a while.

10

Sitting on the end of her bed, Scarlett pulled on the shoes she'd picked out and carefully buckled up the tiny straps so as not to scratch the polish on her nails. She should have done this the other way around, but mistakes had been made, so she was making the best of it.

The high heels contorted her feet, and she knew full well that if she spent too much time standing around talking, she'd be in pain come the end of the night. Hell, she'd be in pain in five minutes!

But they looked awesome.

With her shoes fastened, she got to her feet and checked herself in the mirror, smoothing down the fitted, sleeveless black dress she'd picked out. It was difficult to know what to wear for this. Would her neighbours dress up for the meal, or would it be a more casual affair? Either way, she wanted to make a good impression, and a black dress suited most occasions, so she felt happy with her choice.

Are you ready for this?

Staring into her reflection's eyes, she wondered if this was the right thing for her to do? The two days she'd been back at work had gone well enough, although Rob and the others seemed a little shocked to see her back yesterday.

It was understandable, but there really was no other option. She had to go back. She had to occupy her mind before she went stir-crazy in the house.

Those first few days after Ninette's murder had been horrific, and she'd done a lot of crying and soul-searching. But as the days passed and she got some perspective, her grief slowly turned into anger.

On the face of it, Karl Rothwell had pulled the trigger, even though he continued to maintain his innocence. But ultimately, it didn't matter if he'd shot her or not. He was complicit in everything the gang did, which was just as bad.

She hated Karl and everything he stood for but found that she hated the Mason gang more. Karl was just following orders.

As her ice-blue eyes reflected back at her, all she could think about was how she could get revenge on them. She'd find a way to bring them down, no matter what. It was all she really cared about.

This meal, the dress she wore, and what people thought of her return to work, these concerns paled in comparison to her desire to end the Mason reign of terror, and that's why she'd needed to return to work. She couldn't start down that path at home, staring at the walls.

She'd mourned the passing of her friend, and she'd have one more day of revisiting that grief when the funeral took

76

place, but that was at least another week or so away. Meanwhile, she had work to do.

"Are you ready?" Chris called out from downstairs.

"Just about," she replied, snapping out of her daydream.

"We need to go. We'll be late."

"I'm coming." Chris was not happy about her return to work. He thought it was too soon, and she wasn't taking enough time to reflect and deal with the emotions she was going through.

She saw his point, but she disagreed.

Although, to his credit, he did admit that she wasn't coping well with being stuck at home, unable to work.

I'll work on him. He'll come around. She sighed

With nothing else to do, Scarlett left the bedroom and made her way downstairs, catching appreciative glances from Chris as she navigated the stairs.

"What do you think?"

"Wow," Chris said. "You look stunning."

"Thank you. I'm glad it gets your stamp of approval."

He smiled and nodded. "You don't have to do this, you know. Not if you don't feel up to it."

"But I do," she answered. "I want to do it. You're not going there alone. How bad would that look?"

"I don't care how bad it looks," Chris answered, stepping closer, resting his hands on her arms. "I care about you

77

making careful and rational choices. This is not something to take lightly."

She loved that he cared so much for her well-being, but in this instance, it was misplaced. She took a deep breath. "I know how I feel, Chris, and I'm fine. I'm going, and that's the end of it."

"But…"

"No, stop. Please. I said that's the end of it. I'm going."

Chris sighed and bit his lip. "Okay, but I'm just worried about you, that's all."

Scarlett smiled as she felt her heart melt. "I know, and I love you for it. But you do need to drop it. Let's go and see what kind of people we've moved next door to, shall we?"

"Sure. Don't forget the trifle," Chris remarked with a cheeky smile.

"Oh, crap. Yes," she exclaimed, suddenly remembering. "I'd forgotten about that. That wouldn't have gone down well, would it?" She rushed into the kitchen, carefully lifted the glass bowl from the fridge, and admired her handiwork. The cream looked light and fluffy, and the fruit beneath looked scrummy.

"I'll carry it," Chris said. "I don't think you should while you're tottering about on those heels."

She pulled a face at his comment. "Do you think they're too much?"

"Not at all," Chris replied. "I think they're perfect, just like you."

"Charmer," she said with a smile and then narrowed her eyes. "What are you after?"

"Some trifle for pudding, that's what I'm after." Grinning at the dessert in his hands.

She laughed. "I'm sure there'll be plenty. Come on, let's go."

The moment she walked out of their front door and stepped onto their pea gravel drive, she realised how sensible Chris had been to carry the dessert. She could see herself going over if she wasn't careful. She gripped Chris's arm and used him for balance as they walked out of their driveaway and up the road.

"So, who do we know that's going to be there?" she asked.

"Well, we know Miriam and Charles," Chris answered. They were this evening's organisers and hosts and lived partway up the street. He smiled down at her, offering no more names.

"Is that it?"

"I think so," Chris answered.

"Great. Go us, I guess." They really needed to socialise more.

"I know, we're so on it," he replied as they turned into the driveway of Miriam's house.

Scarlett noted the distinct lack of pebbles. "They have a better drive than us."

"I like our gravel."

"My feet disagree." She noted the lights that were on downstairs and the shadows moving inside. It looked like they weren't the first to arrive.

A swift bell press later, and the door opened, revealing their hostess, Miriam Sullivan.

"Scarlett, Chris. You made it. It's so good to see you again," she said. Her husband Charles was close behind her, smiling.

"And you," Chris said.

"We wouldn't miss this," Scarlett added with a smile.

Miriam gave her a brief, polite hug before moving to Chris, while Charles shook her hand.

She took the trifle from Chris and handed it to Miriam. "One trifle."

"Oh wow, look at that, Charles. Here…" She handed it to her husband. "Can you pop that in the kitchen? And, get some drinks while you're in there." She turned back to them. "Champagne okay for you?"

"Great," Scarlett answered, and Chris mirrored her reply.

"Will do," Charles announced and walked off.

"Come through," Miriam said. "Come and meet everyone."

"We're not last, are we?" Scarlett asked.

"You're fine, don't worry."

Miriam led them through into their spacious front room, where six others were waiting with drinks in hand and smiles on their faces.

"Right, everyone," Miriam said as they walked in. "These are our new neighbours, Chris and Scarlett."

There was a chorus of greetings from the assembled crowd of men and women.

"I think a quick round of introductions is in order," Miriam said. She seemed to enjoy being the centre of attention and taking the lead, Scarlett thought as she started to go around the room.

"This is Barry and Chelsea Wheeler. They live between our house and yours. Barry is a builder, and Chelsea works in the business, right?"

"That's right," Chelsea confirmed. She was around her late thirties with shortish mousey hair and keen eyes. "I'm his boss."

"I would protest, but she's absolutely right," Barry said with a shrug. He was a bald man of a similar age to his wife, with a full beard and a barrel chest, which was currently covered with a check shirt that reminded Scarlett of a lumberjack.

"And this is Gordon Stein," Miriam said, introducing the next person around. "His wife, Nell, was unable to make it tonight."

"She's unwell," Gordon replied with a smile. He was a slim, wiry man, also in his late thirties, with short but wild hair, wearing a shirt and trousers that looked crazily expensive. "Food poisoning, we think, but she's okay."

"She didn't eat the beef casserole you brought round, did she?" Charles asked as he walked back into the room, handing Scarlett and Chris a flute of Champagne.

"Aaah, no. I made that from locally reared produce. Got it from that Deli I was telling you about, Miriam."

"Oh, yes. I remember you saying," she answered and turned to Charles. "I need to go there."

"It's tasty stuff," Gordon said. "We've had their steak a few times. It's lovely. You should try it."

"We will," Miriam confirmed.

"Providing we don't all fall ill from the casserole," Charles added.

"Charles!" Miriam chastised him. "Don't be rude."

"Oooh, I'm in trouble," he joked.

"Ugh." Miriam grunted in disgust at her husband's manners. "Right, well, let's continue, shall we? Next, we have

82

Fern Reeves. She's a good friend of mine and lives in the next street over."

"Hi," Fern greeted them. She looked like she was in her fifties, a similar age to Miriam, Scarlett guessed, with greying hair in a bob, wearing a long skirt and blouse. She offered her hand, which Scarlett shook before Chris did. "Nice to meet you."

"And you," Scarlett said.

"This is Austin Chambers," Miriam said, introducing a man in his early forties with short dark hair and a severe face. He wore a dark suit and merely nodded his greeting.

"Hi," Scarlett said. Chris said the same.

"And finally, last but not least, Ariadne Silk." Miriam motioned to a beautiful woman in her late twenties, or maybe early thirties, with full dark hair, wearing a very fitted dress that showed a little more skin and cleavage than Scarlett's.

Ariadne offered her hand to Chris first and then to Scarlett. "Lovely to meet you both. So, you're new to the area? Like me?"

"We are," Scarlett answered. "We've been here for a few months. You?"

"Same," she replied. "I came up from down south, around London."

"We did too. We came up from Surrey."

83

"A lovely area. I've got friends there," Ariadne said.

"Thank you for inviting us," Chris remarked to Miriam. "We've both been so busy that we've not really had a chance to socialise."

"Yes, thank you," Scarlett added.

"That's okay. It's my pleasure. We have a strong community here in The Park, and we like to ensure new residents feel a part of it."

"That's lovely," Scarlett agreed.

"What is it you do?" Barry asked.

"I work for an investment company," Chris answered. "Our offices are based up here, so it made sense to move."

"Oh, really?" Barry replied. "Austin owns an investment company."

"I do," Austin confirmed, smiling. "Who do you work for?"

Scarlett raised an eyebrow at this small revelation and briefly wondered if Chris worked for Austin without realising it.

"Acorn Investments," Chris replied.

"Aaah, yes, I know it well."

"What's your company called?" Chris asked. He seemed to relax for a moment, and she wondered if he'd drawn the same conclusion.

"Chambers Investments," Austin answered.

Chris frowned. "I don't know it."

"We're small, and we keep to ourselves," Austin answered.

"And what do you do?" Fern asked Scarlett.

She smiled, interested to see how this little revelation went down. "I'm a detective," she replied. "With the Nottinghamshire Police."

"Are you? Wow," Fern answered.

"Miriam, hide the drugs," Barry joked.

Miriam laughed and waved him away. "Don't be silly."

"Fascinating," Ariadne said. "I'm always in awe of the job you do. It can't be easy."

"It has its moments," she confirmed as they settled into the pre-dinner socialising.

Miriam and Charles continued to prove themselves as capable hosts, keeping their wine topped up while Scarlett moved around the room, talking to the other guests and getting to know them. Unable to fully shut off her detective instincts, she couldn't help but observe the group dynamic while trying to figure out people's relationships and personalities.

She didn't see any major red flags, but it was clear that some people here were closer to one another than others. Scarlett watched with interest, enjoying the evening.

A short time later, they were seated at the dining room table and served a Bruschetta starter that Miriam had made.

With the first dish served, she got everyone to smile for a group photo she took with her phone before reassuring them that she'd forward the photo to them all later.

The delicious starter was followed by Gordon's slow-cooked beef casserole, served with Austin's pasta salad, and Ariadne's green salad. All of which were amazing.

And finally, dessert was a choice between Scarlett's trifle and cream or Fern's treacle tart and custard, followed up with Barry and Chelsea's cheese board and crackers.

By the end, Scarlett felt ready to burst and sipped on her coffee while listening to the conversation, which had turned to talk about the youth of today.

"You see, my daughter's a bit of a weird one in that regard," Miriam mused. "She's not really on any social media that I know of, and she keeps very much to herself. I barely see her, do I?" She turned to Charles, who shook his head. "I just wish she'd get out there a little more and find a man, to be honest."

"Maybe she's not into men," Ariadne suggested.

Miriam pulled a face. "You mean she might be... one of them?"

"It's called gay," Chelsea said with a smile.

"Oh, no. She's not *that*," Miriam insisted. "I'd know, I'm sure of it."

Scarlett nearly rolled her eyes but thought she'd best avoid any outward signs of disapproval of outdated attitudes.

As she listened, Chris leaned in close and whispered under his breath, "It's late. Do you want to make a move soon?"

"Yeah," she whispered back and took a final mouthful of coffee. "Thank you for a lovely evening," she said, addressing the table. "But we really should be getting home. I've got work tomorrow, and I need to get my beauty sleep."

"Of course. Don't let us keep you," Miriam said.

"We should head home too," Chelsea agreed, and slowly they all got to their feet.

"You'll all take leftovers, won't you?" Gordon asked. "There's loads left."

"I'm way ahead of you," Charles added while heading for the kitchen. "I've already been portioning it out."

Moments later, he returned with small Tupperware containers filled with casserole.

"Lovely," Chris said, accepting the leftovers with glee.

Scarlett rolled her eyes. "Come on, Guts, let's get home."

11

Climbing out of his car, Bill paused as he gazed up at the small, detached property on Weaverthorpe Road, Arnold, on the city's north side.

It was early, and Bill was due into work soon, but he lived locally to his parents, so it wasn't out of his way, except that wasn't why he hesitated.

It was because he knew full well what he was potentially letting himself in for when he walked through those doors, and part of him just wanted to get back into his car and drive away. He could do without another dressing down by his dad, who would undoubtedly already know from his friends who were still serving in the force about the disciplinary action the PSU had taken against him.

He was always up to date on the latest developments surrounding Bill in the PSU, and that pissed him off something rotten. It felt like his dad, who seemed to disapprove of anything and everything he did, was watching his every move. No matter what he did, his dad always knew about it.

But he couldn't just walk away and not visit. His mother needed him, and she was always supportive and kind. There was no way he could leave her to fend for herself with him in there.

She needed his help, and he would do whatever he could to support her, even if that did mean he needed to brave his father's ire.

With a cold four-pinter of milk in one hand and a loaf of bread dangling from the other, Bill took one last deep breath, walked up the drive to the side door, and used his key to get in.

He found his mother alone in the kitchen—her domain—and full of smiles for him.

"Oh, you brought it. You're a lovely boy, thank you," she said appreciatively and pulled him in for a hug. She took the milk and bread, admiring the groceries as she put them away.

"I'll have some toast this morning, I think," she mused. "A little bit of marmalade on it, it'll be lovely. Would you like to join me?"

"Oh, he's here, is he?" his dad said as he shuffled into the doorway. Both of his parents were old and becoming quite frail, his mother more so than his dad, but he was now at a point where Dad wasn't much use if his mother needed help. So, he came by to help out when needed.

Bill looked up at his dad's sneering face. "Dad," he muttered in a reluctant greeting.

"I've been meaning to chat with you," his dad said. "I heard about your reprimand."

"What?" his mum said. "Are you alright? What happened?"

"It's nothing, Mum, don't worry. I've just been asked to leave a personal issue alone."

"A personal issue?" His dad scoffed. "That's what you're calling this damned obsession with that detective? You're an idiot, William. Leave this Loxley character alone and get on with your life. In fact, get out of the damned PSU while you're at it. There's no career there for a respectable officer. Oh, wait, you're not respectable, are you. You're bloody anti-corruption scum."

"Oh, Bill," his mother crooned, her face full of concern and worry. "You're not still going after Robert, are you? He was such a nice man, and a good friend to you, Bill. He can't help who his family are, and you shouldn't judge someone for things they can't control, either."

"It's not as simple as that, Mum."

She stepped closer and squinted at him. "Are you sure, love?"

"Yeah, I'm sure. He's untrustworthy..."

"God, you're pathetic." His dad scowled at him. "You're a small-minded, petty, pathetic excuse for a police officer, and that Loxley is a hundred times the officer you are. Do you hear me? You should be sacked for what you've been doing. I don't know how you're still in the job, to be honest."

"Fuck off!" Bill yelled.

"Now, Graham dear." His mother turned to his dad, trying to calm him down.

"See what I mean?" his dad pressed, sneering at him. "You're not an officer of the law, you're a spoiled child, playing at it…"

"And why would that be? I'm your child, *Dad*! You raised me. I am who I am, because of you. So if I'm pathetic, what does that make you?"

"Why you little shit…" His dad tensed and balled his fist.

Bill saw the swing coming from a mile off, and caught his arm with ease. His father wasn't the man he once was, and his strength was ebbing away in his old age. Bill held his dad's wrist with an iron grip, while his dad looked on in horror.

"Wha… Let go of me, you…"

With his free hand, Bill grabbed his dad by the collar of his shirt.

"William," his mother screamed. "Don't."

He ignored his mother and shoved his father against the door frame. "I'd be careful how you treat me, Dad. I'm a lot strong than you now."

"You're a bully," his dad muttered. "Little better than a common criminal."

Bill scoffed and laughed. "Whatever. Maybe you need to take a good long hard look at yourself because I'm not the one condoning corruption, am I?" He let go of his dad and backed away. "Sorry, Mum. I'll see you later."

With a final glance at his father, who looked withered and weak, Bill's upper lip curled in disgust before he turned and stormed out, leaving a silent kitchen behind.

His dad hated him. And as he walked away from the house, he was reminded of his sister. She'd been a rebel and hated what their dad stood for. Dad hated her too, and she'd left home ages ago after getting fed up with his behaviour. She'd not come home for ages, and he could understand why.

If it wasn't for his mum, he wouldn't bother.

Storming down the drive, Bill dropped into his car and slammed the door behind him. He gripped the wheel so tight his knuckles turned white as he tried to get control of his breathing, but all he could think about was his dad yelling at him over the last few years, belittling and verbally abusing him.

He hated him for it.

Bill slammed his fist against the wheel in frustration, hoping it might calm him down. He did it again and again, screaming at nothing, shouting and hitting the car until he was too tired to continue.

Finally, sitting back in his seat, with his breathing slowing and his mind beginning to calm, he remembered the email from the sympathetic officer, and his clever reply. Would this mysterious man show up? Would he join him at the pub later?

He hoped so.

12

Spotting Nailer leaving his office and making his way towards the morning briefing, Rob grabbed his laptop and moved to intercept his DCI.

He'd thought long and hard about Guy's suggestion of a team gathering, and the more he turned the idea over, the more he liked it.

The unit had gelled well over the last few months, but there was always room for improvement, and fostering that trust between team members could only ever be a good thing.

Holding the first one at his place was something Rob was less keen on, but he needed to lead by example in the hope that others would offer to host future gatherings. Besides, it was just for a few hours. He was sure he'd be able to get through it.

Briefly, he wondered how Muffin might react. Would he run and hide or enjoy the attention he'd get from the array of guests? It would be interesting to find out.

"Nailer," Rob called out as he drew near.

"Rob," Nailer answered. "Morning. What's up?"

"Morning. I'm thinking about arranging a team social for all of us, plus partners, and I wanted to run it by you first."

"Me?" His DCI smiled. "I am honoured, thank you. That sounds like it could be fun, although I'm not sure how many of us have plus ones."

"It doesn't matter if you don't," Rob replied as they made their way towards the incident room. They walked slowly so they could talk while the other members of the unit made their way by them and into the room. "I'll be alone."

"Okay then. Sounds good. Where would this be?"

"At my place."

"Your place?" Nailer narrowed his eyes, suspiciously. "Are you sure someone didn't put you up to this? What do they have on you?"

Rob grinned. "It's fine. I'll do the first one, and then hand it off to… Whoever wants to do it next."

"Alright. It sounds like you've got it all planned out. I'm in. When will this be?"

"I don't know. This weekend, maybe?"

"Saturday night?" Nailer suggested. "That would work for me."

"Sounds great," Rob replied, with a smile, pleased that his suggestion had gone down so well. As he turned towards the incident room where they held their morning briefings, Guy wandered over.

"Are we on?"

"We're on," Rob confirmed with a nod and a smile. As he walked into the briefing room. "Saturday night."

"What the hell's going on Saturday night?" Tucker asked.

"I'm having a gathering at mine," Rob announced. "You're all invited, partners too. I think it would be good for us to see each other outside of work and build on the trust we've already fostered."

"So, this is one of those God-forsaken team-building events?"

Rob shrugged. "I suppose you could say that, except this will have more alcohol and fewer trust falls."

"But, I'm fucking excellent at trust falls," Tucker remarked.

"No, you're not," Ellen protested. "You dropped me when we tried it at that conference."

"I wasn't ready," Tucker answered. "You went too damn soon."

"He literally counted you in."

"I know, but I wasn't ready," Tucker explained. "You should have warned me by shouting something… like, timber or something."

"I'm not a tree."

Tucker gave her side-eye. "Are you sure? You're pretty heavy."

"Piss off."

"Children, children," Nailer said, raising his hands for calm before he turned to Rob. "Thank you for the kind offer of the evening round at yours. It'll be fun."

"My pleasure," Rob replied. "I'm not sure what to do about food, though."

"We could just get a takeaway," Nick suggested. "Nice and easy."

Rob nodded. "I like that idea. I'll sort something out and get back to you. But you need to be at mine at seven PM on Saturday night."

"It's a date, sweety," Tucker commented with a suggestive smile and wink, making several people in the room laugh while everyone else confirmed their attendance.

"Right then, Rob," Nailer spoke up. "I think we've had something come in, right?"

"We have, sir," Rob answered and opened his laptop. He queued up a video before he spoke. "We've been informed about a violent robbery up in Worksop yesterday evening, which might be of interest to us. It seems that a group of four youths entered a shop and attacked the owner, before making off with a little over three hundred pounds of cash. I've got some CCTV footage here, so I'll play that first." He pressed play and turned the laptop to the team, who watched with interest.

The view was from outside, but they could see in through the window. It wasn't clear what was going on, but there was clearly movement inside the shop. Moments later, four youths, who looked to be in their late teens rushed out and ran for it, disappearing out of shot.

"Okay, there you go," Rob said. "Unfortunately, the camera inside the shop that would have caught the attack itself, was suffering from some technical difficulties, and failed to record anything. We've been through the footage we have, and there isn't a clear view of the attacker's face. But, he is wearing a fairly distinctive hoodie."

"So, we have no idea who they are?" Nick asked.

"Actually, we do. Earlier this morning, the attacker was identified as Curt Gates. The victim of the attack, Leroy Benson, claimed he didn't know who attacked him, but Leroy's wife, who found him after the attack, has said that the attacker was Curt Gates. It seems Leroy was reluctant to identify Curt, and has remained vague about what exactly happened."

"How is this shopkeeper? Is he okay?" Scarlett asked.

"He's fine. He's been in hospital overnight as a precaution due to the headwounds he suffered from the attack, but he's basically fine."

"Gates?" Nailer mused out loud. "As in...?"

98

"Aye," Rob confirmed. "He's part of the well-known Gates family and is Emory Gates's nephew."

"Now, that is interesting," Nailer confirmed. "And you're sure of that identification?"

"As sure as I can be," Rob confirmed. "Leroy's reluctance to speak to us and identify Curt only supports the idea that this is the Gates family." Spotting several blank faces in the assembled team, he thought he should explain himself. "Emory Gates is why this robbery, which would usually be handled by local CID has been handed to us. Emory is a high-ranking member of the Mason gang. We believe he works directly for one of the Mason brothers, probably Sean, and he's someone we've been after for a very long time. He's suspected of moving and selling drugs, people trafficking, blackmail, extortion, kidnapping, the list goes on. However, he's also a very slippery man, and we've never been able to pin any of these things on him. He works through others, directing from on-high without getting his hands dirty."

"So, what are you proposing?" Guy asked.

"Well, given that he's related to Emory and engaged in criminal activity..." Rob paused to see if anyone would catch on.

"You're hoping you can use Curt to get to Emory," Scarlett piped up, taking the words out of his mouth. "And strike a blow against the Masons."

99

"Exactly. From what we know about Curt from previous encounters, he's something of a loudmouth, always boasting about his family and who he knows."

Scarlett's smile was brimming with enthusiasm. "Alright, let's do it. Where is he?"

"We have a known address which is confirmed by the Bensons," Rob replied. "Scarlett and Nick, I want you two with me. We'll go and pick him up. Ellen, Tucker, Guy, I need you to do some digging. I want to know anything and everything about Curt. I want to know if there's any kind of leverage there that we can use to turn him into an informant."

"On it," Ellen confirmed.

"Will do, boss," Tucker added.

"Not a problem," Guy agreed. "What about the others who were with Curt. Do we know who they are?"

"Not yet," Rob answered. "But you might find that out during your research."

"I'll see what I can find," Ellen confirmed.

"Alright, let's go," Rob said, and within moments, they were marching out of the office and making their way to the carpool.

"Are we doing this alone?" Nick asked as they made their way through the station.

"We'll call in some uniform on our way over to back us up," Rob replied. "There's always a risk of us walking into something we didn't plan for."

"Good shout," Nick agreed.

"And you think this guy can lead us to this Mason gang member?" Scarlett asked. "Emory?"

"I hope so," Rob answered. "He's Curt's family, so I think we have a chance. I just don't know how close they are."

"Hopefully, very." Scarlett's face was a mask of determination, with her jaw set and her brow furrowed.

Within ten minutes, they were in the car and heading north, making their way towards Worksop and the home of Curt Gates. As they pushed through the country roads, Nick called to organise a patrol car, making sure it would meet them close by so as not to arouse any suspicion too early.

They needed the element of surprise to make this go as smoothly as possible.

Pulling into a residential street lined with terraces and semi-detached houses, Rob put on some speed to get partway along the road as quickly as possible while still being safe. The marked car kept pace behind them, pulling up close as Rob skidded to the stop.

He jumped out and checked the house numbers, doubled checking he had the right one by glancing at the neighbours to confirm the sequence.

"Number nine," he said, pointing as a uniformed officer pulled an enforcer from the boot of their car. The black-clad officer jogged with the big red battering ram up to the front door, where he paused and checked behind him, waiting for the go signal.

After a quick check to ensure everyone was in place, Rob nodded, and the constable went to work.

Three loud bangs later, and the door was open.

Rob rushed inside with Scarlett and Nick hot on his heels. Shouts of "Police" echoed through the small house as Rob ran into the front room to find a surprised-looking woman sitting up on the sofa, her mouth wide.

"Where's Curt?" Rob shouted as Scarlett pressed on. She pointed towards the back of the house. Rob nodded as shouts and yells echoed from the back room. Rob rushed in to find Scarlett gripping Curt by the neck.

She slammed him against the wall. "You're screwed now," she growled.

"Get her off me," Curt yelled.

"You wish." Rob watched in shock as Scarlett pulled him forward and twisted his arm. He dropped to the floor with a grunt, face down, before Scarlett jumped on him, pressing her knee into the side of his face and neck. "Don't you bloody move."

"Damn, girl," Nick exclaimed.

"Aaaagh, she's hurting me," Curt gasped. "Get her off."

"Constable," Rob yelled. "What the hell?"

"He's with the Masons," she said while fitting a pair of cuffs to Curt as if that explained why she was sitting on top of a man dressed only in a t-shirt, socks and boxers. It was quite the sight, but more concerning to Rob was Scarlett's behaviour.

Rob scowled at her but said nothing more about it. "Alright, get off him. He's not going anywhere."

"You're damn right," she hissed, standing up. She dragged Curt up too.

Curt scoffed at her. "Fucking feds, doing whatever the fuck you want."

"The feds?" Scarlett asked, amused. "This is Britain, not the USA."

"Whatever," Curt replied as they moved him into the front room.

"Curt! What the bloody hell have you done now?" his mother asked.

"Nothin'," he protested. "I ain't done shit."

"I bet."

Rob set him on the sofa. "We're arresting you on suspicion of robbery and assault…"

"What?" his mother exclaimed. "You bloody idiot. What the hell did you do that for? Jesus Christ!"

103

"I didn't do it," Curt replied. "You won't find nothin' in here, either."

"Sir?"

Rob turned as one of the uniformed officers appeared from upstairs and handed him a photo. It showed Curt standing dramatically, holding a realistic-looking firearm. "Well, damn. Where's the gun, Curt?"

"There ain't no gun," Curt shot back before he turned to his mum. "He's lying."

"You really are an idiot," his mum said in despair.

"I... I didn't..." He sighed. "Fuck. I'll be fine. You'll see." Curt turned to Rob. "I'm not going down for this. Just you watch. I have friends."

Rob grinned. "Oh, I hope so."

Curt frowned. "What?"

Taking a breath, Rob moved closer to Curt, where he sat on the sofa's edge and crouched before him. "The man you attacked in the shop? His name is Leroy, and he's in hospital now. His wife is distraught and worried sick. She can't work, which means they have no money coming in, and then there are their children. Leroy has two kids, a boy and a girl. Can you imagine what this is doing to them?"

Curt grimaced and looked away.

"You utter bastard," his mum hissed at him. "I don't even recognise you anymore. You'd better not turn out like..." She trailed off with a sigh.

"How do you think you'll cope in prison?" Rob pressed. "Do you think you'll enjoy it? You've never been, have you?"

Curt's eyes darted around. Rob could see the fear in them, and knew he'd touched a nerve.

"Yeah, I thought so. Not looking forward to an encounter in the shower then, I take it?"

"That won't—"

Rob gave him a look that cut him short. "What? Won't happen to you? Is that it? Do you really believe that? Do you think they care who you're related to? But hey, let's say they do... The Masons have enemies too, you know, and you could become a way for them to send a message, if you catch my drift."

"What do you want?"

Rob smiled. "We'll talk at the custody suite." He turned to Scarlett. "Caution him."

Curt flinched as Scarlett took a step closer. "I want my lawyer."

"Of course you do," Rob muttered.

13

Slumped into a chair, Rob waited with Scarlett and Nick as Curt was put through the system, ready for his interview. They just needed his solicitor to show up before they could begin the questioning.

"He was terrified of you," Nick said off to his left, on the other side of Scarlett.

She shrugged. "Yeah. Sorry about that. I just saw red."

"You need to be careful," Rob said, turning to her. "You can't just attack suspects if they have a possible links to the Masons."

"I know. I'm sorry."

Rob sighed. "I trust you, Scarlett, you know that, and I'm trusting that you'll get a handle on this impulsive behaviour. I know you've got a bone to pick with the Masons, just like the rest of us, but you can't go around assaulting people."

"And if you do, don't do it in front of a senior officer," Nick added with a smile.

Scarlett smirked.

Rob let out a dramatic sigh. "Jesus's hairy bollocks."

"You sound like Tucker," Nick remarked.

"Where is that solicitor? We need to be in there," Scarlett groused. Fidgeting in her seat, she was clearly frustrated. "I think you hit a nerve with him back at the house."

"Maybe," Rob answered. "We'll see how this develops. I've laid the groundwork, so we just need to build on that. I think we can turn him."

"Mmm," Scarlett grumbled. "But what if his hotshot lawyer gets in the way?"

"Then we'll deal with it," Rob answered, doing his best to sound unconcerned. "Let's see how this pans out, shall we?"

"Well, well, well, you three do look like a motley crew," said a familiar voice.

Rob looked up to see Matilda Greenwood, a duty solicitor they regularly worked with. She carried a bag over her shoulder and a leather-bound notepad and clipboard in her hands. She stopped a few feet away and smiled down at him. "Lovely to see you again, Rob. How've you been?"

"Yeah, okay, thanks. You're not here for Curt Gates, are you? We're waiting on his solicitor."

"No, I'm not." She shrugged. "Sorry to disappoint."

"That's okay," he replied, glancing at Scarlett and Nick, who were both aware of the flirting between them. Talking to her with them watching made him uncomfortable. "How's things with you? I've not seen you since..."

107

"A couple of weeks? I've not gone anywhere, Rob. I am around. Are you sure you're not the one playing hard-to-get?"

"Err," he stammered, aware that his colleagues were listening.

Matilda smiled. She seemed to be enjoying this. "Anyway, I can't hang around and chat all day, I've got a client to… Oh…"

She watched a man walk by, wearing a tailored suit while carrying a briefcase. He paid little attention to them and moved deeper into the building.

"What's wrong?"

Matilda frowned at Rob. "Who did you say your suspect was?"

"Curt Gates, why?"

"Not a Mason, then?"

Rob glanced after the lawyer and then back to Matilda. Should he disclose some of the details surrounding Curt's arrest? He debated it with himself for a second, before choosing to throw caution to the wind. "Our suspect has links to them."

"Right. Well then, I think that's your lawyer." She nodded towards the man.

"That guy?" Rob asked.

They all looked.

"Chance Bentley," Matilda said. "He's the new hotshot solicitor that's joined the law firm the Mason family always use. Word is, he's good at what he does."

"Shit." Rob watched as Chance disappeared through a door.

"That's not good," Nick remarked. "Looks like someone's pulling some strings."

"Well, I'll leave you guys to deal with him. I've got an appointment to get to. See you later. Call me if you fancy a drink again, Rob."

"Will do," he replied, feeling his cheeks flush with embarrassment before they all said goodbye.

Sitting back in his seat, Rob caught Scarlett giving him a questioning look with her eyebrows raised. He smiled back but said nothing and looked away. At a guess, she wanted to talk about Matilda, but he wasn't having that conversation right now.

They all slumped back into their seats until, ten minutes later, Rob's phone rang, and the screen identified the caller as DCI Nailer.

Rob answered the call. "Hey."

"Are you in the interview yet?"

"Not yet," Rob replied. "His lawyer's arrived, though."

"Okay, then you need to leave the interview to someone else. We've had a walk-in at Central. She's asking for you and Scarlett. She won't talk to anyone else."

"Who?" Rob asked.

"Vivian Aston," Nailer answered.

"Vivian?" The name rang a bell, but he struggled to place it.

"She was a witness in the Peter Orleton case," Nailer explained. "You put her up in that hotel."

"Oh, crap, yes, we did. Has she said why she's there?"

"Apparently, she's witnessed a murder and will only talk to you and Scarlett. So I want you to get down to Central and see what all the fuss is about. Nick can take over the interview. I'll send Guy over to help him."

"Alright," Rob answered, annoyed that he wasn't going to see this arrest through. "We're on our way." He hung up.

"What's going on?" Scarlett asked.

"Do you remember Vivian Aston, the homeless woman we put up in a hotel?"

She smiled. "How could I forget?"

"She's turned up at Central, saying she's witnessed a murder. Nailer wants us to check it out because she'll only talk to you and me."

Nick gave him a look. "And what do I do?"

110

"Guy's coming over. You need to work on Curt for me and see if you can get him to see sense. Okay? We need him as an informant if we're going to get to Emory."

"Will do," Nick confirmed. "Have fun."

"Not likely." Scarlett rose from her seat with a huff. She didn't seem happy. "Right, come on then, let's get this over with." She led the way out of the building, and Rob followed.

"I know you wanted to be in there."

"Yeah, well, shit happens." As they reached the car, Scarlett paused before opening the door. "But if she's wasting our time..."

"Yeah, I know." Rob nodded in agreement before he climbed into the driver's seat beside Scarlett.

"She didn't last time, though."

"No, she didn't," Rob answered as he pulled out of the parking space and set off into the city.

"I take it nothing happened between you and Matilda," Scarlett said partway to their destination.

Rob grinned. "I was wondering when you'd bring that up."

"I bet."

He took a moment to organise his thoughts. "Well, no. Nothing happened. We had a drink, but that was all." Rob sighed. "After everything that happened with my family recently, I just... I can't put her through that. It's not fair." He paused, but when he sensed Scarlett was about to answer

111

him, he decided to get in first. "And yes, I know. It's not for me to make these choices for her. She deserves to make them for herself, but that would mean I'd need to be brutally honest with her about everything, so..."

"Yes, it would," Scarlett confirmed. "But, does she not deserve that? She's clearly interested in you. Do you like her?"

"I don't think about it much."

"Liar," she snapped. "It's a simple question, do you like her?"

"Alright, yes. I do, but..."

"But what?" She took a breath. "You need to talk to her, Rob. You need to bring her into the conversation and let her know what's going on with you. Relationships are built on trust, you know?"

"But what if my brothers get wind of it, and target her?"

"Again, that's her choice. But if she knows the dangers and what to look out for, she's pre-warned and pre-armed. I'm sure she can take care of herself."

"Yeah, probably."

"Then do me a favour, talk to her."

Rob grumbled. "I'll think about it." He sighed. "I've missed these pep talks from you."

She smirked. "Yeah. Sorry. I know I've not been around, and I've been distant these last two days since coming back but… I just… I have a lot on my plate right now."

"You don't need to explain yourself to me," Rob answered. "I understand."

"Thanks."

It didn't take them long to reach Nottingham Central, Rob's old station, and make their way inside. Within moments, a uniformed officer showed them through to a side room.

"She won't say anything else," the officer explained. "Only that she's witnessed a murder and will only speak to you two. That's it."

"Alright, thanks," Rob answered and gave Scarlett a look before he walked into the room.

"Hey, Viv," he said to the woman perched on the edge of one of the soft seats. Her fingers were interlaced, and her right leg bobbed up and down like a nervous jackhammer.

"You took your time getting here," she complained, annoyed.

"We don't work in the building anymore," Rob explained. "We're north of the city these days."

"Oh, right…" She looked sheepish. "Sorry."

"How have you been keeping?" Scarlett asked as they both took seats opposite.

113

Vivian shrugged and pulled a face. "Alright, I guess."

"We've been told you've seen something, right?" Rob asked. He didn't want to put words in her mouth in case something had been lost or changed as the message was passed from person to person before it reached them.

Vivian nodded. "Yeah, I did. I saw a murder. I saw someone get their throat cut."

"Really? Where and when was this? Run me through what happened."

"Alright," Vivian answered. "It was a couple of nights ago, on Sunday. Me and Aaron were under the Trent Bridge, in one of the tunnels there, when this kid came and sat with us. I got talking to him, but Aaron didn't like him and stormed off. So I went after Aaron to talk him around. I wasn't gone long, but when we got back to the bridge, there was a van on the other side. The kid was inside the back of it, bleeding from his neck. I only saw the back of the man that must have done it as he closed the doors and drove off." Vivian shrugged. "That's it."

"Right, so let me get this straight," Rob said. "You saw what you think was a murder on Sunday night, but you waited until Wednesday to report it. Is that right? Why?"

"I know," Vivian moaned. "I should have come sooner, but Aaron, he… He convinced me not to come. He said you'd already know and that I was wasting my time, you know? He doesn't trust you guys."

"Okay, and you said this happened under the Trent Bridge?"

"That's right. There was so much blood. It's still there, actually. I can show you."

"Alright, let's go for a drive. You can show us where it happened, okay?"

"No problem."

14

With his hands stuffed into his pockets, Tucker walked along the central path through the Forest Recreation ground, just north of the centre of Nottingham. It was a spring day, and the trees were already sporting fresh green leaves, while the massive grassy fields looked lush and welcoming.

People walked and cycled along the path, going about their business as Tucker spied the benches up ahead, looking for a familiar face.

He'd not seen the guy for a while and was honestly surprised when he agreed to meet. But Tucker wasn't about to look a gift horse in the mouth and got down into the city as quickly as he could.

Partway through the park, he spotted a familiar hunched-over, skinny figure sitting on a bench, waiting.

As Tucker approached, the skinny man glanced his way before quickly looking away and shifting uncomfortably. Tucker made his way over in a lazy wander before finally lowering himself onto the bench and sitting back. He didn't look at the man beside him, and he didn't look at Tucker.

To the outside observer, they were two random people with nothing in common who didn't know each other.

Tucker scanned the field for a moment, looking over the various people sitting on the grass, reading or talking, before finally saying something.

"Alright, Kev-o?"

"Tuck," Kev-o answered. "Yeah, I'm alright. What's this all about?"

Straight down to business then, was it? Alright, he thought. "I'm looking for some info, and I think you might be my guy."

"Do you?"

"You're up on the Masons, right, and what they're up to?"

"I might be. Depend on what's in it for me," Kev-o answered. "Make it worth my while, and I might be your guy."

"I've got five tons that say you're my man. But if it's good info."

"Five? Alright, go on then, lay it on me."

"Curt Gates. What can you tell me about him?"

Kev-o glanced at him with a furrowed brow, before turning away again. "Curt? Don't you mean Emory?"

"Nope. Curt."

"Shit. Alright then. Curt, yeah. He's a nobody playing at being a somebody if you know what I mean. He's Emory's nephew, and he's riding on his uncle's coattails. Thinks he's Mister Big and all that. He keeps showing off, thinking his

117

family will always get him out of trouble. Frankly, he's a liability."

"Why? Because he's throwing his weight around?"

"No. He ain't got no weight. He's a liability cos' of his mouth. He's always going on about what he knows, like."

"Anything current?"

Kev-o leaned a little closer and inclined his head. "Yeah. He says there's a big deal going down between the Masons and one of the cartels operating out of Columbia. It's about drugs and shit. I don't know when, where, or with who, but Curt says he knows. Could all be bullshit, of course, but that's for you to work out."

"Are you sure about this info?"

"I'd bet my life on it. What do you reckon? Is that worth five?"

Tucker had been listening with interest, and his mind was already racing with possibilities about what this could mean. "Aye," Tucker answered. "That's worth five, alright." He pulled an envelope from his inside pocket and placed it on the bench beside him. Kev-o reached out and took the packet.

"Lovely-jubbly. Thank you very much."

"My pleasure. Take care of yourself, alright?"

"Will do, matey. Kev-o's getting high tonight."

118

With that, he was up and off, striding away from Tucker, who remained on the bench. A tingle of excitement about what this could mean rippled up his spine as he pondered how they might take advantage of this info.

He needed to get back and inform the team.

***

Madeleine sat on the slope, close to a tree, less than a hundred metres behind Tucker. Various groups and individuals spread out over the hill, allowing her to easily blend in. There was no reason to suspect she was anything other than a local taking a break in the park, just like all the others.

With Tucker's contact gone, Madeleine turned off the parabolic mic concealed in the shadow between her and her bag and removed the attached earbud.

She'd heard some of what they'd discussed, enough to get the basic gist, but that wasn't the focus of her investigation.

Instead, she stuffed the equipment back into her bag and waited for Tucker to be on his way.

So far, she had no reason to suspect him as anything other than an honest police officer… But she'd been wrong before.

119

15

Rob drove south along Maid Marian Way before turning east onto Canal Street and then south again, taking London Road towards the Trent Bridge. The route was intimately familiar to him, as he'd driven home this way for years while working at Central. In fact, the location of this supposed murder could be seen from his apartment on the other side of the river. But how many people would notice a white van going about its business?

They were so common these days that they just blended into the background. It was like the idea that if you wanted to go unnoticed, you just put on a high-vis vest, and everyone would assume you were there officially and doing your job.

Rob had heard multiple accounts of people being able to walk into places that you either needed a ticket for or were barred to the public just by wearing one of these luminous vests.

"Thank you for bringing this to our attention," Scarlett said to Vivian as Rob navigated south. "I know we're not the most trusted organisation for the homeless, so…"

"Yeah, well, you treated me right the last time," Vivian answered from the back seat.

"And we'll do right by you this time, too," she reassured their witness. "But we need to confirm what you've told us."

Rob saw Vivian shrug in his rearview mirror and swapped a sideways glance with Scarlett. "It's not that we don't trust you," he added. "But, there is a process to all this."

"Aye, I know," she said, reassuring him. Vivian sniffed and wiped her nose. "You know, we deal with his kind of shit every day. We get abused and hurt all the time, but no one cares."

"I care," Scarlett cut in. "We both do."

"Scarlett's right," Rob added. "No one should have to put up with abuse, no matter what your social standing is."

"Yeah, nice sentiment, but it don't hold up to much scrutiny, does it? If a rich bastard gets robbed, you're all over it, but if I get robbed, no one cares. We're just ignored."

"Have you been robbed?" Rob asked, curious to know how she'd answer.

"Not recently," Vivian answered. "But what I saw Sunday night, I've heard whispered about before. Others have told me about people going missing. It's just like last time with that hunter. It's been going on for a few weeks at least."

"You should have come to us," Scarlett suggested. "We'd listen. We know you're trustworthy."

"Are you sure?"

"Of course."

121

Vivian seemed to think about this for a moment. "Okay, well, there's also been some local teenagers causing trouble on my patch too. They're a nightmare."

"Anti-social behaviour is a crime. You should have reported it."

"I just did."

"Fair point. However, it's not something our unit deals with. I can pass it along, though, if you like?"

Vivian laughed. "Sure, go for it. It won't make much of a difference, though," she groused.

"You don't know that," Rob replied. "You came to us with this murder kidnap you witnessed."

"That's a bit different to kids being a nuisance, though, isn't it. It's in a different league."

"You're right, it is, and with our lack of personnel and resources, we do have to prioritise," Scarlett replied. "We shouldn't have to in an ideal world, but we don't live in one of those."

"In an ideal world, I wouldn't be living on the sodding street." Vivian sighed. "Thanks, though. I know you're just trying to help."

"No worries," Scarlett replied. "I'll make sure Rob passes along your details and complaint to the relevant department."

As Rob drove over the Trent Bridge, he looked left towards the Forest ground and a side road along the river. "Down there, right?"

"Yeah," Vivian confirmed.

"Alright." Rob took the first left at the end of the bridge and drove along the narrow road down to the river's edge. He pulled in and turned the engine off at the first gap in the parked cars. "Right then, Vivian. Lead us to it."

They climbed out and crossed onto a footpath that led down, back towards the bridge. Vivian led the way. As he followed Vivian, Rob looked back up the river and picked out his apartment on the opposite bank, his block being one of four squat modern buildings right on the river's edge.

As they walked, Rob spotted tyre tracks in the patchy grass beside the river, where a vehicle of some kind had driven. He stopped to take a better look and crouched down beside them.

"Were these made by your van," he called out to Vivian, pointing to the tracks.

"Shit, yeah. The van did that," Vivian confirmed. "It's where they went."

"Alright." Rob pulled out his phone and took a few snaps in case anything happened to this evidence before they managed to get Scene of Crime down here. He turned to Vivian. "What else is there?"

"It's over here," she said and walked them along the pathway to the bridge. The tarmac passed through a round tunnel that threaded through the bridge beneath the road. To that tunnel's left, further from the river, was a second tunnel. It seemed marginally smaller than the first but still big enough to stand up in, and you needed to walk up a shallow incline of muddy grass to enter it.

Rob could already make out some scattered debris inside it that the council had yet to clear away.

"We were in there when we met Malcom."

"Malcom. You know the victim's name?"

"Oh, yeah. I forgot to say. He told me when we spoke."

"Useful to know," he remarked.

"Rob," Scarlett called out. She was standing at the entrance of the main tunnel, looking at the floor.

"What's up?" As he approached, she crouched and pointed. He could make out a dark stain, like a splatter mark on the pavement that had been mostly worn away by passing pedestrians and the elements. But this brownish-red stain hadn't been totally destroyed.

"Is this what I think it is?" Scarlett asked Vivian.

She nodded. "That's it. There's more over here on the cardboard. I moved it into the tunnel to protect it from the rain."

"Good thinking," Rob remarked.

124

"There's some splatters on the wall too, look." She pointed.

"Shit, it's everywhere," Rob muttered, feeling a chill race down his spine. Vivian, it seemed, wasn't lying.

"We need to call this in and get it cordoned off," Scarlett said, standing up.

"See, I told you," Vivian said, looking smug.

"You did," Rob admitted as he pulled out his phone again.

"So, how about it, then? Hmm?"

Rob glanced up and frowned at her. Was she angling for something? "How about what?"

"That hotel room. You need to find me again to talk to me, right? So I'll need a room somewhere."

Rob smirked at her self-confidence. "We'll see. But you're coming back to the station, that's for sure. We need to talk more about what you saw."

"Sure, no problem."

Rob placed the call.

16

"Miller," Guy said as he marched into the custody suit and nodded to Nick. "Hope I didn't keep you too long. Traffic's a nightmare."

"No, you're good," Nick replied.

"So, Curt Gates, right?"

"That's right," Nick confirmed. "Do we have much on him yet?"

"No," Guy replied. "Just his criminal record and what we have on file. Ellen's pulled some stuff off social media, but there's nothing incriminating yet, and Tucker's yet to come back to us about these informants he knows."

"And nothing more on the robbery itself?"

"We've got officers out going door to door, but so far, we don't have anything to corroborate the victim statements from Leroy and his wife. No one's talking, it seems."

"The fucking Masons," Nick muttered under his breath, frustrated by the fear their gang members fostered in the local community. "He'll end up released pending further investigation, and then we've lost control of him."

Guy shrugged. "We're bound by the law."

"Shit. Right, we'll see what we can do," Nick groused. "Curt's spoken to his lawyer, so he's ready to see us."

"Lead the way then," Guy replied.

Nick nodded and walked deeper into the building towards the interview suites, leading Guy through the security doors. "I hear that you were the one to suggest this group meet-up to Rob. Is that right?"

"Yeah," Guy confirmed. "I thought we should all get to know one another, and when I saw Rob's apartment the other day, I knew it would be perfect."

Nick nodded in agreement. "Yeah, it is nice, right?"

"Lovely. Very modern. His neighbour's a bit of alright too."

"Oh, you met Erika, did you?" He'd seen Erika a couple of times and was quite taken with her himself. She was a good-looking woman, and he was a little jealous that Rob lived next door to her.

"Aye. I certainly did."

Nick grinned at the knowing look on his colleague's face. "You like then, I take it?"

"I wouldn't say no, put it that way," Guy replied. He smiled and then paused for a moment and raised his hands. "Although, I wouldn't want to step on your toes."

Nick laughed and then shook his head. "I don't think I'm in any position to request such a thing."

"So you've got no objection to me asking her out?"

"Not if you get there first."

"Challenge accepted," Guy said with a grin and a point of his finger.

Nick shook his head at Guy's comments. He wasn't Erika's boyfriend or anything, and all three of them were single as far as he knew, so he couldn't ban him from asking her out. Besides, Erika was quite capable of making up her own mind about who she'd date, and it might be that she preferred him anyway. Guy seemed quite keen on the idea, too, which caused a seed of jealousy to take root deep inside and start scratching at his brain. He'd been admiring Erika from afar for a while and found himself cursing his hesitancy to ask her out.

He wasn't sure what it was, but for whatever reason, he'd just not got around to popping the question, and now it looked like Guy might beat him to it.

Nick ground his teeth in frustration, but he had no one but himself to blame.

"Anything else I should know about this interview before we head in?" Guy asked.

"Only that our goal is to try and turn Curt into an informant. We made headway with this at the arrest, but he's been with his hotshot lawyer for a while now, so I'm not sure how he'll be. This could be futile, but we'll see what we can get."

Guy nodded. "Alright, lead the way."

They soon reached the interview room and walked in to find Curt sitting at a table with his lawyer, Chance Bentley.

"Afternoon," Nick said.

"Officers," Chance said in clipped tones, he sounded like he wasn't a fan of the police.

"I'm Detective Nick Miller, and this is Detective Guy Gibson."

"Mr Bentley," the solicitor said. He didn't seem keen to chat, but he offered his hand which Nick shook eagerly.

"A pleasure, I'm sure."

Guy merely nodded before settling himself into one of the chairs. Nick took the remaining seat and stole an appraising look at the pair opposite. They couldn't be more different. Chance was groomed, confident and displaying good posture, while Curt seemed sullen in his baggy clothes, slumped into the chair with his arms crossed, scowling at them.

Rifling through his notes to ensure he was ready, Nick looked up to see Chance waiting with a calm serenity that Nick found unnerving. He looked away and focused on the job at hand. They needed Curt to talk.

Once the machine was on and he'd run through introductions again for the benefit of the recording, he settled into his questions.

"So, what were you doing out on Retford Road in Worksop, Curt?"

He shrugged. "No comment."

Nick narrowed his eyes at the young man on the other side of the table, wondering if this was how this would go. "You were out with your mates, right?"

"No comment."

"Were you bored? I bet you were bored, weren't you. There's not a lot to do around there, is there?"

"No comment."

Nick stiffened at the third use of those two words, feeling frustrated. But he needed to continue. "Yeah, I thought as much. Who were you out with? Anyone we might know?"

"No comment."

"I see." Nick sighed. "Well, we know you were out there, Curt, because we have video evidence of it." Nick pulled out a printed screenshot from the CCTV camera that had recorded the group leaving the shop. "That's you, isn't it?"

Curt glanced down at the printout, but remained calm and repeated his favourite phrase. "No comment."

"Well, I think I recognise your hoodie. Look," Nick pointed to the image, "you're wearing the same one today."

Curt seemed to chew on the inside of his cheek. "No comment."

"Really? No comment? That's clearly you, Curt. Look, you can even see the date on the footage." Feeling his confidence grow, Nick adjusted his position as he settled into the role of the interrogator. He had no idea if he could get through to Curt, especially not with his lawyer right there. "It's obvious, and it will be to any jury. Here, look at this." Nick grabbed his tablet and opened up the queued video. He pressed play, and the exterior footage of the attack played on the small screen. "That's you, isn't it, in the shop. You and your mates attacking that poor shopkeeper. You put him in hospital, you know. You did some serious damage to him."

"No comment." Curt looked away, taking a particular interest in the wall.

"His wife and children had to see him in hospital, beaten and bruised. Can you imagine how stressful that would be, how upsetting it is for children? This won't be a day they easily forget."

Curt sighed and glared at Nick. "No comment."

"I'll tell you something else, too. I'll tell you how we know it's you. Would you like to know?"

Curt said nothing, and just stared back at him with dead eyes.

"We have a statement from the shopkeeper saying that he recognised you. They knew it was you because you live locally and you're a regular in that shop." Nick gave Curt a knowing look. "You didn't think this through, did you? You robbed the local shop, not realising that even with a mask on, they knew who you were. Was this a dare or something?"

"No comment."

"Alright," Nick said, leaning a little closer. It was time to lay it on thick, and see what he could get out of him. "I can see we're boring you, so let's get down to brass tacks, shall we? Because we know you did it, and no amount of 'no comments' will change that. In fact, it's only hurting your defence." Nick noticed Curt glance at his solicitor. "It's obvious you're guilty, and any jury will send you down for this. If this gets to court, you're going to jail, have no doubt about that. And I know you think this man here will get you off," Nick waved at the lawyer, "because of your uncle, Emory. But the evidence we have is damning, and we'll only find more. It won't matter how good your representation is. It'll be down to the court to decide what happens to you, not Mr Bentley, and not Emory. And believe me, we will make sure you go down for this."

Watching Curt closely, Nick could see him mulling it over as he contorted his lips in thought. Interestingly, he didn't say 'no comment' this time.

"That is," Nick continued, "unless you talk to us. Because it might be that we can work something out, you know?"

His lawyer tapped his shoulder and leaned in. Curt sat back, and Chance whispered something into his ear. When he was finished, Curt adjusted his position and coughed. "No comment"

Seeing the influence Chance had over Curt boiled Nick's blood. If he was Mason's new star lawyer—as Matilda had suggested—then frankly, he was phoning it in, in terms of legal representation. But, it didn't matter. That wasn't why he was here. He was here purely as a reminder to Curt as to where his loyalties should lie, and Chance would most likely report back to his employer after this interview. And Curt knew this.

If he agreed to cooperate with the police, Chance would likely tell the Masons, which could lead to dire consequences for Curt, family connections or not.

Nick silently grumbled to himself, feeling utterly frustrated and annoyed. This was probably a lost cause, but they had to try.

Glancing right, he met his partner's concerned gaze. Guy shrugged. Nick turned back to the two men opposite and pouted, annoyed. He glanced through his notes. There was so much more yet to talk about, such as the photo of him holding a gun, but first, Nick wanted to address his family connections more. "Tell me about Emory," Nick suggested, returning to his questions. "What's he doing these days? Working for the Mason brothers?"

"No comment."

17

Rob dragged himself into the EMSOU office on aching feet, silently grumbling that there was still most of the afternoon to go. They'd spent the last hour or so at the Trent Bridge, coordinating the Scene of Crime response team, cordoning off the area, and ensuring that the Crime Scene Investigators could do their job to the best of their ability.

It was full-on work, but once things were up and running and they had enough people on site, Rob was able to step back and let them get on with their job.

The scene suggested that whatever happened there involved a violent attack that resulted in massive blood loss. The sheer distance some of the blood had travelled hinted at either a struggle, arterial spray, or, most likely, both.

Whoever this Malcom was, Rob had severe doubts he was still alive.

After leaving the scene, they brought Vivian back to the station to make a statement to one of their civilian investigators about what she'd seen. As for the hotel, he didn't think they needed to put her up in another one when there were various homeless shelters that were better equipped and staffed.

As he wandered into the office with Scarlett in tow, he noticed that Nick and Guy's desks were still vacant, but Ellen was at hers, concentrating on her work.

She waved as they entered but didn't look up from what she was doing.

Scanning the scene for Tucker, Rob spotted him in the corner of the DCI's office, where Nailer was waving him over.

"Aye up," Rob remarked, turning back to Scarlett as she scraped her blonde hair into a fresh ponytail. "Looks like Nailer wants to talk to us,"

"Oh, alright," Scarlett replied and followed.

As he approached the door, Nailer made some odd gestures suggesting both come here and go away. Rob wasn't sure what he wanted, so just carried on and walked into the office with Scarlet close on his heels.

"What was all that about?" Rob mimicked Nailer's hand waving with a smile.

"I was trying to get just you to come over," Nailer explained before looking past him to Scarlett. "Sorry."

"No worries. That's okay," she said before turning to leave. "I can crack on with the paperwork."

Tucker sighed. "Actually, it's fine."

Rob frowned, glancing between the three of them, wondering what the issue was.

"Are you sure?" Nailer asked.

"I don't mind if you need me to disappear," Scarlett remarked.

"No, don't worry about it," Tucker reassured her. "You're good."

"Only if you're sure," Nailer said.

"I am," Tucker replied. "Close the door behind you."

Doing as he was told, Rob glanced across the room at Ellen and the smattering of civilian investigators in the main office as he closed the door, wondering what the secrecy was about. He turned back to the room. "What's up?"

"Tucker's informant came through for us," Nailer explained. "But we're keeping it quiet for the moment. Need to know only."

"I'm pretty sure I don't need to know," Scarlett said and backed towards the door.

Tucker smiled. "The very fact that you're saying that and offering to leave tells me everything I need to know. You're good, don't worry."

"Okay, if you're sure," Scarlett said with a shrug.

"So, what did you find out?" Rob asked, moving to a seat. The others followed suit, getting comfortable.

"It turns out," Nailer started, "that our friend Curt can't keep a secret."

Tucker continued, "My informant said that Curt has been blabbering about a meeting the Masons are having with a

136

Columbian cartel representative. There's talk of it being a big drugs deal."

"When?" Rob asked.

"That, I don't know, but apparently, Curt has been bragging that he knows."

"Shit," Rob muttered. "Okay, so how reliable is this informant of yours?"

"He's in the know," Tucker answered. "He's given me good information in the past."

"So, you trust him," Rob asked. He needed to be sure that whoever Tucker's informant was, he wasn't leading them on a wild goose chase.

"I do," Tucker confirmed, his voice even and confident.

"Good. So what's our next move?"

"For a start, we keep this quiet," Nailer replied. "We've had leaks and corrupt officers in the past, so it's need to know only." Nailer smiled at Scarlett. "Present company accepted."

Scarlett smiled, pointed, and made a clicking sound in her cheek. "Way to make me feel valued, Guv."

"Any time."

"Need to know only, sound good," Rob answered. "What about Nick? He's been leading the interview with Curt, and I'd trust him with my life. I would suggest he needs to know."

"If you think that's a good idea," Tucker replied.

"I think it might be."

"We could call Nick," Nailer suggested. "We could let him know and see if he can use this info in his interview with Curt."

"That's not a good idea," Rob replied.

"How come?" Nailer asked. "He might be able to use it."

"He might, but there's other issues."

"Like what?"

"While waiting for Curt's solicitor, Matilda Greenwood was talking to us. She pointed out Curt's lawyer as he walked in, saying he was the Mason's latest hotshot employee. I have no idea if she's right, but if she is, this lawyer can't find out what we know about this deal."

"Point taken," Nailer agreed. "Okay, let's wait until Nick is back, and we can talk to him properly."

"When you do, I think you should make him the lead on this case. He's doing the interviews, and he's one rank below me. I'll do my best to keep abreast of this, but I think Sergeant Miller would be a solid SIO."

"What about you?" Tucker asked Rob.

"I'm going to have my hands full."

Nailer shifted in his seat. "The walk-in I sent your way?"

"Aye," Rob confirmed.

"Did you speak to her about the murder she said she witnessed?"

"We did. Turns out that she was probably telling the truth. She witnessed something, and whatever it was, it was violent."

"Go on," Nailer urged.

"Apparently, she met a young man by the name of Malcom in the tunnels that pass through the base of the Trent Bridge. They talked for a while, but Vivian was pulled away for a few minutes. When she got back, she saw Malcom with his throat cut, in the back of a van, on the other side of the bridge. He was driven away by an unknown man. There's evidence of massive blood loss and tyre tracks at the scene, backing up Vivian's story. So I think we're onto something."

"Alright," Nailer replied. "So we know what we're doing. When Nick comes back, I'll get him to work with Tucker while you two focus on this Trent Bridge attack."

"Perfect," Rob replied. "I'll get Ellen on board and grab Guy too."

"Sounds like a plan," Nailer agreed. "Off you go then."

Filing out of the office, Rob wandered over to his desk and noticed Ellen looking up.

"Everything okay?" she asked, clearly curious.

"Fine, yeah. We were working out what we're all doing. In fact, why don't you come over here? You, Guy and Scarlett, are with me."

"Sure," Ellen replied and sauntered over. Rob collapsed into his chair, and Ellen perched on the edge of a desk while Scarlett took her seat, one desk over. Rob then explained the discovery of this possible murder site to Ellen, bringing her up to speed.

"So, right now, the only lead we have is the name, Malcom. So I suggest we start there. We'll also need to see what traffic cams and CCTV we can find to see if this van was caught on any of them, too. So, let's get hunting."

"Way ahead of you," Scarlett replied. "Looks like we had a misper report the day before last. The name of the missing person is reported as Malcom Hooper, a fifteen-year-old from Hyson Green. I have a description of what he was wearing and a photo too. The report was filed by his mother, Tess."

"Excellent. Print that all off. We'll go and have a chat with Viv, and see if she recognises the photo. Ellen, while we do that, can you start digging into Malcom's life to see what you can find?"

"Will do," she confirmed. "How about a press release to try and get some attention on it?"

"Go for it. Can't hurt," Rob agreed as he got to his feet, feeling a little more energised. "Right, let's go and see what Viv has to say."

"Looks like it's all kicking off again," Scarlett remarked as they walked through the Lodge.

140

"Aye," Rob agreed. "I reckon someone said the Q word, and now we're paying the price."

Scarlett smirked as they approached the room where Vivian was making her statement.

"How's it going?" Rob asked as he walked in.

"Good," the Civilian Investigator, Annie Faulkner, said from where she sat to one side of Vivian. "We're almost done."

Rob nodded and briefly wrinkled his nose as he noticed Vivian's stale smell in this enclosed, poorly ventilated-space. She could do with a shower. "Okay, good. Vivian, we need you to take a look at something for us. But before I show it to you, can you describe Malcom to us again?"

"Yeah. He was young, maybe fifteen or sixteen, with dark brown curly hair. Good looking boy, actually."

"And what was he wearing?"

"Dark clothing, I think. Tracksuit bottoms, trainers and a black puffer jacket."

Comparing her words to the print-off in his hands, Rob was satisfied that the description matched and showed her Malcom's photo. She took a moment to peer at it before she nodded. "Yeah, that's him. Christ, poor kid. He didn't deserve that."

"No one does," Rob agreed and turned to the investigator. "Right, we'll leave you to finish off. See if you can arrange somewhere for her to sleep tonight. There's probably a shelter nearby that can have her for a few nights and get her cleaned up."

Annie nodded. "Will do."

"See you later, Viv. Thank you for everything you've done today, and look after yourself, alright?"

Vivian nodded. "Will do."

"What now?" Scarlett asked as they marched back along the corridor.

"I think we'll go and talk to his parents, see what they have to say for themselves."

18

"Did you sort it?" Rob asked as Scarlett ended the call. He glanced over at her, in the passenger seat.

"Yep, all sorted. They'll send someone over to swab for DNA at Malcom's house later today."

"Perfect," Rob replied, satisfied.

"Nailer's being very cautious about the information Tucker's informant revealed," Scarlett said.

He drove south into Nottingham, heading to Hyson Green, a large residential and ethnically diverse area just north of the city centre, right next door to Forest Fields and Radford. The area suffered from some of the worst crime rates in Nottingham, and several roads were very deprived. It was also home to one of Nottingham's biggest and most violent gangs, the Hyson Green Killers, or HGK for short.

"I think it's a natural reaction to recent events," Rob replied. "We've dealt with several corrupt officers in the employ of the Masons, so if there's any more, we don't want them to get hold of this information."

"Oh, I know, I get it. I'm just not sure why I was in there. I'm hardly key to this operation."

"You're more valuable than you give yourself credit for." Rob glanced her way with a meaningful look."

143

"He didn't *have* to let me into that office."

"But the fact that he did should fill you with confidence. Nailer and Tucker clearly trust you with this."

"I guess. But do they not trust Ellen? She was right outside the office."

"I don't think that's about trust. It's about keeping the pool of people who know small. The fewer people know, the better. It just makes keeping the information hidden easier and the list of suspects, if it does leak, shorter. I trust all of the EMSOU officers…" Rob paused and then decided to qualify that statement, "to one degree or another."

"Oh yeah?"

"Well, I know some better than others," Rob explained with a shrug. "I've known Nailer for decades and would trust him with my life. Nick too. I've worked with him for years, and even though he can be a little reckless at times, I know he's got my back."

"Whereas, you've only worked with me for a few months," Scarlett remarked with a wry smile.

Rob shrugged. "This shouldn't come as a surprise."

Scarlett chuckled. "It doesn't. I'm just enjoying dragging you over the coals. I would never expect you to trust me as much as you trust someone you've known for years. That's insanity."

"Thanks. Although, for the record, I do trust you."

"Even though I hate your family?"

"That only makes me trust you more."

"Aww, thanks," Scarlett replied. "And yeah, you're right, I shouldn't have attacked Curt when we arrested him. I was out of line."

"You were. Have you been taking lessons from Nick, because that's more his style."

"No," she answered.

"Well, Curt seems a little dim, so I think you'll get away with it, but you need to rein that bollocks in, because a more savvy criminal could have you reprimanded or fired over that."

Scarlett blushed, her cheeks going as red as her name. "You've been mates with Nick for a while, haven't you?"

"He was my partner for most of the time I was in Central and always stood up for me. He always went the extra mile."

"He's former military, right?"

"Yeah. He served in Iraq and Afghanistan, I think. He's told me some stories, and it sounds bat-shit crazy compared to what we do."

"Have you had to rein him in over the years?"

"A bit. He knows where the line is, but again, I trust him, and that means everything."

"Of course."

Rob smiled back at her. She'd proven herself several times over the few months he'd worked with her. Not least of which was most recently when Mason-affiliated gang members kidnapped one of her close friends and tried to blackmail Scarlett into working for them. And even then, she'd stood up for her principles and said no when she had every chance to agree to their terms. That choice led to the murder of her friend and her current vendetta, but it spoke volumes about Scarlett's integrity and how trustworthy she was.

Rob couldn't fault her in that regard and didn't know many people who would have done what she'd done, but what Scarlett had understood was that it wouldn't have stopped with one favour or one threat. Once they had you, it was so much harder to break free. She'd be led down a very dark path that could lead to many more of her friends and colleagues getting hurt or even killed.

Scarlett knew that. She'd accepted the dire consequences and said no.

They continued south and drove onto the residential back streets of Hyson Green, pulling onto Hawksley Road and then around onto Maple Street, where they found a spot to pull over, close to Malcom's parent's house.

Hemmed in on either side by rows of three-story terrace housing, each with its own one-metre-deep, walled concrete

146

front yard, Rob took a moment to soak in the atmosphere and chewed the inside of his cheek in consternation. He didn't get a good feeling.

Looking north, down the street, a huge white tower block loomed over them, adding to the feeling of being crushed. In the same direction, at the end of the road, was a small skate park with ramps and half-pipes. Everything in there was covered in graffiti. Not a single surface remained untouched by the local youths wanting to make their mark. Rob could see movement down there as kids played and shouted, their voices echoing up the street.

Looking around, he eyed some of the local residents going about their business, from a stooped old man whose furtive glances towards the skate park spoke volumes about the power dynamic of the area to the two hooded youths who swaggered down the other side of the street.

As Scarlett walked around the car and joined him on the pavement, Rob evaluated the nearby houses and quickly spotted the one belonging to Malcom's parents.

As he watched, a small rickety flatbed truck pulled up outside, and a man climbed out wearing dirty clothing. He slammed the door shut and kicked a crushed aluminium can. He seemed pissed off.

Rob caught Scarlett's eye and nodded in his direction as the man stomped up to the door of the house they were going to.

"Dad, maybe?"

"Let's find out," Scarlett suggested.

Rob started up the street and turned into the front yard just as the man went to shut the door. He stopped, but held the door nearly closed as if he was worried about Rob trying to break it down. "Yeah?"

"We're looking for Tess Hooper. Is she in?" Rob began. "We're with the police." Rob went to reach into his coat and pull out his ID, only for the man to raise a hand.

"Not here, where people can see. Come inside."

"Okay, sure." Rob understood that being seen working with the police might not go down well with some of the locals. He stepped into the house, directly into the front room, and waited for the man to shut the door before flashing his ID. "And you are?"

"Ernie Newton," the man answered. He had rough, weathered skin with stubble that suggested a five-o'clock shadow from several days ago. "I'm… dating Tess."

"I see," Rob confirmed. "Is Tess around?"

Ernie frowned. "Is this about Malcom?"

"It is," Rob confirmed. "Is she in?"

"Nope," he replied.

148

"Are you sure?"

Ernie sighed. "Yeah, I'm sure."

"What makes you say that?"

"You'd better sit down," he answered.

The front room was a general mess with discarded clothes, shoes, bags, coats, mugs and more. It desperately needed a good clean up and vacuum.

Rob waved for Scarlett to go first and then followed to join her on the sofa. Scarlett looked at the state of the sofa with about as much trepidation as he did and didn't seem too pleased that she needed to sit on it.

Ernie, meanwhile, dropped into a single-seater, enjoying its embrace. "The reason she's not here, is because the bitch left me."

"When? Today?"

"Yeah."

Rob raised an eyebrow. What the hell? Why on earth would a woman who'd reported her son as missing, leave her home? That was madness.

"She's run off with another bloke," Ernie continued. "Her bloody dealer, if you can believe it. I don't know who he is, I just know she calls him Keg." Ernie sat forward. "What kind of name's Keg? Huh? Sounds like a ponce to me."

"Her dealer?"

"Yep. If she's not drunk, then she's usually high. She's taken to smoking crack, which she gets from this Keg. I knew about it, but what I didn't know, is that she was bloody banging him, too. She was probably doing it to get free drugs. Stupid bitch."

"But she reported Malcom missing on Monday, right?" Scarlett asked, looking equally as shocked by Tess's actions.

"Yeah. She was out of it Sunday night, but when she sobered up on Monday morning, she got worried and reported him missing. Then she got high again. Whatever, I don't care."

"You don't care?" Scarlett asked, voicing Rob's thoughts.

He shrugged. "She deals with Mal, not me. He's her son."

"I see. Mal being Malcom, I presume?"

"Yup."

"Can you run us through what happened?" Rob asked.

"We had a fight. I found out she was banging Keg, sending him nudes and stuff for free dugs so… I got upset. Anyway, Mal didn't like it, so he stormed out. I don't know why. It's not like we haven't fought before. It's nothing new."

"So, to clarify, you're saying that you and Tess had a row, Malcom got upset and left, is that right?"

"That's about the size of it," Ernie confirmed.

"And this was when?"

"Sunday night," Ernie answered. "Things calmed down a bit after he left, and the next day she called you guys to report him missing. She started drinking and shit again, and then today, while I was at work, she texted to say she was leaving me. I came back home to try and talk to her, to stop her, but she was gone. I called and drove about, searching, but I didn't find her. That's when you guys turned up."

"How long has she been drinking for?" Scarlett asked.

Ernie sighed. "As long as I've known her. It's her way of dealing with things. The crack smoking's a new thing, though."

"And you don't know who this 'Keg' is, then?"

"No idea," Ernie answered, leaning back into the chair again.

"Have you tried calling her?" Scarlett asked.

"She won't talk to me or pick up her phone. I don't know where she is."

"Do you think she'd answer to either of us?"

"I don't know. She might. You can call her if you like. I can give you her phone number."

"That would be a start," Rob replied.

"I can give you Malcom's number, too, so you can call him. Tess tried but, she couldn't get through."

"That would be great, thank you."

Ernie spent the next minute reading the numbers out for Rob, so he could write them down.

"Tell me about your relationship with Malcom," Scarlett asked. "Do you get on with him?"

Ernie shrugged. "I suppose. I let Tess deal with him."

Rob watched as Ernie answered, noting the uncomfortable body language as he discussed his relationship with the boy. Ernie looked away and shifted in his seat. He didn't seem like he wanted to be in the room.

"Do you know anyone who might want to hurt him?" Rob asked.

Scarlett nodded. "How's his school life?"

"I didn't take too much interest."

Rob pressed his lips together, feeling frustrated that Ernie was dodging the questions. He sat back and let Scarlett continue.

"But you must have talked. Did you hear about anything?"

"I think he was having some trouble with some kids at school, but I don't know who. He never came home with a black eye or anything, so it can't have been that bad."

"Tell me about Tess. Does she get on well with Malcom?"

"Look, is this important?" Ernie asked. "Why are you asking about all this feelings crap?"

"Understanding a person's various relationships is often key to solving these kinds of crimes, Mr Newton. Most violent crimes are committed by people the victim knew, not strangers, although that does happen too."

"Are you saying I'm a suspect?" he exclaimed. "Do you think I did something to him?"

"Of course not," Rob cut in, attempting to try and get the conversation back on track. "So did Tess and Malcom get along?"

"Yeah," Ernie replied. "They did. He didn't like it when she got drunk or high, but they got along."

Was he being intentionally vague, Rob wondered? Ernie was dodging questions and dancing around the edge of answers without really giving them much substance. Was this a complete lack of interest in Malcom and getting him back, or was he trying to hide something? He didn't seem too upset about Malcom being missing, as opposed to Tess, who he seemed much more concerned about.

Spotting some photos on the sideboard, Rob got up and wandered over. He peered at them. "Is this Tess?"

"Yeah," Ernie answered. "That's her with Mal."

"I see," Rob remarked and frowned at the image. "I don't mean to be insensitive, but would I be right in saying, Malcom isn't your son?"

"No, he's not," Ernie confirmed, with a hint of venom.

"I thought not." Rob glanced at the photo again, noting Malcom's skin was darker than either his mother or Ernie. He was almost certainly mixed race, which made Rob wonder if there was a race element to this or not.

"Is that why you're not interested in Malcom?" Scarlett asked.

Ernie shrugged but didn't answer. This was going to take longer than he'd like.

19

Rob stuffed his hands into his pockets as Scarlett closed the door to Nailer's office.

"How'd it go?" Nailer asked.

Rob pulled a face. "Not as well as I'd like," he admitted, feeling frustrated at the lack of significant progress that the visit to Malcom's house had given them. "Malcom's mother wasn't there, leaving us with just his mum's boyfriend, who was about as helpful as a wet paper bag. He didn't seem concerned about Malcom's well-being at all and was only really interested in where Tess might be. But even that was debatable."

"I see," Nailer replied. "Did you learn what happened?"

"It seems there was an argument because Ernie found out that Tess had been seeing another man called Keg. I suspect the fight was severe because it made Malcom storm out, but Ernie made it sound like a minor disagreement. That was Sunday night. On Monday, Tess reported Malcom missing, and then today, Tess texted Ernie while he was at work, saying she was leaving him for Keg. Ernie had tried calling and looking for her but with no luck. She's disappeared."

"But, he's not out looking for Malcom?"

"Apparently not, no. According to him, Tess spent Tuesday morning doing that and then getting into a drunken stupor when she couldn't find him. I'm guessing things went downhill from there, but Ernie isn't giving much away. We have phone numbers for both Tess and Malcom, which we've been calling, but Tess isn't answering, and Malcom's isn't even connecting."

"What are your thoughts on this Ernie?"

"That he hates Tess's son," Scarlett said. "After a fair bit of questioning, it seems that Ernie's been Tess's partner for a long time, and Malcom is a son from one of her affairs. Both Tess and Ernie are pasty white, but Malcom is quite clearly mixed race."

Nailer nodded. "Is that an issue for him, do you think? Race?"

"I don't get that feeling from him. I think it's more that Malcom isn't his flesh and blood."

"I'm inclined to agree," Rob added. "His darker skin made it painfully obvious that he wasn't Ernie's, so Tess couldn't hide it, and Malcom now serves as a constant, walking, talking reminder of Tess's infidelity."

"Fair enough," Nailer answered. "So, what's next?"

"I've got Ellen looking into Malcom's friends and school, so I'm going to catch up with her," Rob said.

"Ernie hinted that there might have been trouble at school, although he didn't seem to know what that trouble was," Scarlett added.

"Alright, good. It sounds like you have this in hand." Nailer rose from his seat and motioned for them to stay put. "Right, wait there a moment. I'll call Nick and Tucker in so we can chat about Curt and Emory Gates and that deal. Hold on." Rob waited while Nailer walked to the door of his office and called the two men in, leaving Ellen at her desk.

She looked up to see what she might be missing out on but didn't pursue it any further.

"Where's Guy?" Rob asked as Nick walked in.

"He had an appointment to get to tonight," Nick replied.

Nailer closed the door behind the two men and returned to his desk. "Right then, Nick, how'd the interview with Curt go? Did you get anywhere with him?"

Nick dropped into a chair with a sigh. "No. Nowhere. It was 'no comment' across the board, as usual. I tried to guilt trip him several times, but that lawyer of his is a massive roadblock. Anytime I got anywhere, Mr Bentley whispered in Curt's ear, and Curt went right back to 'no comment'. There's no way we're going to flip him with that lawyer there." Nick looked over towards Rob. "I think Matilda is right. He's working for the Masons, and it's as if one of your brothers is in that room with him, reminding him about what will happen if he puts a foot out of line."

"Bollocks," Rob muttered. It was frustrating, but not unexpected. These days saying no comment seemed to be the default advice from the duty solicitors that attended the interviews.

"But, we need him to flip," Scarlett exclaimed, her tone filled with fire. "We can't give up. We need to get to him."

"I've tried everything," Nick answered, sounding as frustrated as Rob felt, "and I've hit nothing but brick wall after brick wall. I feel like I've wasted hours of my life on a fruitless task, and I can't see it changing while that Chance Bentley is there. So, unfortunately, unless we can come up with something, I'll be heading back there tonight to release him, pending further investigation." He sat back and scratched his cheek in thought. "I can probably have a chat to him when I drive him home, but I think it'll take more than that to turn him at this point."

"He's susceptible, for sure," Rob agreed. "He's not very bright, and I think if we handed him the right shovel, he'd dig his own grave. It wouldn't take much work if we can get him away from the influence of the Masons."

"We'll figure something out," Nick said, with a note of hope.

158

"That may be so," Nailer agreed. "But unfortunately, we don't have much time. Tucker? Care to share what you found out?"

"Of course. I've been talking to some sources, and one of my guys came back with something fucking juicy. It seems that Curt Gates, God bless the loud-mouthed twat, has been indiscreet with a particularly sensitive piece of information. Apparently, the daft wazzock's been bragging that the Mason firm is due to have a meeting with a representative for the fucking Columbian cartels. It seems there will be a big bastard drug deal going down soon, but we don't know who, when or where. But according to my source, Curt does."

"God damn it," Nick exclaimed. "Fuck. Really? Are you certain?"

"My man's always been on the bastard money with his intel," Tucker replied. "If he says Curt's been saying these things, then I have no God-damn reason to doubt him."

"Then we're running out of time," Nick said.

"Yes, we are," Rob agreed, noticing how Tucker's revelation had suddenly lit a fire under Nick's arse.

"We need to know what he knows," Nick said, "and we need to know today."

"What can we do?" Scarlett asked, all animated and keen. "We need to do something. We can't let this chance pass us by. This could really screw up the Masons."

"I know, I know," Nailer replied. "But I don't see how you're going to convince Curt to work with us."

"Not with the lawyer there, we won't," Rob agreed.

"Shit," Nick hissed and got to his feet. He started to pace the room while rubbing his jaw and temples.

"There must be something we can do," Scarlett mused. "Can we scare him somehow?"

"Scarlett," Rob exclaimed, surprised by her outburst. "I didn't take you for a rule-breaker."

"I would never break any rules, but there's a difference between bending and breaking." She shrugged. "Besides, they've got to be stopped. We can't let this slip through our fingers."

Nick stopped pacing and looked. "Curt is a little gullible, isn't he?"

"Yeah," Rob agreed. "He seems to think we can do whatever we like to him, too."

"And I haven't disabused him of that impression, either," Nick said.

Peering up at his friend and long-time partner on the force, Rob could almost see the gears grinding in Nick's head. He had an idea. Rob was sure of it. "What are you thinking?"

"I have an idea based on something you said earlier... and on my time in the Middle East."

"Oh, shit," Rob said under his breath. "I don't like this already."

Nick turned to Nailer. "How badly do you want this info and Curt as an informant?"

Nailer sucked in a long breath. "I don't know what you're thinking..."

"How badly?" Nick pressed.

Nailer sighed. "You know that the Masons have been a pet project of mine for years. I want them arrested and disbanded more than most. But I want to do it within the bounds of the law. We are police officers, after all, and we have a code of ethics."

"The Masons have no such code," Scarlett muttered, darkly.

"What are you going to do?" Rob asked.

"Nothing, really. I'm going to let his imagination run wild, that's all. I won't hurt him or anything, don't worry."

"I don't know if this is a good idea..." Nailer mused.

"Fine." Nick shrugged. "Then we do nothing, and let this slip through our fingers. I can return him home once he's 'released pending', and we'll let this drug deal happen right under our noses."

"Sir," Scarlett urged, her eyes fixed on Nailer. "We need this."

Nailer glanced over at Rob. "What do you think?"

Rob briefly closed his eyes and sighed. "If this had been suggested by almost anyone else, I'd have more reservations. But, Nick is an exceptional officer who I'd trust with my life, and I'd be inclined to trust him on this, too."

Nailer nodded and seemed to withdraw into himself as he mulled the options over. There wasn't an easy answer to this, and Rob didn't envy his DCI at all. They desperately needed a win against the Masons, who were running roughshod over the police whenever it suited them, and this chance was a juicy one, and tantalisingly close if only they could get Curt on-side. But it looked like they needed to play a little fast and loose to get the result they wanted.

"Of course," Nailer said, "if we do this, it doesn't work and the robbery case goes to court, then we're screwed. We'll never get it to stand up in court and depending on what you're planning, you could lose your jobs."

"True," Nick countered. "But if it works, he turns informant, and he's back out on the street, then it doesn't matter, does it?"

"It's a risk," Nailer agreed.

"A calculated risk," Scarlett added. "I'd hate to see that shopkeeper fail to get justice for the crimes perpetrated against him, but if we can stop this drug deal and hurt the Masons, how many other lives are we saving from similar pain and tragedy?"

"The needs of the many," Tucker mused.

Rob watched, fascinated as Nailer wrestled with the choice before him. "Shit," he hissed. "Okay, fine. Do what you need to do. But I don't want to know anything about it, and this conversation never happened."

"What conversation?" Nick replied with a smile.

"Whatever it is you're planning," Scarlett said, leaning in, "I want in. I'm not missing this."

Nick glanced at Rob, asking a silent question.

Rob saw it and knew what he was asking. "Your choice, matey. I trust her, but this is your thing."

"Alright, Scarlett, you're in." Nick got up and Scarlett followed.

"You'd better not make me regret this, Miller," Nailer warned him. "I'm putting my neck on the line here."

"I won't," Nick answered. "Trust me."

20

Sitting upstairs in the Arrow pub in Arnold, Bill lifted his pint and took another sip of his Foster's Lager. He enjoyed the cool sensation as it filled his mouth.

Up here, by the balcony, he had a great view of the pub below and would hopefully get to see his informant—if they turned up—well before they reached his table.

But then, that was the issue, wasn't it? That unknowable 'if'.

If they turned up.

There was no guarantee that the sender understood the hint he'd dropped in his reply. That would require a degree of intelligence, and right now, he had no idea who this person was or what the intention behind their email might be. Were they a genuine supporter of his, who agreed with his perspective on Rob, or were they trying to set him up? Or maybe they were an idiot and had no intention of coming here to meet him.

The possibility there was someone, or several someones, laughing their arses off over their hilarious email was high.

But the bigger question, and the more compelling one, was, what would he do if the person did turn up and wanted to help? He'd been issued a stern warning to keep away from

Rob and not to investigate any further. Just meeting this person was potentially grounds for his dismissal, or at the very least, another dressing down by a superior officer.

How much did he want to bring Rob down?

That's what it ultimately came down to in the end. How far was he willing to go, and what was he willing to sacrifice to get what he wanted? Because if this turned out to be genuine, he would need to make some very tough choices that could end his career in the force if they backfired.

Picking up his beer, Bill took another long sip as he thought things through, letting various scenarios play out in his head. He mulled his ideas over, trying to work out every possible variation until he reached the end of his pint, but finding himself no closer to an answer.

Looking around the room, he saw no sign of this contact, but after quickly checking his watch, he realised he'd not given it very long.

After a few moments, Bill got up and walked down to the bar, where he was served quickly on this quiet Wednesday night. With his fresh drink in hand, he turned away from the bar and scanned the room, realising he'd not paid much attention to it. He'd lost himself somewhere deep inside his head while being served, and forgotten to keep one eye on the room around him.

Seeing no one he recognised, Bill made his way back upstairs to his perch, only to find a figure sitting at his table with his back to Bill.

Bill froze as he stared at the back of the figure's head, trying to work out if he knew them, but he just couldn't be sure. It was a man with short dark hair, but there was little else to give away his identity.

"Come and sit down, Bill," the figure said without looking around.

They knew he was behind them. "Sure," Bill replied and moved around the table, peering at the man, wondering who they were.

The figure looked up and smiled. "Your reply was clever, I liked it. Nice and subtle. Well done."

Bill stared at the man sitting before him in disbelief. He recognised him, but couldn't quite believe that he was an honest-to-God supporter who believed in his cause.

"You're kidding me. You? You believe me about Loxley?"

Guy Gibson smiled back at him. "Sit, please."

"This is a set-up," Bill said and looked around for any hints of the other EMSOU officers. But he saw none.

"I promise you, it's not," Guy replied. He stood up. "Pat me down if you like. I'm not wearing a wire. And in all honesty, I do believe you."

"Is that right?" Bill couldn't quite believe what he was hearing.

"Do you want to search me?" Guy pressed.

"Yeah, sure." The pat down took moments but revealed nothing. Bill eyed Guy suspiciously, wondering what angle he had on all this. "Alright, turn out your pockets, and put your phone on the table."

Guy gave him a brief incredulous look, and then shrugged before doing as Bill asked.

Bill snatched up Guy's phone and asked him to unlock it. He did so and handed it back. Bill checked it for any recording apps that might be running but found none. He turned the phone off and placed it face down on the table.

"What about you?" Guy asked.

Bill stared at Guy for a long moment as he searched for a clever answer, but none were forthcoming. "Okay, fine." Bill pulled out his phone, shut it down, and left it on the table. "Satisfied?"

"For now," Guy muttered, as they both took their seats.

"You said you believed me in your email," Bill started. "And yet, you work with Rob on the unit in the EMSOU office. How on earth can I trust you?"

Guy shrugged. "Ultimately, whether you trust me or not will be down to you, not me. I can't help you there. All I can do is be honest, give you my opinion, and share what I've

167

learned. If, after all that, you want to walk away, that's fine. I'll do this on my own. But if we can work together, then I think we might start to get somewhere... Sheriff."

Bill snorted, aware of the nickname that others had given him, because of his strict nature when it came to corruption. Obviously, it was a reference to the legendary Robin Hood villain, in the same way that Rob had chosen Loxley as his surname because of the legend.

But that was a whole other issue that Bill had with Rob. How dare he cast himself as the hero by taking the name Loxley when trying to hide his criminal past and family.

Bill found it sickening, especially when others cast him as the villain.

Was that another reason why they named him Sheriff because he was going after Loxley?

He'd not thought of that before, but it made sense.

"Having someone to work with who shares my beliefs about Loxley would be nice," Bill admitted, tapping his foot as he continued to scrutinise Guy.

"See. I knew you'd come around."

"I'm a long way off 'coming around' to working with you, Guy, but I'll hear you out." Bill shifted position in his seat. "So you believe me, then?"

"You have a serious point about Rob," Guy answered. "He's compromised. That's clear. I know who his family is, I've

168

known about them for a long time, and I've always had my doubts. I've just kept them to myself. But after seeing how you were treated during the Lee Garrett case, I did some self-examination and realised that I needed to do something."

"Do something?"

"About Rob. I think he could be a serious liability to the unit and the Nottinghamshire Police as a whole. So I've been doing some digging, and I think someone noticed because I was sent this." Guy slid the brown envelope across the table towards him.

Bill watched it draw near. "What's in there?"

"Proof," Guy answered. "Take a look. I have no idea who sent it to me. Although, if I had to guess, I wonder if it might be a journalist?"

His curiosity piqued, Bill reached into the envelope and drew out the small stack of photos. Printed on the glossy paper was a zoomed-in photo of Rob in his apartment. It was clearly taken from a long way away, from outside of his home, and as Bill went through them, the photos showed Owen Mason walking into Rob's apartment and offering him some kind of package."

"Any idea what he handed to Rob?" Bill asked.

"I don't know. This is all I have, and I have no idea where they came from or who sent them."

"Damn," Bill whispered under his breath and continued to flick through the image. Suddenly the next one was from a different time and place and showed Rob meeting with Owen Mason somewhere else entirely. They were outside this time, in what looked like some kind of gravel car park at the back of a building. "What's this?"

"Photos of another meeting," Guy replied. "That's Clipstone from a couple of months ago. I recognise the village hall car park."

"Clipstone?" Bill asked, as a jigsaw piece fell into place in his head. "Oh, crap. These are Vincent Kane's photos."

"Kane?"

"He's a reporter who was investigating Rob for me during the Clipstone case. He said he'd taken photos of Rob meeting with Owen, but he lost them, so… These must be those photos."

"He lost them?"

"He had his camera taken from him by Owen's bodyguard," Bill explained.

"Really? But that begs the question, how did these photos end up being delivered to me?" Guy asked.

Bill frowned as he tried to connect the dots. Were the Masons trying to smear Rob? Or was this somehow coming from Kane? Maybe he wasn't attacked and didn't lose the photos, but instead he chose not to share them. Vincent

170

could be slippery when he wanted to be, so he wouldn't put it past the slimy journalist. But ultimately, the source of these images didn't matter. What mattered was that they showed Rob meeting with Owen on more than one occasion and that some kind of transaction had taken place.

"I don't know where those have come from, but they are damning. I've suspected this for a long time, but to finally have some proof…"

"I'll hang onto these for now." Guy gathered the images up and slipped them back into the envelope. "Remember, they're just photos, so I'm not sure how much proof they'll really be."

"They're the best evidence I've seen so far," Bill said.

"Evidence of what?"

"Rob's corruption. For years he's maintained that he's had no connection with his family, but this proves otherwise. I'm convinced he's working for them, now more than ever."

"I'm inclined to agree," Guy said. "I've suspected that there's a leak in the EMSOU for a while. Someone's passing info to the Masons, and I'm willing to bet it's Rob. But we're going to need more than these photos. They're not enough. We need concrete proof of his relationship to the Masons."

Bill sighed. "Well, that's the problem, isn't it. I've been trying to find that evidence for years, with no luck, so…"

"But, you've never had someone on the inside before," Guy replied before leaning in. "Look, I'm attending a social gathering at Rob's in a few days, so while I'm there, I'll see if I can find anything else. If I can find that package in his apartment, we'll finally have the evidence we need, right?"

Bill nodded. "Right." He felt defeated for now, but a budding flower of hope was starting to open deep inside. Could it be that after all this time, when his dismissal felt so close, he'd finally achieve what he always wanted and prove to the country that Rob Loxley was indeed as corrupt as he'd feared?

21

"Here you go," Gordon said, tipping the bag into the bowl, letting its contents tinkle into the porcelain. "Get them down, yeh. They'll put hairs on your chest, they will."

Chris smiled and plucked one of the pork scratchings from the bowl. It was crunchy and flavoursome.

"Thanks." Chris smiled at his guests. He'd got along well with all of the neighbours he'd met at the meal the other night but found he had the most in common with Barry, Gordon, Austin and Fern, all of whom were keen to meet up again. So when Scarlett phoned earlier on to warn him she'd be back late again, he thought, screw it, why not, and made some phone calls.

Luckily, all four of them were free and were round within the hour. Fern brought wine, Austin brought Champagne, Barry had a six-pack of beer, and Gordon brought snacks. So, within a short space of time, they were sitting in Chris's lounge, chatting and laughing.

It was just what Chris needed after the week he'd had so far, but with his mind preoccupied with thoughts about his wife-to-be, Chris found he needed to share with the group and offload to someone other than Scarlett.

"So yeah, I just don't know if Scarlett should be back to work so soon after her friend's murder, you know? I guess I'm just worried about her."

"But she loves her work, right?" Barry asked.

"Oh yeah," Chris confirmed. "It's her whole life. She loves it."

"It's unsociable, though," Fern suggested.

"Isn't it a thing that police officers get divorced way more than the average or something?" Barry asked.

"Barry!" Fern cried. "They're not even married yet."

"Sorry," Barry muttered.

"That's okay. And I don't know if the divorce thing is based in reality or not. It could just be an urban myth spread by thriller novels and TV dramas. Also, I knew what I was getting into when we got together. It's never bothered me before, but this time feels different."

"Because of her friend's murder," Fern stated.

"Yeah. Is two weeks too soon?" Chris asked.

"How close was she to this friend?"

Chris shrugged. "They were friends at Uni, and it sounds like they went through some tough times together. But, I'm not sure they remained super close or anything after leaving Uni. They went out for drinks occasionally while we were together, but that's all."

"I think you're just going to have to deal with this," Fern suggested. "I'm sure Scarlett knows how she feels, and if she believes that this is what she needs, then the best thing you can do to help is to support her."

"Yeah, I guess," Chris agreed with a sigh. "I'm sorry to dump this on you all. I'm sure you didn't come round to hear me moan."

"It's okay, matey," Barry answered. "I'm sure I'll be moaning about Chelsea before the night's out. We all do it."

"Thanks," Chris replied. "Sorry to be a downer."

"You're not," Gordon answered, chewing on a scratching. "We're happy to help."

"Exactly," Fern agreed. "What are neighbours for if not to help?"

"Is she busy at work?"

"I think so, but that's the thing, I'm worried she's going to go on a vendetta against the gang that did this. I just… Shit, I've done it again. Sorry, I need to get off this subject."

"Of course, of course," Barry agreed and turned to Austin. "Right then, Austin. No more sitting silently in the corner for you. Tell us about the exciting world of investing. Is it like Dragon's Den? Because I'm sure we all want to know, right?"

Austin laughed. "I wish."

"Come on, play along," Barry added, stage whispering. "We need to keep Chris company while Scarlett's still at work."

Austin sighed. "Okay, sure. What do you want to know? Is it a cut-throat business?"

"That's more like it," Barry urged.

"Well, is it?" Gordon asked.

Austin smiled. "You have no idea…"

22

Sitting silently in the back of the pool car behind the driver's seat, Scarlett had never felt so nervous during her whole time in the force. She'd attended gruesome RTCs, she'd been in scuffles and fights with suspects and faced down vetting and dressing-downs from senior officers, but none of that compared to how nervous and on edge she was feeling right now.

Whatever they were about to do was utterly outside of what they should do, and if things got out of hand or it got out, this could very well end their careers.

As they pushed north from Nottingham, driving in the darkness, Scarlett thought back to her first week of training, which seemed to consist of anyone and everyone, from senior officers to Professional Standards, telling them everything that could get them fired.

They watched video after video, showing the silly, stupid or corrupt things that former officers had done that had ended in them being suddenly unemployed.

By the end of that first week, she'd felt utterly demoralised and wondered if the police even wanted new recruits.

Of course, in hindsight, this was just the force setting out their expectations for the new recruits. Forces up and down the country had time and again become embroiled in scandal after scandal, none of which helped the reputation of the police and its founding Peelian principle of policing by consent.

Trust in the institution of the police and transparency about how it worked were key.

If the public didn't trust the police, the whole system broke down.

They had to hold themselves to a higher ideal and not get dragged into the mud when fighting crime, even when the criminals took advantage of it.

And yet, here she was, going against everything she'd been taught and stepping outside the strict guidelines of what an officer should do.

But, as nervous as she was, she also felt utterly justified in bending the rules in order to finally strike a blow against the Mason gang.

They'd kidnapped her friend and used Ninette to try and blackmail her into working for the gang. And when that didn't work, they'd killed Ninette. They had no remorse or ethics that any rational person might recognise and cared nothing for human life.

They were scum, and they needed to be taken down.

Not by any means necessary. No, she wasn't a monster, not yet, at least. The ends very rarely justify the means. But in this instance, and with her particular history with the gang, she felt totally justified in bending the rules, and if this led to her dismissal tomorrow, next week, or next year, then so be it.

Nick turned off the main road and drove along a winding side road, somewhere in the countryside between Nottingham and Worksop.

She had no idea where they were, having not paid attention to where Nick was driving. She'd been lost in thought, poring over the events that led her here, and found that she didn't have a scintilla of regret about the choices she'd made.

She had no great animosity for Curt. In her opinion, he was an idiot working for a morally corrupt organisation. He'd probably had fewer chances in life than many others, which was regrettable, but he had undoubtedly also made several poor choices in life.

But there were so many others who'd come from poorer or more deprived backgrounds, made sensible or intelligent choices, and then gone on to make something of their lives.

So no, she felt no regret for what tonight might bring and had little sympathy for the position Curt found himself in.

Besides, it wasn't as if she would hurt or kill him; although he did deserve a good slap. They were going to scare him, and in that, she felt completely justified.

Three more side roads later, Curt noticed they weren't heading to his house.

"Oi, where you taking me?" he said suddenly.

"I've got an errand to run," Nick replied. "Won't take long."

"Err, no. You're meant to be taking me home, like."

"And home you will go after I've run this errand," Nick answered, his voice calm and even.

"Fucking pigs," Curt muttered under his breath.

Scarlett thought she sensed a tremor in his voice but wasn't sure. Was he starting to feel a little worried?

She hoped so.

Nick took a couple more turns, disorientating her even further. On these unlit back roads, she'd felt so turned around she had no idea where she was or in which direction they were heading.

Nick took one final turn and bumped the powerful 4x4 off the road and onto rough ground.

"What the hell is this?" Curt exclaimed. "Where are you taking me?"

Scarlett held onto the roof handle as the vehicle juddered and rolled over the uneven surface. She could make out trees and undergrowth all around as their headlights cut through the gloom.

"Jesus fucking Christ," Curt exclaimed as they continued to bump along until Nick turned the car, swinging it around before abruptly braking.

"That'll do," Nick remarked.

"That'll do?" Curt asked, sounding bewildered. "Where the hell are we?"

Nick turned to Curt. "Stay there. I'm just going to check it out. But this looks like the perfect spot."

"Check what out?" Curt asked,

Nick nodded to her, and she nodded back.

"Wait," Curt yelled. "You can't leave me here with this crazy bitch. Oi, what are you doing?" But Nick was gone.

Curt went quiet.

Scarlett turned and looked him in the eye. She was surprised to see actual fear there. He kept glancing away, hunting for Nick, who was sweeping a torch around, lighting up the woods outside. She smiled at Curt and waited.

Curt remained silent.

She'd be lying if she said she wasn't enjoying this feeling of power they seemed to have over Curt.

Moments later, her door opened, and Nick beckoned her out. She followed, shutting the door behind her.

He leaned in close. "Are you ready for this?" he whispered.

"One hundred percent."

"Alright, then follow my lead. You're doing the brooding, silent act perfectly. I like it. Keep at it."

"Thanks."

He nodded to her and moved to the car. Scarlett crossed her arms and watched as he opened Curt's door.

"Out," Nick ordered.

"What the hell is this?"

"I said, get out. Now!" His tone brooked no insubordination.

"Alright, alright. Fuck. I'm coming, okay? I'm doing what you asked." Curt climbed out, keeping his hands in plain view while Scarlett watched. Curt kept furtively glancing her way.

"Round to the front, into the light."

"What the hell *is* this? Why? What are we doing here?"

"Move it!"

Curt raised his hands in surrender and started walking. When he was standing in the middle of the sweeping beams of light, he stopped. "Here, okay for yeh?"

"Perfect," Nick replied. "Wait there."

He walked to the back of the car, leaving her to watch Curt. She stared at him, keeping her face neutral and her arms crossed. Curt, however, shuffled about, looking this way

182

and that, stuffing his hands into his pockets and taking them out again while occasionally glancing up at her and scratching himself.

She watched, doing her level best to present a façade of cold but watchful indifference.

Moments later, Nick appeared carrying a shovel. But it was an odd looking one. It had a slightly pointed metal blade and a very long wooden pole but no handle on the end.

He threw it onto the floor at Curt's feet, before putting his hands on his hips.

"What the fuck is this?" Curt asked.

"*That,* is a shovel," Nick answered. "An Irish shovel, specifically."

"It's broken," Curt exclaimed. "Where's the handle?"

"It doesn't have one," Nick replied, and turned to Scarlett. "Do you know what shovels like that are perfect for?"

"No," Scarlett answered, keeping her eyes fixed on Curt.

"Digging graves," Nick answered. "I like to think of it as my grave-digging shovel."

So that's where Nick had disappeared to before they'd headed off to pick up Curt.

"What the hell?" Curt exclaimed, glacing down at the shovel as if it might kill him.

Nick turned back to Curt and lowered his voice. "Get digging."

"What?"

"Get digging," Nick repeated. "It's quite simple. Dig."

"No, man, I ain't doing that."

"I said dig," Nick repeated, and reached a hand into the inside of his jacket and held it there.

Curt's hands shot up in surrender. "Okay, alright, I'm digging." He grabbed the shovel.

Scarlett peered over at Nick as he held his hand beneath his jacket. The implication was clear, and Curt had obviously picked up on it. But would Nick actually check out a gun for this? Was that what he was hiding under there? She had no idea but honestly wouldn't be surprised if he had. He was former Army, after all.

In the headlights, Curt started digging, using his foot to push the blade into the earth before lifting the sod and dumping it to one side.

He kept looking up, deep fear obvious in his eyes. Scarlett started to wonder just how this might go. Would Curt get wise to their tactics, or would his fears run rampant and drag his mind to dark possibilities?

She hoped it was the latter.

Nick moved and leaned against the front of the car, watching. Scarlett started to pace back and forth, both to keep warm and to give Curt the impression of impatience.

Several minutes in, Curt looked up. "How deep do you want it?"

"How deep do you think I want it?"

Six foot, Scarlett though, the obvious implied answer leaping to the forefront of her mind.

Already sweating, Curt visibly swallowed and then got back to work. Scarlett returned to pacing and watching as the cool night air cut through her suit and blouse. She wondered how long this might take.

Curt continued to dig, and without them asking him, he outlined a hole long enough for a person to lie in it. Scarlett found it fascinating that he'd done that without any direction and was actually self-reinforcing the impression he'd jumped to. He was turning his fears into reality.

Forty minutes in, she noticed that Curt was starting to well up. He was actually crying. It began as tears, but as the minutes passed it evolved into outright sobbing.

Scarlett watched dispassionately, wondering where this might go. Over the next twenty minutes, the crying subsided but then returned with a vengeance. Minutes passed with Curt muttering inaudibly to himself until, dripping with sweat, covered in mud, and up to his knees in what he clearly believed was his own grave, he turned to them.

"Please, don't do this," he pleaded, dropping to the floor. "Please. I'll do whatever you want. I tell you anything. But please, don't kill me."

"You'll tell me anything?" Nick asked.

"Anything," he cried, dropping to his hands and knees.

Nick crouched down before him and waited for him to look up. When he did, Nick asked his question. "When, where, and with who is this Columbian drug deal happening?"

"Oh, God," Curt sobbed. "Please. You can't. I can't answer that. They'll… You don't know them…"

Nick stood up. "Dig."

"Noooo," Curt howled.

"I said dig."

"Alright, alright. It's with my uncle, Emory, at his place, in the next few days. I don't know when exactly, but soon.." He collapsed into the mud, looking utterly defeated. "I can't go back now. They'll kill me. You have to help me. You have to protect me."

"What's your name?" Nick asked.

"What?"

"Your name?"

"Curt. Curt Gates."

"Thank you, Curt," Nick answered and reached into his jacket pocket. Scarlett stiffened as she watched, thinking the worst was about to happen and she had made a terrible mistake.

"No, no, no," Curt cried out.

Nick pulled out his phone, which had been recording the audio. He showed it to Curt and hit pause.

"W...What," Curt stammered. "No..."

"You understand what this means," Nick asked. "We own you, now. If this recording gets back to Emory, or one of the Mason brothers, things won't go well for you, will they?"

"No," Curt muttered. "You bastards. I thought..."

"You thought what?" Nick asked.

"You said... I was digging my own grave..."

Nick looked surprised and genuinely offended? "What? No. I never said that. No, no, no. You were helping me."

"Helping?"

"Yeah," Nick replied, and reached into another pocket and pulled something out. He threw it onto the ground beside Curt. "There."

"What's this?" He picked them up. "I don't..."

"They're seeds," Nick explained, as if talking to a child. "We're planting some seeds."

As Scarlett watched, Nick looked over and winked.

You crafty bugger, she thought.

***

In the darkness, far enough away that there was no chance of DC Scarlett Stutley or DS Nick Miller seeing or hearing her, Madeleine watched them through a scope as they spoke with the utterly broken suspect.

She took photos and made notes.

23

Slumped into his sofa, tapping out a rhythm on the arm, Ernie stared at the TV screen but wasn't paying any attention to it. Instead, his mind wandered through the last few days' events, wondering where he'd gone wrong and when Tess would return to him.

He kept returning to that moment on Sunday, when he'd seen the text come in from this Keg and snooped into her phone. He knew the code from watching her unlock it, so he'd grabbed the device and had a look.

Even that, he was partially regretting. He'd looked at her phone a few times before, but he didn't make a habit out of it and didn't go hunting through her messages, but there was something about that notification that just pricked his curiosity and drew him in.

What he'd not expected to see was a long thread of messages that included several nude or revealing selfies that Tess had taken and sent to Keg.

He remembered the shock and utter dismay he'd felt as he scanned through. She'd been buying drugs from Keg, and as part payment, he'd started asking her for selfies. Then more recently, based on the texts he'd read, it looked like she was actually having sex with him in return for more drugs.

Tess getting high was no surprise. She'd been indulging in that, on and off, for years. And on occasion, Ernie joined in, although he often didn't have time for it while trying to work.

Coming home to find Malcom upstairs and Tess passed out or high on the sofa was not uncommon. He'd learned to accept it and move on.

But this was a step too far.

Part of him regretted how he'd let the rage build up and explode out of him and how he'd spoken to Tess and Malcom. He half wished he'd dealt with it in a more measured way and perhaps sat Tess down to have a calm talk about what was going on and why she was doing this because maybe then she'd still be here with him.

There was another part of him, though, that wondered what on earth she thought would happen?

She was cheating on him, again!

How did she think he'd react when he found out, which he obviously would eventually? Did she think he'd ignore it and brush it off as one of those things?

Hell no! He was furious with her and hated that she was making him feel bad about being upset. He had every right to be angry, offended and betrayed by her actions.

And yet, here he was, alone in his house, having been questioned by the police who were looking for her delinquent son.

He'd felt bad answering the filth's questions and admitting to his complete lack of interest in Malcom. He didn't like that he hated the kid so much, given that it wasn't Malcom's fault. Malcom had no say in this at all, and yet he was also a constant reminder of Tess's infidelities, and Ernie found that difficult to get past.

He'd tried, and there were times when things were better, and he forgot that Malcom was the result of Tess shagging some other bloke, but inevitably he would always return to it and remember that he really wasn't Mal's dad.

Someone else was, and they'd abandoned Mal completely.

Christ, things were a mess. Where had everything gone wrong?

Ernie picked up his phone to recheck it, hoping that Tess had been in touch since he'd last looked at it five minutes ago. But no, she hadn't, and she still wasn't picking up the phone, either.

There was a short, sharp knock on the door.

Ernie jumped up, kicking the remains of his drink over.

"Shit," he cursed but didn't stop to assess the damage and ran to the door. "Tess? Is that you?"

In hindsight, he should have checked through the window or put the chain on, but in his desperation to see Tess, he forgot about the various safety precautions he usually ran through when answering the door.

The moment he'd turned the latch and released the door, it flew open with a bang, smashing into his chin and arm as four people barged in.

"Grab him!"

"Get him down."

"Shut the fuckin' door."

Ernie was bundled to the floor of his front room by three of them, two guys and one young woman, who held him down. The last guy closed the door behind them and stood guard. They wore gloves, and bandannas over their nose and mouth to hide their identities, but they were quite clearly young. In their teens, maybe, or early twenties at the oldest.

"Get off me," Ernie yelled.

"Shut the fuck up." One of the three that had thrown him to the floor, got up while the other two held him down. The one who stood up was possibly the oldest of the bunch and was undoubtedly the broadest.

"What do you want? Let me up," Ernie yelled.

"After how you treated Tess? Fuck off. No one does that to my girl," the bigger man spat.

"Your girl? What the hell are you talking about?" Ernie answered, confused. He frowned at the man for a moment until it clicked. "Keg?"

192

"The man's a fucking genius," Keg exclaimed. "And yeah, she's my girl now, and I ain't standing for no one dissin' her. Only weak ass, nonces with tiny dicks do that. And I think you fit the bill."

"Fine, she's yours. She's nothing but trouble anyway. Good riddance to yeh."

"Nah, man. Nah. You ain't getting off that easy. No way. I gotta teach you a lesson right here. No one fucks with me or the Killers."

"No one!" one of the other guys joined in, much to the delight of the others.

As Ernie watched, Keg reached under his jacket, pulled out a long, dirty-looking machete, and admired it for a moment.

"What the hell are you gonna do?"

"I gotta take something, man. I gotta show people that no one fucks with K-Boy."

"Please, don't," Ernie pleaded, knowing there was little chance of him getting out of this now. He knew who the 'Killers' were, the Hyson Green Killers that is. They were a local violent gang that loomed like a shadow over the area. They were the reason you had a chain on the door and checked before opening it.

Why did he answer the door? He was such an idiot.

193

On his right, the girl and the second guy grabbed his arm and held it out on the floor, using the weight of their bodies to keep him pinned.

"No, please," Ernie cried, tears running down his cheeks. "Don't do this. I'll do anything. Please."

"Too late, fuck face," the last guy mocked as Keg raised the machete and brought it down hard.

Pain lanced up his arm. Incredible, unbearable pain. Ernie screamed.

"Fuck me," the girl said. "Look at that. It's spurting everywhere."

"No more jerking off for you, you limp dicked twat," the last guy continued to mock him.

"That was awesome," Keg said, "I wanna do it again. Move. I want his whole arm."

Ernie wailed and shouted, crying out for help, but knew none would come. Everyone on the street knew not to mess with the Killers, not unless you wanted them to come looking for you. Ernie had heard screams and wails of pain several times in the past, and his only response was to turn up the TV or put music on.

Whatever you did, you did not call the police or get involved.

You only did that if you had a death wish.

He regretted that now.

Keg swung the massive blade again, and more pain flooded through him. It took three swings before Keg and the others cheered the successful removal of his right arm.

But by then, he was delirious and swiftly descending into shock.

"Cut his dick off," the girl shouted.

"Take his head," another suggested. "Kill him."

But that was the last Ernie heard or understood anything as his attackers continued to have their way with him.

24

Driving back onto Maple Street the following day in his beloved Ford Capri to find it a familiar hub of chaos was an odd feeling. Rob had been called here straight from home, which was only a short distance away and was not looking forward to his return visit.

The familiar scene of police vehicles, blue and white tape, and flashing lights filled his vision as he pulled over and got out. Uniformed officers in high-vis vests were standing around the edges of the cordon, keeping an eye on the hobnobbing locals and ever-vigilant press.

Rob marched through and approached the nearest officer. He flashed his ID, and the woman waved him through the outer cordon. Moving deeper, past the various houses and cars, Rob spotted DC Ellen Dale in a white forensic coverall standing outside Ernie Newton's house. She saw him coming and walked over to meet him.

"Morning, guv," she said. "Sorry for the rude awakening."

"That's okay," Rob answered. "I was up anyway." He'd not yet heard back about how Nick and Scarlett's mission had gone, and was keen to find out. He presumed no news was good news, though. "I'm guessing it's Ernie?"

"Aye, it is. Do you want to take a peek?"

196

"Sure," Rob agreed and walked with her to a nearby van, where he removed his coat and pulled on the barrier suit. Once he was fully covered, they made their way inside, walking through a tent erected over the front of the house and into the living room, where Scene of Crime officers were already hard at work.

In the middle of the room, which had been turned into a veritable bloodbath, lay Ernie, but he was no longer whole.

His right hand had been severed and lay a few feet away, and the rest of the same arm had also been chopped off, just below the shoulder. Additionally, Ernie's head had been severed, and placed on a nearby table with an empty mug set on top, upside down, like a hat.

It looked like he'd also been stabbed several times, with a concentration of wounds and shredded clothing around his groin.

"Poor bugger," Rob muttered. "I don't care what he did to Tess or Malcom, no one deserves this."

"No, they don't," Ellen agreed, her tone sombre.

As they gazed down at the corpse, one of the Crime Scene officers walked over. Rob recognised her eyes. It was Alicia, one of the Crime Scene Managers they regularly worked with.

"Morning, sir," Alicia said in greeting. "Thanks for coming out."

"Of course," Rob replied. "What do we know?"

"It's early days," Alicia answered, but from what we can see, I think this took place late last night. There's no sign of forced entry, but there are traces of blood on the door, suggesting it was violent. And then, of course, we have Mr Newton himself. I'd say he suffered quite badly during this. From what we can see, it looks like he was alive when his hand and arm were severed, judging from the blood patterns and bruising. It looks like he was struggling at first, but from the footprints and smears, I think he was held down while they did this. The last thing was cutting his head off. That took several hits to complete. You can see the ragged cuts into the soft tissue of the neck, here."

"I see," Rob confirmed. "Thoughts on the murder weapon?"

"A large blade," Alicia answered. "A kitchen knife or something? A machete, maybe?"

Rob pointed to the head and how it seemed to have been displayed. "Any thoughts on that?"

Alicia sighed. "Not really. My guess is they were messing about, mocking him or something."

"Okay. Anything else?"

"One other thing. From what we can see, we think there were between three and five people in here with the victim. That's it for now, though."

"Okay, thank you," he said and let Alicia get back to work as he stepped away with Ellen. "What do you think? Any thoughts on who did this?"

"Could it be gang related?" Ellen asked.

"Yeah, it could be. But Ernie did have a fight with his partner, Tess, on Sunday. That led to Tess's son, Malcom, running away, and then Tess herself disappearing yesterday while Ernie was at work. Apparently, he caught her cheating with some drug dealer called Keg, and that was what led to the fight. So the obvious first assumption then, is that Keg did this. Maybe he was angry with Ernie?"

"That fits," Ellen agreed. "But we need to do some digging into Ernie's life."

"Agreed," Rob said as they stepped outside into the early morning light. "On the other hand, could this be related to Malcom's disappearance? Are the two linked, maybe?"

Ellen shrugged. "If Keg is Tess's dealer, we should check aliases and see if we get a hit? He might be known to us."

"Good idea, keep me informed," Rob said as they reached the van and started to remove their barrier clothing. He gazed out at the small crowd at the edge of the outer cordon and spotted several knots of youths in hoodies watching closely. The very sight of them was intimidating.

"Yeah, they've been hanging around since we got here," Ellen said, noticing where Rob was looking.

"The Hyson Green Killers," Rob stated, chewing his lip before turning back to Ellen. "What do you know about them?"

"Not much. I've *heard* of them, but I've not *dealt* with them."

"They the biggest gang in Nottingham, but a fairly recent phenomenon compared to old school firms, like the Masons," Rob explained. "These guys are moulded on the crack dealing gangs of the USA, along the lines of MS-13. They go by various names. The Hyson Green Killers, HGK, The Hoods, The Radford Crew and more."

"I've heard some of those names," Ellen remarked.

"Yeah. They're actually not just one gang. They're a loose alliance of several regional gangs in the city, and they fight amongst themselves almost as much as with other outside gangs. But the one thing they're united on is their iron grip on the local drug trade. They're the biggest threat to the Masons, who they do *not* get along with, and they're a nightmare for us, too. Not just because they're violent in the extreme."

"How come?"

"Because there's no central leadership. The gangs that identify as HGK are in constant flux, with old leaders getting killed or thrown into jail and new leaders taking over. Every time we think we've struck a blow or beheaded the group, they get right back up and keep on going."

"Do you think they did this?" Ellen jabbed her thumb towards the house.

"They are certainly capable. They've done worse, for sure. Killing Ernie is small fry for them."

"Wonderful."

***

Standing on the pavement with her cap on and hands in her pockets, Madeleine watched the scene, focusing on Rob and Ellen as they chatted beyond the inner cordon.

She wished she could get closer and hear what they were talking about, but there were too many police around. Narrowing her eyes, she peered at Loxley, trying to weigh him up. She'd heard the stories and rumours surrounding him and his relationship with organised crime, but she didn't like to pre-judge as most of it was likely inflated or untrue.

But he would require a more in-depth investigation and much more surveillance.

25

Rob walked into the office with Ellen to find the team already in and at their PCs. As he approached his desk, Rob locked eyes with Nick and then Scarlett, silently asking a question that didn't need voicing.

He'd slept terribly last night, wondering and worrying about how their drive with Curt had gone and if it might get them into trouble. He had no idea what had happened, and neither Scarlett nor Nick had been in touch.

Seeing them both here, alive, well, and employed, seemed to bode well, although it didn't negate his concerns entirely. Doing something that broke the code of ethics could get you fired quickly and easily, but so could knowing about such a breach and not reporting it. In fact, that could be even worse.

Whatever it was Nick and Scarlett had been up to last night, he hoped they'd been careful and intelligent about it. The last thing they needed was Curt blabbing or an unseen witness reporting it.

As Rob watched, Nick nodded and gave a surreptitious thumbs up. Rob nodded back and glanced at Scarlett, who smiled knowingly at him.

A smile broke out on his face as relief washed over him as if a great weight had been lifted from his shoulders. He wasn't sure what might happen, but a small part of him had expected to come in and find the pair of them arrested.

He was thrilled to discover that this was an unfounded fear and not the case, but now found himself feeling incredibly curious as to what they had been up to.

Although, maybe it was better if he didn't know.

With thoughts and feelings of all kinds rampaging through his head, Rob turned to the corner office, looking for his DCI. Had they already talked about this?

Spotting Nailer through the windows, Rob walked over and knocked on the door.

"Come," Nailer called out.

Rob stepped inside and closed the door behind him. "Morning."

"Morning Rob. Everything okay? How'd the trip to Hyson Green go?"

Rob ignored the question. He was too curious to find out how Nick and Scarlett's evening drive had turned out. "Have you spoken to either of them yet?" He jerked his head back towards the main office.

"Nope," Nailer answered brightly. "I was waiting for you, and you've not answered my question."

"Oh, sorry. Yeah, Hyson Green was a mess. The man I spoke with yesterday, Ernie, the boyfriend of Malcom's mother, was killed and butchered last night."

"Butchered?"

"Viciously attacked by several people, he had his arm chopped off, and eventually his head."

"Jesus. That's not good."

"No, it's not, and I have no idea where Malcom or his mother are. We'll follow up a bunch more leads, focusing on Malcom for now, and see what shakes down."

"From what you describe, it sounds like a gang-style attack."

Rob nodded in agreement. The presence of the youths watching the response, and the general style of the murder, all suggested gangs. "That was my impression too. We'll look into it."

"Alright, well, we have another complication on that front, but I'll tell you about that shortly during the morning briefing. In the meantime, let's get Nick, Scarlett and Tucker in here." Nailer nodded past him towards the room outside.

"Sir," Rob replied and opened the door. "Nick, Scarlett, Tucker, can you join us for a moment?"

Seconds later, the three officers filed in and settled into the office while Rob closed the door. Outside in the office, Ellen and Guy went about their work.

"Morning," Rob greeted them and was met with a chorus of replies. "So, how was the drive with Curt?"

"Lovely," Nick replied. "It was a very serene drive across Nottinghamshire. No dramas at all, were there?" Nick asked Scarlett.

"No, nothing," Scarlett agreed. "Curt was very agreeable, and we even got to do a bit of gardening."

Rob did a double take. "Gardening?"

"Absolutely," Nick confirmed. "I had some seeds to plant and asked Curt to help by digging me a hole. My back isn't what it used to be, so it was useful to have some help. He got a little over-enthusiastic, but it all worked out in the end."

Rob regarded Nick's smiling face and wasn't sure what to make of his explanation. For a brief moment, he considered enquiring deeper but then decided against it. "So, did we learn anything?"

"Definitely. Curt very kindly admitted to knowing more about the Columbian deal. He says that it will take place between the cartel representative and Emory, at his home, in the next few days. We recorded this confession, and when Curt found that out, he naturally agreed to help us. He also requested protection, but we said no, suggesting instead that he return home and lie low for a few days. If he disappeared, that would arouse suspicion and could lead to Emory changing his plans."

"Good thinking," Rob complimented them.

"That was Scarlett's realisation," Nick answered.

Scarlett beamed at him.

"Good work, both of you," Rob complimented them.

"Now," Nailer said. "We need a plan on how to proceed. Thoughts, please."

"What about the undercover officer?" Rob asked. "The one embedded in the Masons. We could speak to Philip and see what he can find out."

"Agreed. But we're not guaranteed to get what we need."

"Can we bug the house?" Scarlett asked. "If we can listen in, we can find out when and how the drugs are coming into the country."

"Do we have that capability?" Rob asked.

"We have the technology," Nailer confirmed. "That's not an issue. The problem is getting the bug into the right place in the limited time we have available. Bugging operations can take weeks of planning."

"Actually," Nick cut in, "I might know someone who can help us there."

"Oh? Like who?"

"Back in my Army days, I worked with some highly trained units and people, and I'm still friendly with several of them. How about I make some inquiries?"

"I've worked with some squaddies before, so that sounds perfect," Nailer answered. "Let me know how it goes. If they are up for it, I'll do the paperwork."

"Will do, sir."

"Okay, I think we're done here." Nailer got up from his chair. "It's time for the morning briefing."

26

"Morning briefing, everyone," Nailer called out as he exited his office, making for the meeting room in the opposite corner. Rob followed as Guy and Ellen rose from their desks and joined them.

"What was all that about?" Guy asked, stepping closer and keeping his voice down.

"What?" Rob asked and then pointed back to Nailer's office. "You mean the meeting?"

"Aye."

"It was to do with the investigation that Nick's heading up into the robbery in Worksop. Nothing for you to worry about. You and Ellen are with me on the Malcom case, which got a little more interesting overnight."

"Oh?"

"I'll go over it in the briefing," Rob replied as they walked into the side room, and everyone picked out a seat and started to make themselves comfortable with notepads at the ready.

"Morning all," Nailer began, standing at the head of the table. "Alright, so let's go over where we are, shall we? We've got Nick leading the investigation into the robbery and assault over in Worksop. We had a suspect in yesterday, but there wasn't enough to hold him, so he's been released pending further investigation. Nick, along with Tucker and Scarlett, are on that one, and apart from the usual bumps in the road, they're making good progress. Right?"

"Aye, Guv," Nick confirmed. "We've got some research to do, so we'll see where that takes us."

"Excellent," Nailer replied.

Rob nodded appreciatively at how Nailer had presented the information to the group, keeping the details vague so much of it remained on a need-to-know basis.

"Sir," Guy said, leaning forward. "But, shouldn't CID be looking into this robbery? Surely we have more serious crimes to be looking into?"

"Normally, I'd agree with you," Nailer answered. "However, this case was initially being looked into by CID, but they passed it onto us when they realised there was a link to organised crime through one of the main suspect's relatives."

"Aaah, okay. Fair enough," Guy said, sitting back in his chair.

Rob gave him a look, wondering what that outburst was really about.

"Now then, let's talk about the missing teenager, Malcom Hooper, as we've had a couple of developments overnight. So, Rob, where were we with this at the end of play yesterday?"

Rob nodded to his DCI before launching into his speech. "This came in on Wednesday when Vivian Aston, who was part of my Orleton corruption case before I joined the EMSOU, came to us saying she'd seen a teenager called Malcom being thrown into the back of a van with their throat cut. Vivian is homeless and can be a little excitable, but we took her at her word and investigated. To her credit, it looks as if she was telling the truth. We found tyre tracks and dried blood at the scene, which backed up Vivian's story. When we looked into it further, we found a missing persons report from Malcom's mother. Vivian saw the attack on Sunday, and Tess, Malcom's mum, reported him missing the next day. We immediately visited Malcom's and discovered Tess was not home. Only her long-term partner, Ernie, was in.

"We spoke to him and he seemed distinctly uninterested in Malcom and the fact that he'd not been seen for three days. He was much more interested in Tess and her whereabouts. It turned out that Malcom was Tess's son from an affair, and Ernie had never liked Malcom for that reason. From talking to him further, it seems that Ernie recently discovered that she was having another affair with a dealer called Keg, and the resulting argument caused Malcom to run away. Then, on Wednesday, Tess left after dumping Ernie over text.

"Ernie was vague about the details of their argument, but I got the impression that they had a fiery relationship. Anyway, we didn't get too much out of him and left him be. Then last night, his house was stormed by several people, and he was attacked and killed. He had his head, hand, and the rest of his arm severed, but not in that order. It looks like he suffered, which means they were making a statement. We're following various lines of enquiry to try and piece this together." He glanced over at Ellen and nodded.

"Actually, on that note," Ellen interrupted. "I've called the PNC guys, and I can confirm that there's no local drug dealer going by the name of Keg. At least, there's no one on our systems by that name, anyway."

"Great, thank you," Rob replied.

"Do you think Ernie's killers and Malcom's kidnapper might be the same person or people?" Scarlett asked.

Rob took a moment to think about it. "That's possible. Vivian only saw one person, but that doesn't mean there weren't more in the van."

"And this attack on Ernie was on a residential street?" Guy asked.

"Correct, Maple Street."

"Any witnesses?"

Ellen coughed before she answered, "We've had officers interviewing residents since we got there, but so far, no one's talking. No one dare say a thing."

"Which suggests it was a gang," Nailer added.

"It is HGK territory," Rob explained.

"And we're pretty sure they were there, watching the investigation," Ellen added. "They weren't hiding."

"Of course they weren't," Nailer answered. "They were watching you, sure, but they were also there for the neighbours. Reminding them about who owns that street. No one will speak to you while the gang is watching."

"Exactly, even Ernie was nervous about talking to us at the door when we got there. Refused to see our ID until we were inside," Rob agreed.

Scarlett spoke up. "Is this gang the HG...?"

"HGK," Rob explained. "Hyson Green Killers."

"Are they linked to the Masons?"

"No," Nailer answered. "Well, not in a positive way. The Masons and HGK are bitter rivals and have been since the beginning. They hate each other."

"Oh okay," Scarlett replied.

"Right now," Rob continued, "we're still no closer to finding Malcom. We've been briefing the press and doing our best to get the word out, but with no luck so far. We're hoping to find Tess soon, but in the meantime, our next step is to delve deeper into Malcom's life and speak to his friends and teachers to see if we can build up a picture of his life."

"Excellent work," Nailer stated. "But it seems our investigation has not gone unnoticed."

"Oh?" Rob asked.

"As part of the drive to get information out, we gave a phone number and email address that people could call, and last night, we had a call that has me concerned."

"The killer?" Rob asked, feeling the hairs on the back of his neck stand on end.

"We think so. This is the message he left." Nailer grabbed the tablet he'd brought into the meeting and played an audio file.

"Well, hello there, Nottinghamshire Police," said a digitally altered and distorted voice. "You know, when I saw this hunt for Malcom on the news, and the phone number that people could call with information, I just couldn't pass it up. It was too tempting. I just had to call. I'm a little disappointed that its messaging service. I'd have much rather spoken to a real person, but hey-ho, I guess that's the reality of budget cuts and austerity, right? But honestly, the fact that you've only just cottoned on to what I'm doing, after so long, tells me everything I need to know. You're nowhere near finding me. Not even close.

"Malcom has made a fine victim, he really has. I thought that he was just another homeless kid living under Trent Bridge. But imagine my surprise when I saw the news report because, you know, I didn't think he looked homeless in his Nike puffer jacket. But this explains it, doesn't it. He was so young, and supple, and tender. And you know what? It's given me the desire to up my game, especially now that you're aware of me. I mean, why hold back now? Dear little Malcom has given me a taste of something better, and I want more, because this is about more than just me.

"Oh yes, did you think that's all this was? Did you think I was just killing for the fun of it? How naive of you. Now, I will admit to taking pleasure in my work, but this is not just fun and games. No, this is my calling. This is my mission. Society has to change, my friends. I want to break down our taboos and introduce you all to new experiences. I want you to discover the same things I have. And you know what? Do you know what the best part of that is?"

The man on the recording laughed. "Yes, that's right. It's already begun. Many of you have already had your first taste, and you have no idea. Oh, I'm going to enjoy this. It's going to be wonderful and revolutionary, and delicious. Oh, so delicious." He laughed again. "But I think that's enough for now. I've dropped enough hints for you, I think. I have work to do. Goodbye, for now, my friends. I will see you soon."

214

The line clicked off.

"Well, if *he's* not bat-shit cuckoo, then I don't know who is," Tucker remarked.

"Aye," Nailer agreed. "But don't take crazy or disturbed to mean stupid. If, as he hints, he's been killing people for a while, then that speaks to a calculating mind."

"His suggestion that he's ramping up is also worrying," Rob added.

"Indeed. So, next steps?"

Rob nodded and turned to the team. "Ellen, Guy, I need you two to visit Malcom's school and interview his friends, teachers, and classmates. You're looking for anyone who might want to hurt him."

"That didn't sound like a classmate," Guy stated, pointing to the tablet.

"No, I agree, but we do our due diligence anyway. For all we know, the person who left that message is just a crank caller who got lucky, and the real kidnapper or killer is his best mate's older brother."

"Sure thing," Ellen replied. "We're on it."

Rob nodded. "Meanwhile, we need to keep looking at CCTV, calling his mother, Tess, pull their phone and bank records, etcetera, etcetera. We need a full work-up to look for any hint of who his kidnapper might be. Alright? Okay, let's get to work."

215

27

Standing at the window, Ellen gazed out at the fields behind the school, where teenage kids were being put through their paces on the football pitch and the nearby netball court.

Running and jumping, the youngsters called out to their friends while the teachers ran around after them, refereeing the games and keeping score.

She'd only left school about nine years ago, but it felt like an age ago. These kids looked so young to her now.

Back then, when she'd been their age, she felt so grown up, and yet now, in hindsight, she realised how wrong she'd been. And yet, here they were, questioning these kids about the disappearance of one of their peers. It didn't get much more adult than that.

When they'd first arrived, they'd been shown into the headteacher's office, where they'd discussed their observations surrounding Malcom and his friends with him, the head of year, and Malcom's form tutor. It seemed he hung around with three others, Zeke, Jordan and Angel, most of the time, although he did have other friends, too. There hadn't been any major issues within this friendship group that the staff were aware of, but there had been some issues with a couple of boys in Malcom's class, who'd been a little rough and verbally abusive. They'd also made a couple of threats, which the staff insisted they'd dealt with.

For the interviews with the kids, the staff had been making phone calls to their parents, calling them to let them know and allow them to sit in on the interview if they wanted.

Holding a small stack of business cards in her hand, she ran her thumb down the side of them, riffling the stack, before taking the top card and turning it over in her fingers, glancing at the Nottinghamshire Police logo, her name and phone number.

They'd just finished speaking to Jordan Anderson, who was apparently Malcom's closest friend at the school, according to the teachers. He'd been sullen but cooperative and, with his mum sitting beside him, talked about how the group had hung out on Sunday. Jordan related how an argument had broken out between Malcom and Zeke, in which Zeke accused Malcom of leering at Angel.

According to Jordan, Zeke seemed to quite fancy Angel and didn't like Malcom looking at her.

Once they'd finished their questioning, Ellen handed Jordan her business card and asked him to call if he thought of anything else. He'd said he would and left. Zeke was next on the list.

A troublemaker, Zeke often played truant, rarely did homework, and was frequently in detention. The staff saw Zeke as a bad influence on Malcom, and from the sound of it, Ellen might have to agree.

"Fool's errand or valuable research," Ellen stated as she continued to watch the kids outside.

"You mean this?" Guy asked.

She could see his reflection in the glass, sitting at the table, checking through his notes.

"Yeah," she confirmed and looked back at him.

He pulled a face and shrugged. "Don't know. We barely know anything about Malcom so far and what his life was like. We've not even found his mum yet."

"True," Ellen agreed. "Hopefully, that will change today."

"That would be good, providing the staff don't keep us waiting too long between each child." Guy grunted. "You're close to Tucker, right?"

"We've worked together a lot, yes."

"Has he told you anything about what he's looking into with Nick?"

Ellen shook her head. "Nope. I figure it's got nothing to do with me, and that's fine. I've got enough to work on right now without adding to it. Why?"

"They're just being a bit secretive. I was just wondering what they're up to."

"Tucker's not said anything to me since he went to speak to one of his informants."

"One of? He sounds like a modern-day Fagin, with eyes and ears everywhere," Guy commented.

"He spent time on the streets before joining the force, so he's got a few friends," Ellen remarked. "It's useful."

"Have you ever met any of them?"

Ellen pulled a face as she looked over at Guy. He seemed indifferent and only half concentrating on what Ellen was saying. "No. He keeps them to himself. He'd lose their trust, otherwise."

"Aye, I guess so," Guy agreed.

"You must have some informants of your own, right?"

Guy grumbled something. "I don't tend to get too friendly with criminals," he remarked. Ellen picked out a note of disgust in Guy's tone.

"To each his own," Ellen muttered before an uneasy silence settled over the room. Was Guy casting doubt on Tucker's loyalty and commitment to the police?

The door opened, and three people walked in. The two teachers and a student. The staff, Mrs Duke and Mr Kendrick wore smart clothing with ID badges around their necks, while the boy wore the school's blue uniform and carried a bag over his shoulder. As the young man walked in, he glanced nervously at Ellen and Guy before taking a seat where Mrs Duke directed.

"So, this is Zeke Ward, and he's one of Malcom's friends," Mrs Duke said, introducing him.

"Nice to meet you, Zeke," Ellen said.

"Y'alright?" Zeke replied, his eyes still nervously glancing around the room.

"We've been calling his mum," Mrs Duke said, "but we've not been able to get through."

"Okay," Ellen replied and then nodded to the male teacher who'd taken a nearby seat. "With the pair of you in here, we'll be fine."

"That's what I thought," Mrs Duke answered.

"What's this about?" Zeke asked.

"Your friend, Malcom."

"Oh…" Zeke seemed to think about this for a moment. "Have you found him yet?"

"Not yet," Ellen answered. "That's why we're here. We were hoping to speak to people who knew him, and might be able to help us with our inquiries."

Zeke huffed but said nothing as he glanced around the room.

"May we have a look in your bag, please?"

Zeke sneered. "Yeah, sure. Go for it."

He kicked the bag over, and Guy grabbed it. He lifted it onto a nearby table and started to empty it.

"Do you know Malcom well?" Ellen asked.

"Dunno," Zeke answered.

"But he's a friend, right?" Ellen pressed.

"I guess."

Ellen took a breath, seeing already how much work this was going to be. "Do you hang out with him?"

"Yeah," Zeke agreed.

"Just in school or outside of it as well?"

"Both," Zeke replied, his voice clipped and grumpy.

"Who else do you hang out with? Who's in your group?"

Zeke seemed to pull a face at the question as he thought about his answer. After a moment, he crossed his arms. "I ain't grassing on no one."

"You aren't grassing anyone up, because we already know who you hang out with. Jordan and Angel, right?"

"Yeah…"

"So when was the last time you saw Malcom?"

"Sunday," Zeke answered, dejectedly.

"You were hanging out together, right?" Ellen pressed as Guy continued to hunt through the backpack.

"Yeah."

"And how was that? Were there any problems or anything?"

222

Zeke shrugged. "Dunno."

"You don't know? Are you sure about that? Was there any kind of argument, maybe?"

Zeke gave her a look. "If you already know, why are you asking?"

"Because I want to hear it from you, Zeke, that's why."

"Do you? Well, I don't need to tell you shit!"

"Zeke!" the teacher exclaimed. "That's enough."

"It's okay," Ellen said, waving the teacher off as she continued to focus on the boy. "You're right, Zeke. You don't have to say anything. That's your right. But may I remind you, Zeke, that Malcom is still missing after several days, and there are signs that he was hurt. Anyone who's acting suspiciously or is hiding things from us could be a suspect. Do you want to be a suspect? Do you have anything to hide?"

Zeke seemed to deflate where he sat. "No..."

"Then tell me about the argument you had, what happened?"

"I don't know, it was over some stupid shit—"

"Zeke!"

Ellen raised a hand to get the teacher to stand down. "It was over Angel, wasn't it? Angel Green?"

"Maybe."

"Did it get physical?" Ellen pressed, keen to push him and get him to talk.

"If you already… Ugh. Yes. Alright. We got into a bit of a fight, and then Mal stormed off. I didn't see him again."

"But, you sent him some messages, right?"

"Fuck me," Zeke hissed. Beside him, his teacher bit her lip in annoyance. Ellen could almost see the steam coming out of her ears. "Yeah, alright. We swapped some messages. So what."

"Then, may I see your phone, please? I'd like to read them."

Zeke sighed and scanned the room, looking very uncomfortable, but after a moment, he dug his phone out and unlocked it, handing it to Ellen. She checked his texts, WhatsApp messages and emails, soon finding the most recent messages between them. Filled with abbreviations and text speak, it took a moment for her to decode them.

It started with Zeke accusing Malcom of being a coward, which caused Malcom to hit back. After that, there was a curse word laden back and forth, with Zeke accusing Malcom of fancying Angel and Malcom denying it, until Malcom called Zeke 'a fatherless fucking bastard'.

Zeke didn't take kindly to this and replied with a racism-filled rant, calling Malcom a 'half monkey' who'd never even met his real dad.

The next few messages were a litany of insults between them until it stopped in the early evening. One of the last things Zeke sent was a warning, saying, 'You're fucked'.

"That's some fairly ripe language," Ellen remarked. "Racist, too."

"What?" the teacher exclaimed.

"He deserved it," Zeke replied.

"For calling you fatherless?" Ellen asked.

"Yeah," Zeke answered and seemed to calm down. "My parents split up a few years back." He paused as a sneer spread over his face. "But at least I know who my dad is."

"And what did you mean by, 'you're fucked'?"

"I don't know," Zeke answered. "I was angry, so…"

"So you threatened him," Ellen answered while Guy took photos of Zeke's text messages.

Zeke grunted.

28

With his fingers interlaced and elbows on the desk, Rob leaned his chin against his hands and stared at nothing. Focused on the middle distance, Rob tried to link the various aspects of this curious case together, because right now, they almost seemed like separate incidents.

First, Malcom disappears, apparently kidnapped in what seems like a violent altercation on the banks of the Trent that was at least partially witnessed by Vivian Aston. The Scene of Crime officers had been investigating the area and sent DNA samples off for sequencing. They'd been to Ernie's house the day before to pick samples from Malcom's bedroom, and based on the early results, it was an obvious match.

The blood they'd found at Trent Bridge had been Malcom's, and they'd taken samples from several places. All of it matched, which meant he'd lost a lot of blood. An awful lot.

With a tightening knot in his stomach, Rob knew what that meant. And if he ever managed to get in touch with Malcom's mother, he'd need to have a very careful chat with her. He couldn't say for certain that Malcom was dead, but it seemed highly unlikely that he would be alive after suffering such massive blood loss.

All of which meant, they had a killer on the loose.

But then they had Malcom's mother, Tess, disappearing and leaving Ernie. That seemed easy enough to explain and was probably the reason why Malcom ran away in the first place.

But then there was the mess this morning. Ernie's murder came out of nowhere and was arguably even more brutal than Malcom's kidnapping. Was this the same killer or something new? Was there a link between Ernie's murder and Malcom's kidnapping?

Right now, they seemed very different, and Rob had a strong suspicion that Ernie had been killed in a gang-related attack. But why?

The obvious conclusion was that this had as somehow to do with Tess and their break up, but why? Was it this boyfriend, Keg? Had he chosen to take revenge on Ernie? That made sense, and if true, meant it wasn't linked to Malcom's kidnapping.

Maybe it wasn't, but Rob couldn't discount the possibility that whoever had killed Ernie was the same person who kidnapped and probably killed Malcom.

And then there was the creepy phone message. Whoever had called in seemed very knowledgeable about the kidnapping, providing details that they had not released, such as the make of puffer jacket Malcom had been wearing.

227

It was possible that the caller had just made a guess and somehow managed to get it right, but it was also possible that the caller was just a weirdo who'd done their research into Malcom, trawled through his social media presence and seen the jacket in another photo.

Either that, or it really was the killer, and they had two murderers to find and arrest.

Shaking his head, Rob ran his fingers through his hair as his mind boggled with possibility. Like a crazy puzzle, he kept turning it over and over in his mind, looking at it from different points of view, trying to link the various parts in new ways. But so far, while he had several possibilities, he couldn't pin it down.

This was going to take some time and further investigation.

With a grunt, Rob leaned back in his chair and lifted his phone. It had been nearly thirty minutes since he'd last called Tess, so he figured he'd try again and hit redial.

Rob waited. On instinct, he almost pulled the phone away from his ear and ended the call before he realised that Tess's phone was actually ringing.

"Oh," he gasped and stiffened in anticipation. Would she pick up?

Five rings later, and with Rob's hopes starting to fade, it suddenly connected.

"Urgh, hello?" The female voice on the end of the line sounded weak and strained.

"Tess? This is Detective Loxley from the Nottinghamshire Police. I need to speak to you regarding your son, Malcom. I left you some messages."

"Ma… Malcom?"

"Yes. Your son. We need to talk to you about his disappearance. Can you come in? Or I could come and get you?"

"Aaah…" she gasped and groaned. She sounded badly intoxicated or maybe even high.

"Tess? Are you okay? Can we come and pick you up?"

He heard movement on the line, but she said nothing.

"Tess. Are you there? Shall I come and pick you up? Tess?"

"Pick… Up…" she muttered, struggling to get her words out.

"Where from? Where are you?"

"Hyson… Skate park…" she grunted. "Help…"

"We will," Rob answered. "Stay there, we're coming."

The line went dead halfway through his reply, sending a note of concern shooting up Rob's spine.

"Tess?" Scarlett asked from her nearby desk. She'd leaned in and overheard bits of the call.

229

Already up, Rob grabbed his coat. "Yeah. Come on, we need to go get her. She sounded strung out."

"Drunk? High?"

"Both?" Rob answered as they darted from the EMSOU office down to the carpool, only to find none available. Annoyed, they rushed into the car park with Rob leading the way to his pride and joy.

Belle. His black 1985, end-of-the-line Ford Capri 2.8 injection, gleamed in the late afternoon light. He loved driving this car, which he'd managed to keep in excellent condition over the years, but he had to admit to a hint of worry deep in his mind about bringing an intoxicated woman back to the Lodge in the car.

If she threw up over the back seat, he'd be having words with her later, that was for sure.

Within moments they were blasting their way south into the city, making for Hyson Green, just north of the centre of town. When they finally pulled into Hawksley Road and found a place to park, he'd filled Scarlett in on the one-sided call and his impressions about the state of Tess.

Getting out, Rob locked the car and peered up the street.

At the end of Hawksley Road, the street made a ninety-degree right-hand turn onto Maple Street, with the skate park on the outside corner of that bend.

As they approached, Rob could make out a few knots of youths, many of them in hoodies and tracksuits with gleaming white trainers, standing around talking. A couple of them were even skateboarding.

As they neared the park and the bend, Rob looked up Maple Street, towards Ernie's house, where he could see the police cordon still in place with a smaller group of officers guarding it. Ernie's body would have been removed by now, but the Forensics Team would be going over that front room in great detail, looking for any hint of a clue that might point them toward the killer.

Dismissing the crime scene, he focused on the park and scanned around, hunting for any sign of Tess.

Several of the teenagers were already looking their way with 'mad dog' stares, trying to intimidate them.

"This looks like it'll be fun," Scarlett muttered.

"Watch your back," Rob replied, keeping his voice low. "We get in, find Tess and get out."

"You've got no argument from me," Scarlett replied as Rob reached the gate and turned in. Pausing for a beat, Rob took a moment to identify the areas he couldn't see from the street.

"What you doin'?" one of the nearby youths said.

"Looking for a friend," Rob replied and marched in.

Calling it a park was incredibly generous, Rob thought. It was little more than a few areas of grass and concrete with a few permanent skateboarding ramps, and everything was covered in graffiti. Colourful stylised words covered every surface of the ramps and surrounding walls, including the whole side of the end terrace house of Maple Street that adjoined the park.

This was clearly a focal point for the local youth. A place for them to hang out that, in no uncertain terms, they had made their own.

"Fuck off," the kid muttered as Rob strode in with Scarlett on his heels. He needed to look behind the ramps to see if he could spot Tess anywhere.

He hoped she was still here. He didn't want this to be a wasted trip.

"Ay up, you're a bit of alright," one of the others called out to Scarlett.

"Oi, fuck face, get the fuck out of 'ere," another remarked to Rob, swaggering closer as he spoke. Most others in the park watched, their eyes tracking them as they marched by, wondering what these two smartly dressed adults were doing here.

They were in clear view of the uniformed police further up the road, but they didn't seem to care.

"Rob," Scarlett said, leaning in and pointing. "There."

Rob saw it too. A single, slight figure slumped up against one of the ramps. A couple of teens were standing close by. Rob walked over as one of them gave her a gentle kick.

The other spotted them and urged the kicker away, leaving the woman on the floor.

"Tess?" Rob said as he crouched beside her, ignoring the fleeing youths. "Tess? Is that your name?"

Barely conscious, with lank, unwashed hair and dirty clothing, she groaned but didn't answer. She had a cheap phone in her hand with a cracked screen. On instinct, Rob tapped the power button, and a selfie of her and Malcom appeared on the screen, smiling through the cracked glass.

"It's Tess," Rob said. "Help me get her up."

Between them, they managed to get her up and onto her feet. She moaned as they moved her while the kids in the park laughed, jeered and insulted them.

Rob ignored them as they carried her to the pavement and made for his car. Nearby, the police at the crime scene looked on but didn't leave their posts.

"Are you…?" Tess croaked.

"I'm Rob, and this is Scarlett. We're with the police."

"Police?"

"Don't worry?" Scarlett reassured her. "We'll get you somewhere safe where you can sober up."

"Thank… you…"

233

Tess stumbled to the car, dragging her feet half the time. She'd have been flat on her face if it wasn't for them holding her up. She babbled the whole way back to the vehicle, making very little sense, although Rob made out the names of Malcom and Ernie in there.

Between them, they managed to get her into the back of Rob's car, although that was no easy task with it being a two-door vehicle.

Scarlett got into the back too. Tess promptly collapsed onto her and started to cry.

"Malcom," she sobbed. "Where's Malcom?"

"We're looking for him," Rob answered, catching his breath in the driver's seat. She was heavier than she looked.

"I lost them both," she wailed. "I lost them."

"Let's get her back," Scarlett suggested.

"Aye," Rob agreed. "She'll need a night to sober up. We can talk to her tomorrow." He gave Tess another look, grimacing at the snot and tears leaking from her face, and hoped no other bodily fluids would join them. He didn't fancy cleaning the upholstery.

Rob turned the key, firing up the engine with a roar.

29

"We've spoken to your mate, Boyd Dunn," Ellen said, leaning in towards the fifteen-year-old sitting opposite. "He told us what you've been doing to Malcom."

"I ain't been doing nothin'," Ted Preston replied. "I don't care about Mal."

"That's not the impression we got from Boyd." Ellen fixed Ted with a glare. "He was very forthcoming, actually. He told us all about what you've been doing. Your teachers told us, too, about the shoulder barges and the threats of violence."

"So what?" Ted protested. "We didn't mean it. We weren't going to do shit."

"So, you weren't going to hurt him, then? Is that what you're saying?" she pressed, feeling sceptical.

"No."

"But you were rough with him. You pushed him around and got physical."

"I never hit him," Ted said defiantly. "He's not worth it."

"You didn't punch him," Ellen stated.

"Nah, man. No way."

Ellen eyed him for a moment, wondering how far to push it, before choosing to throw caution to the wind. "How about... slitting his throat? Would you do that?"

235

Ted gave her an incredulous look. "What? No. Of course not. What the hell?"

"Are you sure?" Ellen asked, still carefully leading him up the garden path.

"Yeah, I'm sure. Are you insane?"

Ellen smiled. "But, you were given detention for doing this, right?" Ellen extended a finger and drew it across her neck in a threatening manner.

Ted rolled his eyes. "Yeah, so what? That don't mean nothin'."

"Is that right," Ellen replied.

Beside them, Guy reached over and grabbed Ted's backpack. "I'm just going to have a quick search through, okay?"

"What? No. You can't do that."

"I can, and I will," Guy replied. "I'm searching your bag in accordance with Section 1 of the Police and Criminal Evidence Act, because you've displayed threatening behaviour towards a fellow student who's since gone missing, to see if there's anything in your bag that we need to be concerned about. Okay? Do you understand?"

"Yeah but, that's my stuff."

"Exactly," Guy replied, and started to rummage.

Ted seemed aghast, and glanced over at Ellen. "Is he allowed to do that?"

"He is," she replied. "Unluckily for you. Why, is there something in there we should be concerned about?"

"Err, no… nothing."

Ellen didn't believe him for a moment. Suddenly, Guy yelped.

"Ow! Aaah, what have you got in here," Guy asked as he held the pocket open and peered inside. "Well now, that is interesting."

Before her very eyes, Ted seemed to sink into his chair, almost folding in on himself, as beside her, between thumb and forefinger of a gloved hand, he pulled out a pen knife with the blade extended.

The teachers in the room gasped.

Ellen gave it a long hard look before she turned back to Ted and met his gaze. "You were saying?"

30

Pulling open the dishwasher, Briana dropped her used plate, cutlery and glass into the rack before cleaning up. She wiped the table and washed off the baking tray she'd used, and within moments, everything was done and clean. Satisfied, she glanced over at the handful of items in the dishwasher and wondered if it was worth turning it on. It would probably be quicker to hand wash them, and it would likely use less water too.

She stared at it for a moment more, then dismissed the idea.

Cleaning the dishes was not what she wanted to do after working all day. The only thing she desired right now was to collapse in front of the TV and watch the latest Chris Evans film while munching on something sweet.

The thought of a treat made her glance up at the fridge, where she'd placed several reminders about joining a gym. She sat on her rapidly growing arse all day long for work, and it simply wasn't doing her any good. She needed to get out, move, work up a sweat, and shed some of the extra pounds that had started to build up. She'd already noticed that some of her clothes were beginning to feel a little tight, and it wasn't as if she could afford to buy a new wardrobe of outfits to wear.

Sighing to herself, she closed the dishwasher and opened the cupboard, eyeing the snacks she kept in there. The bag of chocolate eclairs was calling her name, and she couldn't think of anything better than a mouthful of delicious chocolate and caramel while watching Chris's bulging biceps.

She reached for the bag, only for her phone to start buzzing in her back pocket.

She knew who it was without looking, but pulled the phone from her pocket and checked, just to be sure.

"Mum," Briana groaned. She stared at the vibrating phone for a moment, weighing up the pros and cons of answering the call, before deciding she simply wasn't up to listening to her overbearing mother drone on for an hour about how she was wasting her life, or how her body clock was ticking.

Her mother was desperate for Briana to find a man, settle down, and pop out a few sprogs for her to dote on.

Well, she didn't feel like listening to that familiar rant tonight and rejected the call with a roll of her eyes.

"Not tonight, Mother," she muttered, casually dropping the device onto the counter before grabbing the eclairs. She tipped about a third of them into a bowl, knowing full well that if the packet was beside her for the movie, she'd chomp her way through the whole thing without even thinking about it.

Satisfied with the portion she'd allocated for herself, she returned the packet to the cupboard, grabbed her phone, and walked through to her modest front room.

As she sat on her sofa, folding her legs beneath her, she felt her phone buzz twice, alerting her to a text message. She knew before looking that this was her mother again.

Sure enough, a quick glance confirmed her suspicions. She opened her phone and read the text.

'Don't make me come over there, young lady. Answer your phone.'

Briana pulled a face. 'Not tonight.' She wrote. 'Been a long day. We'll talk later in the week.' She hit send. That would ward her off for a while.

Satisfied with her reply, she placed the phone face down beside her, so it wouldn't beep or buzz and grabbed the remote.

A few minutes later, she was comfortably chewing on the first of her chocolate and caramel treats as the production company logos played at the film's start.

As the handsome face of Chris Evans appeared on the screen, she forgot the worries of her day and the attentions of her mother and lost herself in the film, until it was rudely interrupted by a knock on her door fifteen minutes later.

The sudden noise jerked her out of the trance she'd fallen into and back into reality.

"Wha... Ugh. Christ, Mum," she muttered to herself while getting up off the sofa. "Can't you just leave me alone for one night?" she whispered before raising her voice. "Hold on, Mum."

Storming out of her lounge, she braced herself for the torrent of well-meaning but bloody annoying comments she was about to face. She loved her mother, but she really did need to learn to keep her nose out of her affairs. It was why Briana had been so keen to move out as soon as possible, because she was so fed up with it.

Her mother might very well be a social butterfly who thrived on being around people, but she needed to realise that not everyone was like her. Some people just needed their own space and found social gatherings to be exhausting affairs that could only be tolerated for a short time.

That probably made her something of a disappointment to her mum, but it was what it was, and nothing was going to change that.

Turning the key, she pulled the door open to find that it wasn't her mother out there at all.

Briana frowned briefly at the strange man standing in her doorway.

"Err, hello? Who are you?"

"Hello, Briana," he said, before striding inside.

Hearing her name caught her off guard, and caused her to hesitate. "Wait, no. What are you…" But he was inside.

Slamming the door behind him, he grabbed her with his gloved hands and forced her to the floor.

Briana screamed, but it came out muffled through his hand as she grabbed his arms, trying to force him off.

He grimaced and grabbed her hair, then jerked her head up and slammed it back down. Pain exploded through her skull, and her vision swam as he did it again.

She cried out, sobbing, begging him to stop.

"Please… No…," she yelled, but it sounded muffled through his hand.

A third slam into the floor, and she lost all sense of where she was or what was happening. Moments later, she realised he was rolling her over, and a horrific thought appeared in her fuzzy mind.

Was he going to rape her?

Weakly, she bucked her body, trying to throw him off, only for him to grab her again and slam her face into the wooden floor.

Something cracked as hot pain blossomed from her nose.

She cried out as he grabbed her hair again. This time, he yanked her head back. That's when she saw the blade.

"No!"

242

It bit deep into her throat, causing a torrent of pain and panic to consume her every waking thought.

The man stepped off her back as she watched her lifeblood gush out of her. She tried to scream or cry out, but only gurgles bubbled from her ruined throat. As her strength faded, she collapsed to the floor, letting shock take her into the veil of endless night.

"Lovely," the man crooned from somewhere behind her, sounding satisfied with his work.

31

"I'm going to have to stop having these late nights with you," Scarlett said as they drove into Worksop town centre. "Chris is going to start asking questions."

"It's all for a good cause," Nick replied with a smile. "Did he not understand what he was getting himself into by getting engaged to a detective?"

"Yeah, he knew. He likes his own space, so I don't think he's too bothered."

"Good thing, really," Nick said as they pushed through the darkened streets. It might only be Thursday night, but there were still plenty of people out and about, drinking and socialising. The glow from the bars and pubs helped to light up the town, turning night into a neon day as they approached midnight.

"You found Malcom's mum, then," Nick remarked.

"Tess? Yeah," Scarlett confirmed. "Rob got through to her, and we picked her up from the Hyson Green Skate Park. She was a mess."

"Damn. What did you do with her?"

"We put her in a cell. It was the safest place for her, really. She had some wraps on her too, so... I don't know if we'll charge her with possession. Probably not with everything she's going through. Depends what shakes down, I suppose."

"How bad was she?"

"Pretty bad. We had to carry her to the car. She couldn't walk. Hopefully, by tomorrow she'll be ready to talk."

"That'll be fun. I don't envy you and Rob at all."

"I know," she agreed. "I wish we had some better news for her about Malcom, but it's not looking good."

"So, you've still got nothing?" Nick asked. He'd been busy all day, working on something for tonight, but he'd played it all very close to his chest, and she still didn't know where they were going or what they were doing here tonight.

"Nope. Nothing. We've got no idea where Malcom is. We're still trying to track the van over CCTV, but there are too many blind spots, and we're not sure which is the right van. We've got several options right now. We know Malcom was at Trent Bridge from the blood we found, but judging by the amount, I can't see him surviving."

"So, you're chasing a dead body."

"Probably. And an elusive one at that," she answered while thinking about their chat with Tess tomorrow. Somehow, they needed to tread a fine line and not get her hopes up too high but not dash them completely. It was possible—unlikely, but possible—that Malcom was still alive, although she'd be shocked if he was at this point.

245

Scarlett gazed out the passenger side window and watched the people stumbling through the shadows after one-too-many drinks and lamented the morbid nature of her job. Once again, they were picking up the pieces after someone had taken a sledgehammer to someone else's life.

"Thanks for letting me join you on this," she said, grateful to Nick for including her in this investigation.

"That's okay," he replied. "I get the impression you need this."

"Yeah, I think I do," she agreed, comforted that Nick recognised this in her. "Chris and Rob want to wrap me up in cotton wool and protect me, but I can't just sit by and do nothing. These monsters killed my friend. I have to do something."

"Of course you do. I get it completely. You don't need to explain yourself to me."

"Thanks."

"Besides, cotton wool's not your style."

Scarlett smiled. "Go on then. Why are we out here?"

Now it was Nick's turn to smile, before replying in a conspiratorial tone. "That's a surprise." He winked.

Scarlett furrowed her brow in frustration as Nick pulled up to the side of a random road close to the centre of Worksop. There were people walking around, stumbling home in small groups. The men spoke loudly and cat-called the women, who tottered about in high heels, wearing dresses that revealed more skin than they covered.

Scarlett eyed them all suspiciously, looking for whatever it was Nick might be waiting for, while trying to dismiss the parallels between the people around her and the night out she'd had with her mates when one of them had been kidnapped.

After several minutes, Scarlett started feeling anxious and shifted position in her seat. She was about to ask Nick what the hell this was all about when the back door behind her suddenly opened, and someone jumped into the car.

Startled, Scarlett jumped in fright and turned on her seat to look behind her.

A scruffy-looking woman with bleached blonde hair that needed its roots done stared back at her. She had no make-up on and wore an old, stained, ripped denim jacket and jeans. For a moment, Scarlett thought a homeless woman had got in, but something about her bright, piercing blue eyes gave her pause.

"Miller," the woman said, still staring at Scarlett.

"Black," Nick replied.

"You didn't say this was gonna be a menage a trois." The woman Nick referred to as Black glanced at Nick.

"Not a problem, is it?"

247

The woman looked back at Scarlett, meeting her gaze without a hint of fear or concern. She sniffed, wrinkling her nose, before she answered, "Nah, it's cool."

"Excellent," Nick replied and pulled out into the road. "Everything's in the case beside you. You have a fifteen-minute drive to get familiar with it all before I drop you at the target site."

She nodded once, never taking her eyes off Scarlett.

Still shocked by what was going on, Scarlett had yet to sit back in her seat and continued the stare-off with the strange woman. She looked short but stocky, with nails trimmed all the way down and grubby fingers.

"Problem, sweet cheeks?" the woman asked.

"Scarlett," Nick said, his voice soothing. "Trust me."

The woman smiled. "Do as the boss says." She smiled a final time before grabbing the case, placing it on her knees, and opening it.

With the woman now ignoring her, Scarlett relaxed a little, turned back around, and stared at Nick. After a few moments, he glanced her way and met her glare. He did a double take, then raised a finger and mouthed one word to her.

"Later."

Scarlett pouted in annoyance but had little choice but to trust him as they raced out of Worksop and into the surrounding countryside.

Nick's statement about how long it would take to get wherever they were going was accurate. They pulled up on a road through a village. Scarlett wasn't sure where they were exactly, but when she looked back to the woman sitting behind her, she'd finished going through the case and was sitting calmly.

Nick turned to her too. "You know what to do."

She nodded and, without another word, got out. She closed the door behind her and strode off through their headlight beams before she turned right and disappeared.

Scarlett stared out the window for a moment before turning to Nick. "Are you going to explain what the hell that was all about?"

Nick sighed. "While in the military, out in Iraq and Afghanistan, I worked with a special forces unit and their team. There were a few of us who were chosen for a variety of reasons. We were given extra training, and I took part in some missions that are still top secret to this day. Calico was part of that team."

"Calico?"

"I have no idea if that's her real name, but that's who I know her as. She's very highly trained and well connected."

"Oh," Scarlett replied, starting to get an idea of what was going on. "Is she former SAS or something, then?"

"No. There's no women in the SAS. I don't really know who or what she is in that regard. I just know that she was part of the military, was very highly trained, and worked with the SAS boys when needed. We got to be friends over the course of a few missions, and we've remained in contact since I got out."

"So, what's all this then?" She waved her hands at the car they sat in. "What was in the case?"

"The bugs. We're quite close to Emory's house, and Calico will get them where we need them."

"She will?"

"Yep. This is well within her skill set."

"I bet," she replied, her head filled with questions about this curious Calico Black. But she refrained from inquiring further about her, sensing that Nick either wouldn't know the answer or simply wouldn't tell her. Everyone had secrets, after all. "How long do we wait?"

"She won't be long," Nick reassured her.

Thirty-five minutes after Calico had disappeared from view, there was a sudden knock on Nick's window.

Scarlett turned to see Calico's face there.

Calico moved to the back door and threw the case inside. "Bugs planted," she said.

250

"Right," Nick replied and reached into Scarlett's footwell. There was a small flat bag there, which Nick grabbed and lifted onto his lap. He unzipped it to reveal a laptop inside. The machine came to life as he opened it, revealing a bank of wireless feeds from the bugs that had been planted. There seemed to be a mix of video and audio, and the signal from them all was strong.

"Perfect," Nick said. Scarlett looked up with Nick, but Calico was gone.

"Alright," Scarlett muttered, impressed. "So, she's Batman."

"Bat-Woman," Nick corrected her.

"Whatever."

32

Rob noticed Scarlett as she wandered into the office, looking like death warmed up. She sported large dark rings beneath her bloodshot eyes, and there was a lethargy to her movements that was unlike her. Everyone else was in, including Nick, who he knew she'd been out with as part of the operation against the Masons.

"Late one?" Rob asked as she reached her desk and dumped her stuff.

"Yeah," Scarlett confirmed. "I didn't get to bed until well after two in the morning. It was probably closer to three by the time I was in bed. And then I didn't sleep very well, either. I need another coffee."

"I was going to say, it's not like you to be the last one in."

"I know, sorry. Didn't miss anything, did I?"

"Nope," Rob confirmed. "We'll have the morning briefing soon."

"Okay, cool", she said, taking her seat. She leaned back and closed her eyes. "Can I just go to sleep here? You'll wake me if anything happens, right?"

"So, how did it go last night?" Rob countered with a question of his own.

Scarlett opened her eyes and glanced around. She scootered the chair out from her desk and rolled around to Rob, coming in close. "I guess I can tell you."

"Aye," Rob agreed. "There's a coffee in it for you, if you do."

"I think that's the best thing I've heard all morning," she said with a satisfied sigh. "So, we met up with one of Nick's Army mates. Some woman called Calico Black. We picked her up and dropped her close to Emory's place with a case full of bugging equipment. She took them and, half an hour later, reappeared, having placed them in Emory's house. I've never seen anything like it. I have no idea how she did it, but the bugs are all good, from what we can make out."

"That's great. Now we just need to wait until we hear something," Rob said with a smile. "With any luck, we can catch these guys in the act."

"Here's hoping," Scarlett agreed. "So, how about that mug of black gold?"

"Right then, boys and girls, let's have a chat, shall we?" Nailer called out as he crossed the office, making for the meeting room.

Rob turned to Scarlett and shrugged. "Sorry, it'll have to wait."

"If I fall asleep in there, I'm blaming you."

"Noted. I'll grab you a coffee as soon as we're done, okay?"

"You'd better."

"You can count on it," he replied, before getting up, wandering over to the conference room and taking his seat with the others.

"Okay, let's get into it," Nailer remarked. "The Hooper case, where are we?"

Rob nodded. "Well, we have a DNA match between the blood we found at the bridge and the samples that Forensics got from Malcom's bedroom, which is about as close to confirming Malcom was there as we're going to get. This probably means we can assume that he was brutally attacked at the bridge and taken away by this white van that Vivian witnessed."

"I agree," Nailer confirmed.

"In addition, we've been looking into Malcom's school life and friendships. Ellen and Guy spent the day interviewing Malcom's teachers and classmates at his school yesterday." Rob turned to Ellen. "Do you want to run us through what you discovered?"

"Sure," Ellen agreed. "We spoke to a whole bunch of people, and it appears that Malcom had a troubled school life. There are three friends that he hangs about with, Jordan Anderson, who's his closest friend, Zeke Ward and Angel

Green, but that's about it. From what we could find out, his friendship with Zeke seems strained, at best, and we know that Malcom got into an argument with Zeke on Sunday while out with his friends. I think this was the catalyst for him running away."

"How bad was the argument?" Scarlett asked.

"Both Jordan and Angel said that it got physical. They didn't throw punches, but they did rough each other up. After that, Malcom went home, but they continued to send insulting and threatening messages to each other over the next few hours. We saw Zeke's phone and the thread of messages on it. They were brutal, with Zeke being openly racist and Malcom insulting Zeke's broken family."

"Okay," Nailer commented. "What else?"

"While we were there, the staff told us about some issues that Malcom had with two boys in his class. Again, they'd occasionally been rough with him, as well as making threats, such as drawing their finger across their throats from across the class."

"They threatened to cut his throat?" Rob asked.

Ellen shrugged. "I know. It sounds like it's linked, given what we know of the attack, but I'm not sure. That said, however, we did find a knife in one of the boy's bags. We confiscated it and sent it for testing but chose to let the school deal with him for now. Both boys had alibis for the night of his death that we're looking into."

"Okay, let me know what you get."

Ellen nodded. "Will do. But that's not the only thing we got. Overnight, Malcom's friend, Jordan, contacted us with some screenshots taken from his phone. They show a message from Malcom to Jordan. The message contained images of another message that Malcom got from Zeke's older brother, Wayne. It seems that Zeke told his older brother about the fight and disagreement, because Wayne messaged Malcom that night, and threatened to kill him."

"Kill him?" Rob asked.

"Yep," Ellen confirmed. "He wrote, 'I'll fucking kill you, you...' and then spouted off a string of racist expletives."

"And what do we know about this Wayne?" Nailer asked.

"Well," Ellen replied, "we've done a little digging this morning, and it seems that Wayne is indeed known to us. He's been picked up for a few minor offences, and we suspect that he has some links to the gangs. But he's very low level."

"Alright, then, I think it's time for a chat with this Wayne."

"I agree," Rob said, and turned to Ellen. "You and Guy pay him a visit and see what he has to say for himself."

"Will do."

"Sir," Guy replied.

Nailer turned to Rob. "Have you spoken to Tess yet?"

256

"No, that's first on my list for today, though. I'll head down there with Scarlett this morning. Hopefully, she'll be sober and ready to speak to us."

"Not before I've had my coffee," Scarlett said.

"Absolutely, we need to keep our priorities straight," Nailer agreed. "Okay, and I've already had an update on the Curt Gates situation, which is good, so I think we'll adjourn here and see what turns up today."

Rob got up and made for the door with all the others. As he left the room and made for his desk, Scarlett poked him in the arm.

"Oi, the coffee machine's over there."

33

Pulling to a stop on Collison Street, Ellen gazed up at the three-story, flat-fronted terrace house that lined one side of the road and picked out the Ward household just a few doors further up. The dwellings were bland, red-brick affairs that were little better than a box. It looked like a grim place to live.

"Let's go and see if Wayne's got anything to say for himself, shall we?" Ellen remarked.

"Do you think this is going to come to anything?" Guy asked from where he sat. "Given what we know of the killer driving a white van and leaving that taunting message, I mean."

"I don't know," Ellen answered honestly. "With Malcom's friends yesterday? No, I was fairly sure that wouldn't come to anything, but this? I don't know. Maybe. Wayne's certainly old enough to drive, and he does have gang connections and a record, so..."

"If he did it, he's an idiot if he thinks he could get away with kidnapping his brother's friend after their argument."

"If he did it," Ellen repeated. "Hmm. Stranger things have happened, that's for sure. I guess we'll see. Hopefully, he's in."

"We've got him down as unemployed as of a couple of months ago, when we last spoke to him."

"Maybe we'll get lucky, then?" Ellen remarked before climbing out of the car. "He did threaten to kill Malcom, after all."

"That's a big step up from petty crime," Guy said as he joined her on the pavement. He sighed. "I don't know. I just think we're chasing ghosts."

"Would you rather be somewhere else?"

He shrugged. "I just don't want to waste my time, and... I think the Gates case is more my style."

"Well, tough," Ellen remarked, smiling at him. She thought he'd seemed a little distracted and dismissive towards this case, so maybe that was it. He liked the look of the Gates case and chasing down some gangs. But Rob and Nailer had chosen their teams for the two investigations, so he was shit out of luck.

"Right, come on then. Let's get this done, shall we?" Guy said, taking a deep breath.

"That's the spirit," Ellen remarked and started off down the street.

She knocked on the door to the Ward household and then rang the bell, before stepping back to observe the windows for any twitches.

Several seconds later, the door opened, revealing a young man who seemed barely out of his teens. "Yeah?"

"Wayne Ward?" Ellen asked.

"Who's asking?"

"Notts Police," she answered, showing him her ID. She already recognised him from his mug shot. "We'd like to ask you a few questions."

Wayne pulled a face and then leaned his shoulder against the door frame. "About what?"

Ellen grimaced. He looked like he was getting comfortable. "Shall we head inside?"

"Nah," he replied, with a shake of his head. "I'm happy here. What have I done now?"

Ellen gave him a look before deciding to roll with the punches and do as he asked. She pulled her phone out and brought up the screenshot of his message to Malcom. She showed it to him. "Do you remember sending this message?"

Wayne peered at the phone, curling his lip up in disgust. "Aaah, right. Fuck me, took you long enough to get round 'ere, didn't it? I sent that ages ago. And yeah, I saw the news. Let me guess, you think I did him in, right? You think I've got him in my basement or something, yeah?"

"You threatened to kill him," Ellen replied. "So yeah, the thought had crossed my mind. Is he in your basement?"

"I ain't got a basement."

Ellen wasn't a fan of the games Wayne was playing. "Where were you on Sunday night?"

"Here, obviously. Otherwise, how would I have spoken to my little bro and found out what had happened?"

"And you have a witness that can attest to that?"

"Yep. Zeke and my mum. You can ask them if you like. Zeke's at school, mind, but my mum's in. You wanna talk to her?"

"Absolutely," Ellen replied before Wayne stepped back into the room, letting them in.

The front room was set up with a large sofa facing a giant, wall-mounted TV, with several consoles below it. Wayne walked into the front room and pointed to the door leading deeper into the house. "She's through there."

Ellen glanced at Guy and then nodded to the door. "Do you want to do the honours?"

"Why not." With a final quick look at Wayne, Guy walked through to the back room.

Wayne gave her a disapproving look before swaggering around to the sofa and dropping into it. Ellen watched him and then moved into his eye line.

"How about you tell me how you came to send that message?"

Wayne shrugged. "Zeke was all upset, like. Slamming doors and shit, so I came out and just asked him why he was acting like a dick. He told me about this mate, Mal, and showed me the texts he'd sent." Wayne shook his head. "It was fucked up, man, and it got me all angry, like. So I copied the number and told him to fuck off. Otherwise, I'd fuck him up."

"You said you'd kill him," Ellen clarified.

"Yeah, so. I wouldn't actually kill him, obviously. I just wanted to scare him, like."

"Scare him?"

"Yeah. No one fucks with my little bro, not like that. It's fucked up." He shrugged again. "I didn't know he was gonna catch some feels over it and do a runner, did I?"

"Do you drive a van?" Ellen asked, trying to catch him off guard.

"A van? No. Fuck off."

"Do any of your friends drive a van?"

"Do they fuck-as-like. I wouldn't be seen driving round in a bloody transit. Nah, mate. No way."

"Not even when you're doing jobs for the Masons?" If she was going to push his buttons, she might as well hit the massive glowing red one, she thought.

He gave her an incredulous look. "Masons?"

"Yeah, that family you do stuff for. Surely you know who they are."

She watched as Wayne screwed his face up in disgust and looked away.

"Nothing to say?"

"Not to you," he muttered as Guy walked back in.

Ellen gave Guy a look and walked round to meet him. "Any luck with her?"

"I didn't get much out of her. She's barely conscious as it is. So I asked her if Wayne had been in on Sunday night, but she said she had no idea. She'd been drinking and had no idea if he was in or around."

"Not much of an alibi," Ellen replied.

"Nope."

In truth, it wasn't much of anything. They couldn't prove he was innocent, and they couldn't really prove he had anything to do with it, either. Apart from the text, they had nothing.

Ellen grunted in annoyance.

34

"How many is that now?" Rob asked as he climbed out of the car.

Scarlett glanced at her takeaway coffee. "Of the day, or since I got to work?

"My point exactly," Rob remarked. "You'll be on the loo all day at this rate."

"At least I'll be awake."

"I guess." Rob laughed as they set off across the small car park towards the custody suite. It was by far the safest place for Tess while she slept off whatever concoction of drugs she had in her system.

"How do you think she'll be?" Scarlett asked.

"I have no idea, but I know that I'm not looking forward to this. She's potentially lost both her son and her long-term partner in one week, so I'm expecting her to be a mess."

"Yeah, I can't even imagine what that's like."

"We'll tread carefully," Rob stated. They needed Tess on their side, and didn't want her working against them or resenting them for how they'd treated her. "I have no intention of charging her for possession. What she's been through is enough to drive anyone to drugs."

"Agreed. We'll take it steady."

They walked into the building and, after passing through security, soon found themselves waiting in an interview suite. It wasn't long before Tess walked in, accompanied by a custody officer who checked they were all okay before leaving them to talk.

Rob was glad to see Tess up and about, no longer under the influence of drugs or alcohol, but it looked like she still had a ways to go before she fully recovered. The rings beneath her red eyes, her poor skin condition, and the sores around her mouth betrayed how little care she was taking of herself. She also sported what looked like a black eye, small cuts, and several bruises on her arms that suggested she'd been hurt.

As good as it was to see her sober but hungover, Rob was under no illusion that she was in any way clean or free of whatever addiction she was battling. Tess had a long road ahead of her if she wanted to clean up her act.

"Morning," Rob started, wondering if she remembered them from last night. "I don't know if you remember, but I'm Detective Loxley. We brought you here last night."

"Yeah, I think I remember," she answered.

"How are you feeling?"

She gave him a look that betrayed her disdain for his question. "How do you think I feel?"

"Not good," Rob stated.

"Too fucking right." It looked like she'd been crying.

"Hi, I'm Scarlett. I'm afraid we need to talk about everything that's been going on."

"I know," Tess muttered, with a heavy sadness to her voice. "Just get on with it."

"What are you aware of? How much do you know?"

Tess took a deep breath. "My son went missing on Sunday, and you lot did jack-shit until Wednesday. Is that about right? Oh, and my shithead boyfriend is dead, right?"

"Ernie? Yes. I'm afraid so," Rob replied, a little surprised by the venom in her voice when she spoke about Ernie. "I'm sorry for your loss."

"My condolences," Scarlett added.

Tess sniffed and wiped a tear away. "Thanks. I... So, have you found Malcom yet?"

Scarlett shook her head. "I'm sorry, no, we haven't, but we think we know what happened to him on Sunday night."

"Fucking hell. I'm going to need a drink. Go on then, what? What happened to him?"

"We have a witness and DNA evidence that suggests Malcom was attacked and abducted close to the Trent Bridge on Sunday night. However, we don't yet know what happened after that, or where he might be now."

"Attacked!?"

266

"Yes. I'm sorry," Scarlett answered, her voice low and soothing.

Tess took a breath and suppressed a sob. It broke out, and for a moment, she cried quietly, before slowly getting herself under control. "I'm sorry. Ernie can go fuck himself, but Malcom… I… I don't know what I'd do if…"

"I understand. But that's why we're here. You might know something that can help us."

"I'll try to help."

Scarlett pointed at her face. "What happened to your eye?"

Rob frowned, wondering where she was going with this.

Tess went to answer, but hesitated and sighed. "That was Ernie. He hit me."

"When?"

"A few days ago. It's nothing too bad, but… It's fine."

"It's not fine," Scarlett pushed back. "Don't dismiss this. Has he done this before?"

"Yeah. This isn't the first time he's hit me." She sighed. "But it was the first time he hit Malcom."

"Ernie hit Malcom?" Scarlett clarified. "On Sunday night?"

"Yeah. He was just trying to defend me. He's a good kid, really, and I think it shocked him."

"So Ernie was attacking you, and Malcom tried to intervene?"

267

"Yeah. It's probably why he ran."

"I think there were other factors at play," Rob remarked. "But I can understand that this probably shocked him."

"Absolutely," Tess agreed. "But, what other factors?"

"Well, when we spoke to Ernie, he said that Malcom had been having a tough time with friends. Is that right?"

A sadness fell over Tess. "Yeah. He's been having friendship issues for a while with that Zeke and a couple of boys in his class. It's been affecting his mood and causing all sorts of problems. He wouldn't go to school and would just skive off. I spoke to the teachers, but they didn't do a lot." She paused and then looked up. "Do you think his friends had something to do with his disappearance?"

"Well," Scarlett said. "Our team have been talking to his school friends and teachers. There are certainly issues, and from what we can ascertain, Malcom had a confrontation with Zeke on Sunday. They argued. It got a little physical and continued over text once Malcom had left. We also know that Zeke's older brother joined in and sent a threatening message to him."

"Did he kidnap him or hurt him? Is that why he didn't come back?"

"We're still looking into it," Rob explained. "I wouldn't want to jump to any conclusions at this point."

"So where is he?" Tess cried. "What happened to him?"

"We don't know. We'll keep you up to date," Rob reassured her.

"Tell me about Keg," Scarlett asked.

Tess gave her a look. "What about him?"

"Well, he's what all this is about, right? Ernie discovered you were having an affair with this Keg and got upset."

She seemed to deflate. "Yeah. He found out."

"And, Keg is your drug dealer." Scarlett phrased it as a statement rather than a question.

Tess shrugged. "He's a mate, and he helps me out sometimes, that's all. He treats me right and doesn't hit me, either."

"Unlike Ernie," Scarlett remarked. "I get it."

Tess nodded.

"We found some wraps of crack cocaine on you when we brought you in," Rob said. "Are they yours?"

"I just… I found them."

"Found them?" Rob didn't believe a word of it. "What, just on the street or something? Were they just discarded by the side of the road?"

"I… I can't remember. I wasn't going to take them."

"I see. Do you know Keg's full name? His real name?"

"Aaah, no. I just know him as Keg."

"Are you sure about that?" Rob asked. "You're having an affair with him, and you don't know his name?"

269

"What is this?" Tess exclaimed, raising her voice. "My son is missing, and you're interrogating me about a man I'm seeing? What the hell!"

"Calm down," Scarlett soothed, her hands raised. "It might help us find your son if we can eliminate Keg from our investigation. That's all we're trying to do. So, are you sure you can't remember his name?"

Tess looked away. She looked sheepish and worried. "No. I can't."

"Do you have a photo of Keg?" Scarlett pressed.

"No."

Rob sighed, annoyed. It was obvious she was trying to protect Keg, and if Rob had to guess, this Keg had probably warned her about saying anything to the police if she were ever taken in. Getting anything out of her about Keg would be a battle, to say the least.

Rob leaned in closer. "Do you think Keg might have anything to do with Ernie's murder?"

Her eyes widened, and Tess seemed frozen to the spot. "Err, no." But the wobble in her voice betrayed her.

"So he wasn't angry that Ernie had hit you?"

"Well, he didn't like it, but... No, he wouldn't..."

"Are you sure?" Scarlett insisted. "I'd be wary about protecting him. Do you think he'd lie for you if things were reversed?"

"He didn't do it," she snapped and crossed her arms.

Rob sat back in his seat, frustrated. "Alright, let's go over this again…"

35

Seth pumped the dumbbells again as the dude who'd been using the leg-extension machine finished up. There were other machines he could have used, but only that one gave him the perfect viewpoint.

The man wiped the machine down and moved on while Seth placed the weights back onto their rack. He smiled and walked over with his stuff, pleased with his choice and timing.

As he climbed on, he quickly glanced at the beautiful Candy across the way on the running machine. She'd only just started and would be there for a while, allowing him to enjoy the hypnotic spectacle of gravity and its effects on her body.

He climbed onto the machine, chose a weight that wouldn't tax him too much, and started his workout.

Over the years of coming here, he'd become quite adept at secretly enjoying the display of these fit young women working out while wearing body-hugging lycra.

It wasn't the only reason he came, of course. He loved working out and feeling the burn as he pushed himself to the next level, but he didn't want to do that every time.

Sometimes, he preferred to work at a more manageable level and enjoy the view, and today was one of those days.

After a hard week at work, he deserved to gaze at Candy's gravity-defying boobs. It was just what the doctor ordered.

Of course, he didn't stare like some of these other idiots. Nor did he invade their personal space. No, he kept his distance and was careful to take notice of any mirrors or phones that might be recording him in the background, and enjoyed the show from a distance.

He had no desire to get caught and thrown out.

Seth allowed his gaze to wander over the rest of the room, curious to see who else might be here.

He noticed a new girl he'd not seen before. She must be new. She certainly looked like she worked out regularly, that was for sure. He watched her from afar until he noticed Candy finish her run and step off the machine.

She glanced his way, and they locked eyes for a second. He picked up a hint of disgust in her glare and cringed. He shot Candy a quick smile as the new girl approached Candy's machine.

"Are you done?" the new girl asked.

"Yeah, I'm done." She sighed. "...with the machine *and* the audience." Candy shot him a look filled with daggers.

The new girl glanced his way, but he wasn't looking.

"Noted," she replied as Candy walked away, moving onto something else, far away from him.

He'd pushed it too far and silently chastised himself. He should have been more careful. He really didn't want a complaint lodged against him.

Several more reps later, he looked up at the new girl jogging on the treadmill. She wasn't quite as jiggly as Candy. Instead, she had a trimmer, taut physique that Seth appreciated. She'd worked hard to look like that.

As he stole a second glance at her, she looked over, catching him looking.

Damn it, what's wrong with me? Am I losing my touch?

He'd used this machine for countless sessions, pumping his legs and watching without once being called out or even noticed. And yet today, he'd been caught twice.

The girl held his gaze for a moment longer than felt comfortable and then smiled.

The thud of the muscle deep in his chest quickened.

This was new.

Did she like him watching? She looked away as thoughts and possibilities rushed through his head. He'd always daydreamed about coming here and picking up one of these lovely ladies, but that was just a pipe dream. He never thought he'd manage it. But maybe today would be different?

After a few more leg pumps, he chanced another glance, and this time, he caught *her* looking over at *him*.

A frisson of excitement rippled through him.

She'd been eyeing him up.

What on earth was going on?

He averted his gaze, not quite believing this was happening. But when he turned back, again she was looking.

She smiled at him. *What the hell?*

Well, in for a penny, in for a pound. He smiled at her, and she seemed to like it. She winked and then turned away.

This was crazy. Was she actually into him? Where the hell would this go?

He concentrated on a few more leg pumps as he let his imagination run riot.

Suddenly, she stepped off the treadmill and walked over, using her towel to dry herself.

Play it cool, play it cool.

But his heart was hammering out a drum roll in his chest.

"Hey," she said brightly.

Seth looked up and, for a brief moment, enjoyed her heaving chest. He tore his eyes away and forced himself to look into her eyes. "Hi. Are you new here?"

"Yeah," she replied with a smile that sent a thrill up his spine. "My first session. Do you come here regularly?"

"Several times a week," he admitted. "I love it."

"Me too," she agreed.

"You look like you work out. You look good." Was that too much? Would she get creeped out?

275

"Thank you, that's very kind of you to say."

No, she loved it. "Credit where credit's due."

"You look good yourself," she said and briefly stroked his upper arm. The warmth and softness of her skin thrilled him. "Nice. Very nice."

This was going ridiculously well. "Thanks."

"Pleasure," she said, and glanced around. "I might just have a go at lifting that," she said, pointing to a nearby barbell.

"Go for it."

She winked and wandered over. He found himself staring at her swinging hips. He looked away. He was getting far too carried away by all this. This had to be a dream or a trap or something. This never happened.

"Watch this," she said, looking over at him while adjusting her ponytail.

"Alright," he agreed and took a break as she squared up to the weight.

Angled away from him, he had a great view as she crouched, sticking her bum out to reach down and pick up the weight. Was she doing this on purpose? She managed the modest weight easily enough before dropping it back down.

"Well done," Seth said, still enjoying the view.

"I think I'm done for the day," she answered, breathing hard. "It was good to meet you…?"

"Seth," he replied.

She smiled and offered her hand. "Seth. A very manly name. I'm Briana."

"Nice to meet you, Briana."

"And you." She winked at him again. "Keep working on that delicious body."

"Err…" He wasn't sure how to handle that remark and found himself briefly lost for words.

She seemed to enjoy his awkwardness. "See you soon."

And with that, she strode out, leaving him with the memory of her walking away in those fabulous leggings.

He tried to move onto another machine and keep going, but his head just wasn't in it anymore. Frustrated, he gave up, had a quick shower, and walked out of the gym, wondering when he might see the lovely Briana again.

"Hey, Seth."

Briana was outside, leaning up against the wall.

"Oh, hi. I… I thought you'd gone," he stammered.

She smiled. "I was going to, but I just couldn't stop thinking about you, so I waited… I hope you don't mind."

His heart tripled in speed. "No, not at all. That's great."

"So, you don't think it's creepy?"

"Not at all. It's great." Seth couldn't believe it. Was she seriously interested in him? He took a breath while thinking about how to handle it. Best to let her take the lead, he

277

reasoned. Let her choose what they did. There was no need to rush things. "What did you want to do?"

She smiled. "Want to come back to mine?"

Seth stiffened and, for a long moment, found that he couldn't quite breathe. This was madness. "Are you sure?"

"Yeah, why not. Here, we'll go in my car. Jump in."

Seth pulled a face and glanced over at where he'd parked. He could come back and get it later, he reasoned. There was no need to be difficult when he had such a fantastic opportunity.

Surely this was all code, right? Codename coffee and all that? Come back to mine, was code for, I want to bang you senseless, wasn't it?

There was no way he was missing out on this. "Sure."

He jumped into the passenger seat and watched her fiddle with the key. She accidentally set the wipers going before finally getting the car in gear. She giggled, and set off.

She was probably nervous. He certainly was.

"Where's home?" Seth asked.

"Not far. Just a few minutes drive. I live in Lenton."

"Oh, yeah? That's not far." He knew the area of Nottingham well and reasoned that he could walk back to his car after... Well, after whatever it was that Briana had in mind for him.

278

"I hope you don't think I make a habit of picking people up at gyms," Briana said. "Because I don't. This really isn't like me, but…"

"But?" Seth asked, curious.

"But, there was just something about you. I don't know what it was, but I just had to… take a bite, if you catch my drift."

Seth swallowed in a futile attempt to banish the lump in his throat. "Err, yeah. Sure."

She navigated her way through the city into Lenton and pulled up on the side of the road. Seth noted the name. Forsythia Gardens. He wasn't familiar, but it seemed to have an estate of terrace houses and flats packed into a small area.

"Sorry," she said, climbing out of the car. "It's not much, but it's home."

Seth couldn't say he was very impressed, but his home wasn't anything extraordinary either, and right now, he didn't care as long as she owned a bed.

"This way," she said, leading him across the grass to her front door. "Here we are. Home sweet home."

"It's nice."

"Thank you, Seth. I'm glad you like it." After fiddling with the key, she finally got the door unlocked and moved inside. "Come in, come in."

With his heart skipping several beats a minute, Seth nervously followed her, allowing himself a cheeky look at her perfectly formed rear as he went. He was looking forward to getting a handful of that.

He closed the door behind him.

"Can you lock it?" she asked, pointing. "Just turn the latch. You wouldn't want to be disturbed, right?"

With trembling hands, Seth did as she asked and locked the door. She must be planning something wild. This was going to be mind-blowing.

When he turned back, he couldn't see her.

"Briana?"

"Through here," she said. "I'm in the kitchen."

"Oh." He dropped his bag and followed her through. He stepped into the kitchen to find the floor covered in plastic sheeting and Briana leaning up against the counter across the room.

"Hi," she said.

"Hey. Err, what's all this?" He waved towards the sheeting.

She smiled sweetly. "Just in case things get messy."

He raised an eyebrow at her wicked smile and took another step. She pushed off from the counter and closed the gap between them, her eyes locked on his. As she drew close, she reached out and grabbed his wrists.

A floorboard creaked behind him.

An arm reached around from behind and clamped over his mouth as metal glinted. White hot, intense pain exploded across his neck as something cold and sharp bit into his throat. It ripped across, tearing and ripping.

Warm liquid gushed as his mind went wild. He ripped his hands from Briana's grip as she stepped back.

He couldn't breathe. His hands flew to his neck, desperate to stop the flood of blood flowing from his neck.

Why?

He looked up and tried to ask Briana, 'why', but he couldn't talk. He was drowning in his own blood. Ahead of him, Briana grinned wildly. With her hands clasped in excitement, she bounced on the spot, giddy with glee.

It was the last thing he saw.

36

Rob watched the video playing on his monitor with interest. It was a view from opposite Ernie's house, from the window of a neighbour, and showed the moment when a group of four youths barged into Ernie's house.

The video was short, no more than a few seconds long, but it clearly showed the event. It started with the group already knocking on the door. A moment later, the door opened, and the group rushed in, with the last person through closing it behind them. It then cut to about fifteen minutes later, when the door opened again, and they left the property with their heads down, seemingly in good spirits.

Rob watched the video loop a couple of times, focusing on different aspects of the clip each time, trying to take it all in.

After the third cycle through, he felt he had a good handle on things.

"Right," Rob began, sitting back in his chair. "So this came in overnight?"

"Apparently," Nailer answered, standing beside Rob's desk. Scarlett, Ellen and Guy were there also, watching. "It was sent to us anonymously, but I think we could figure out which house it came from."

"Probably, but that doesn't mean the person living in that house sent it to us," Rob answered. "If this was shared on a street WhatsApp group or something, it could have come from anyone."

"Fair point," Nailer agreed.

"Do we know who these people are in the video?"

"Not yet," Nailer answered. "We've already got people looking at the video and comparing it to mug shots, but it's not as if we have a close-up of their faces."

"Could it be this, Keg, character?" Scarlett asked.

"Maybe," Rob answered. "We need to do some digging and see if anyone comes forward."

"Unlikely," Ellen muttered.

"They might if they knew we had this footage," Guy added. "Someone might talk."

Rob shrugged. "It might just tip the balance."

"So, what do we do?" Scarlett asked.

"Maybe if we head back to Maple Street and knock on some doors?" Rob suggested.

"You're not trying to get out of tonight, are you?" Nailer asked.

Rob smiled at the reference to the gathering at his place, scheduled for that night. "Never."

"Are you ready for us?" Scarlett asked.

Luckily, he'd not forgotten about the gathering and had been shopping over the last few days to pick up what he needed. He was feeling confident that he had everything. Besides, they were going to order in. It didn't get much easier than that. "I'm ready," Rob replied. "Don't you worry. You just concentrate on turning up on time."

"I'll be bringing a bottle or two," Nailer remarked.

"Lovely," Rob replied.

"We're bringing drinks?" Guy exclaimed. "No one told me."

"Looks like you've got some shopping to do," Scarlett said, her voice full of mirth.

"Damn it."

"I'm sure they'll be plenty," Rob added. "I've got a fridge full."

Nearby, a phone rang. It was coming from Nailer's office, he excused himself and dashed to take the call.

"Hopefully no one dies suddenly in the meantime," Ellen remarked. "That would be bloody typical."

"Comes with the territory," Rob commented. "We'll just reschedule it to the following night."

"A man with a plan," Guy commented. "I like it."

"Well, I can't let you down now, can I?"

Moments later, Nailer walked back. "Looks like you've got your wish."

"What?" Guy asked. "That someone's died?"

"No, I'm pleased to say," Nailer explained. "We've got someone down at the front desk who says he lives on Maple Street and claims to have seen the house invasion at Ernie's. He wants to chat with someone."

37

Ellen walked into reception and spotted the man waiting in a nearby chair. An older gentleman with mid-brown skin, salt and pepper hair, in jeans, and a jacket that had seen better days sat patiently with fidgeting hands. Every now and then, he'd nervously glance up at the people passing back and forth before looking away and focusing on the ground in front of him.

Ellen approached with Guy right behind her.

"Hi, Mr O'Neal? Marvin O'Neal?"

He looked up. "Hello, yes. That's me." He smiled.

"Hi. I'm Detective Inspector Ellen Dale, and this is Detective Gibson. Would you like to come with us, so we can chat in private?"

"Yes, please," Marvin agreed and got eagerly to his feet.

"Great, this way," she said and led him through a security door and along a couple of corridors to a vacant room with sofas and a nearby coffee machine. He followed right behind her, keeping close. He seemed keen to get out of the reception, and as she waved him into the room, she heard his sigh of relief.

"Here, take a seat," she urged and waved towards one of the soft chairs. He sat, and she did the same on the next chair over.

"Would you like a drink?" Guy asked. "Coffee? Tea?"

"Aaah, just water, thank you," Marvin answered.

"Coffee for me," Ellen added.

"Coming right up," Guy answered and moved to the machine where he busied himself making the drinks.

"Are you okay?" Ellen asked. "You seemed a little nervous out there."

"Yeah, sorry. I've never been here before and speaking to the police... Well, it makes me nervous."

"You have nothing to worry about," Ellen reassured him.

"If *you* lived on Maple Street, you *wouldn't* be saying that," Marvin stated, fixing her with a knowing look.

"HGK," Guy suggested as he brought the drinks over.

Marvin hesitated and then nodded.

"This is the local gang, right?" Ellen asked, just to be sure.

"Yeah," Marvin agreed, taking a breath. He seemed to need a moment, so she sat back and waited for him to open up. After a few seconds, he pressed on. "You have no idea what it's like living there. We live in fear, constant fear for our lives. That gang, the Killers, they rule Hyson Green. They terrorise the streets, and frankly, we feel like hostages in our own homes. I daren't go out at night. None of us does. If they're down at the skate park, at the end of the street, I stay in with my doors locked. They're a nightmare. They're constantly dealing drugs and getting drunk. They play loud music for hours, shouting and making noise for most of the night. They've broken into most of the houses at one time or another or attacked random people walking past, going about their business. They set fires and vandalise anything and everything. The kids round our way don't stand a chance. You're either with them or against them. That's it. And god forbid you ever do what I'm about to do. My days would be numbered if they ever find out that I came to you."

"And yet, you came," Ellen stated.

"I had to," Marvin replied. "I can't stand it any longer. I've had enough. What they did to Ernie is a step too far. Any of us could be next. They need to know that they're not all-powerful."

"I understand. Thank you for taking this risk. What can you tell us?"

"This has been brewing for a long time, but no one wants to step up, so I took the initiative. I want people to be able to report things anonymously, without anyone knowing who was who. So I bought a whole bunch of old, second-hand phones with pay-as-you-go sims and mailed them to neighbours I knew wanted to do something. Then we all joined a new, anonymous WhatsApp group where we could all talk and share things. One of us spotted the group going to Ernie's house, alerted us, and we started filming. You should be getting more videos coming in today, but they'll all be anonymous."

"We got one overnight," Ellen said.

"I know," Marvin answered. "There were four people who broke into Ernie's house, and I can identify one of them right now. The other three, I'm not yet sure about, but the one I know is known as K-Boy. He was probably the ring leader."

"Do you know his real name?"

"Yep. Keegan Baron, although I've heard his friends call him Keg."

Ellen grinned as the jigsaw piece fell into place. "Brilliant, thank you. And the other three?"

"We'll let you know. I can do some digging and get back to you."

"Okay, thank you. So, how do you know this Keegan?" Ellen asked, curious as to why he'd know the youth's name.

"Mainly because of the group. We share all our information. The gang live locally mostly, and have family in the area, so someone usually knows them. But also because of Tess." Marvin sighed. "Tess was never a part of the Saviours, mainly because of her drug use. We can't trust her, so we watch her instead."

"The Saviours?" Guy asked.

"Oh, yeah," Marvin chuckled. "It's what we call ourselves. If they're the Hyson Green Killers, then we're the Hyson Green Saviours."

"Nice," Guy said with a smile.

"Very good," Ellen added.

"Thanks. Yeah, so we noticed that Tess keeps having Keg over to her house during the day while Ernie is working. We know who Keg is, so we had our suspicions about what Tess was doing with him."

"Which is what?" Ellen pressed.

"Do I need to spell it out for you? She's a drunk and a drug user, and Keg deals drugs. I think you can put the rest together yourselves."

"Fair enough," Ellen replied. Marvin's confidence was growing.

"But we think that Tess was doing more than just buying drugs. We think they were having an affair. So it was only a matter of time before it blew up, what with Ernie's temper."

"How do you mean?"

Marvin sighed again. "He hits her. We all know it."

"You knew Ernie was hitting Tess?"

"We did. Tess always denied it, of course. We reported it, but Tess would never do anything about it and refused any investigation, so it went nowhere. There was nothing we could do."

"Shame," Ellen remarked, feeling sad for Tess. "Can you tell us anything about Malcom's disappearance?"

"Sorry, no," Marvin answered apologetically. "I saw that report on the news, we all did, but we don't know anything about it."

A thought occurred to her. "Do you think the gang might have anything to do with it?"

Marvin frowned and pulled a face as he thought it through, but he didn't seem convinced. "I wouldn't put any kind of depravity beyond them. They'd kidnap someone in a heartbeat, I'm sure. But I don't see how this would benefit them."

"No problem. And if this moves forward and goes to court, would you be willing to take the stand?"

Marvin took a deep breath. "I honestly don't know. I'd rather not. We need to remain anonymous to be effective… and alive."

"I understand. We'll see what we can do."

"Thanks."

They went over what Marvin saw a few more times, ensuring they got everything they needed, before letting him head home and returning to the EMSOU office, where Rob and the others were waiting.

"We got a name," Ellen announced to Rob as she walked over.

"It was Tess's drug-dealing boyfriend, Keegan Baron, better known as K-Boy, but Keg to his friends."

"And he's sure of that, is he?" Rob asked, as he turned to his PC and started to type in the name.

Ellen watched as Keegan's criminal record appeared on the screen, listing a litany of violent and criminal behaviour that went back years. Keegan was deeply embedded into the Killers, having worked his way up from a petty street thug to a respected but violent dealer within the gang. He wasn't one of the leaders yet, but he was not someone to be trifled with.

"So what's next?" Ellen asked, curious.

Rob turned and looked up at her. "It looks like we have an address, so I think we should pay Keg a visit."

38

"How do you think Tess will react?"

Rob glanced at Ellen sitting beside him in the car's passenger seat and grunted at the question. He knew full well how Tess would react to them storming Keg's house and arresting him. She'd be pissed because he was both her lover and her dealer. She'd gone out of her way to protect him in her interview, refusing to accept that Keg had anything to do with Ernie's murder, even though the evidence was now starting to stack against him with the videos that had been coming in.

Since the interview with Marvin, they'd had seven other anonymous emails appear, each one with an attached video or two, showing the group, led by Keg, either storm into the house or leave. Often both.

One of them, filmed on the same side of the street as Ernie's home, had a close-up view of the four of them walking away from Ernie's house. It very clearly showed Keegan Baron, and the faces of the others, some of which were uncovered by this point. Keg was the first, but with evidence like this, he felt sure the identification of the other three was just a matter of time. They already had a working theory about who one of them was, which also gave them hints about the other two.

The net was closing in on Keegan and his mates. However, this sting operation was risky, as they might alert the others by picking up Keg. By the same token, it might also force them into making rash choices, which could be beneficial.

They'd just have to wait and see, but given Keegan's penchant for violence and the risk he posed to others, it was decided they needed to bring him in. They couldn't wait until they located the other three. It was too big a risk.

"Tess?" Rob asked. "I think she'll be pissed off, but she'll get over it."

"I love your optimism," Ellen remarked.

"I'm overflowing with the stuff."

"Now we just need to find Malcom and whoever kidnapped him."

Rob nodded, aware that this complication with Keg was taking their focus away from Malcom's kidnapping. That was unless Keg was somehow involved in all this. Would he have any need for Tess's son? He might make a useful county lines drug runner, or a street dealer, but kidnapping him wasn't really the best way for them to bring someone on board.

Could they be missing something? Was there more to this Keg than met the eye? Perhaps there was an, as-yet, undiscovered piece of information that would explain Malcom's disappearance too?

It was possible, sure, but it was just as likely that the kidnapping was unrelated to Keg and his issues with Tess and Ernie, and it was all just a great big coincidence. But if that were true, they were decidedly short of evidence and clues that might lead them to the killer, which worried Rob.

Every day that went by without Malcom being discovered reduced the chances of him being found alive, and it was nearly a week since he'd disappeared.

But he couldn't think about that right now. They had a job to do and a murderer to catch.

With the radio blaring in Ellen's hand, Rob drove them south into the city, making for Hyson Green and the address of Keegan Baron.

The plan was simple, but it had taken them a couple of hours to get organised and ready back at the Lodge with a firearms unit and a handful of uniformed officers. But they were on their way now, and they wouldn't be hanging around once they got there.

Word would spread like wildfire that they were raiding someone's house, and it would be a matter of minutes before members of the Killers descended on them and started to cause trouble.

That in itself wasn't an issue. They could handle some trouble. But if that happened, then they'd need more officers on the cordon, leaving them short-handed on the arrest. Plus, there was the issue of any officers keeping the crowds at bay getting hurt in the line of duty.

They needed to be quick.

The radio squawked as they drew near their target, with the teams coordinating their ingress towards the property. Around a minute out from Keg's place, Rob and the other units were forced to pull over and wait for one of their vans to get into position after being held up by traffic.

Moments later, the affirmative came through, and they were off again, racing towards their destination. Seconds later Rob banked the car round into Cope Street, a cul-de-sac just a short walk from the Hyson Green Skate Park, and pulled in behind the two vans that were already disgorging their armed officers.

Rob jumped out and followed them towards a mid-terrace house on the northern side. He could already see one of the lead officers carrying a crimson battering ram, affectionately known as the Big Red Key. Moments later, it was being slammed into the house's front door, which gave way after two hits.

"Armed Police," the men and women repeatedly shouted as they rushed inside. Rob moved up with Ellen and Guy right behind him.

There was a sudden deafening gunshot, followed by yells of pain. Then two more gunshots echoed out half a second later.

"Bollocks," Rob muttered as he ducked back.

"Gordon Bennet," Ellen exclaimed in shock. "They were armed?"

"Bloody hell," Guy added.

"He's down," a man shouted. "We're clear."

Rob jumped up and rushed into the front room. He hoped to whoever was listening that they hadn't shot Keegan. In the doorway, through to the back room, a body lay on the floor, twitching, and to his left, an officer was hissing in pain, while two others tended to his bleeding arm.

"He's running," shouted someone from the back of the house.

"Bollocks." Rob scowled and darted from the room. He jumped over the supine body finding the stairs to the first floor between the front and back rooms. The shooter must have run down the stairs with the gun and opened fire.

Without hesitating, Rob dashed into the back room, where an officer was on the floor with a bloodied nose. She pointed to the kitchen.

297

"That way."

"Thanks," Rob answered. He ran into the kitchen and banged through the rear door into the garden. He caught a glimpse of Keg shimmying over the rear wall as another officer jumped up to follow. Seconds later, Rob did the same and clambered up. He glanced back at Ellen and Guy, who'd followed him out.

"Check for other exits," he yelled and flung himself over the wall. "He's running south, towards the field."

Ahead, Keegan was charging down the snicket towards a spikey green metal fence and, beyond that, a small grassy park, less than half the size of a football pitch, dotted with trees.

"Stop, or I shoot," the armed officer yelled, only for a child to pop their head out of a rear gate several houses up. "Shit." The officer lowered their weapon as Rob charged past.

He raced along the narrow alleyway, dodging wheelie bins, bags of rubbish, a discarded and rotten soft chair and other assorted debris. Keegan reached the fence seconds before Rob got there and jumped, climbing over a length of carpet draped over the spikes, certainly it had been placed there on purpose. The lanky teenager was fast and soon clambered up and over.

Rob reached it the moment Keg rolled over the top and leapt to follow.

On the other side, Keegan tried to pull the carpet off, but Rob was already there and held it in place as he climbed.

"Shit," Keegan hissed and ran.

As Rob pulled himself over, he saw Ellen charging across the field with Guy close behind. She intercepted Keegan, and in an impressive display, rugby tackled the young man to the floor.

It was all the delay Rob and Guy needed.

Dropping down into the field, Rob rushed over to join his fellow detectives.

"Get off me," Keegan yelled, furious as Ellen wrestled with him to keep him subdued. "Get the fuck off me."

Rob rushed in and added his strength to the mix, helping to hold Keegan down. Guy whipped out his cuffs and between them, they got him secured.

"I'm arresting you on suspicion of the murder of Ernie Newton," Rob began, before proceeding to read him his rights, while Keegan scowled and spit at them.

"I ain't done nothing wrong," he bellowed. "Fuckin' pigs. This is harassment. You can't do this. What proof do you have, huh?"

"Be quiet," Rob stated, "before you dig yourself a deeper hole than you're already in."

Keegan grumbled as they started to march him back towards the street.

"You took your time catching up," Ellen remarked.

"Oh, you know," Rob replied with a shrug, "I stopped to ponder what we were going to order tonight."

"Thought as much," Guy replied. "Always thinking with your stomach."

39

"Well, well, well," Rob said, standing in the corridor of the custody suite as Matilda Greenwood walked towards him. "Fancy seeing you here. You're not representing Keegan, are you?"

She smiled. "We must stop meeting like this."

"I know, what would people think. It's good to see you again."

"And you," she agreed, with a twinkle in her eye. He always relished time spent with Matilda and wished things were different, so he could have more of it. "Well," she continued, "I don't want this to drag on for too long. I've got plans tonight."

"Join the club. Me too."

"Go on then, you first," she urged, tilting her head to one side in a manner that Rob found endearing.

"Oh, it's nothing stunning. Just getting together with the team at mine for some drinks and takeaway. It'll be fun, though."

"Sounds good to me," she reassured him but didn't volunteer her plans.

"And you?" he asked, keen to find out. Was she reluctant to share her plans, or was she luring him into asking?

"Well, actually, I have a hot date tonight." She smiled as she spoke, but seemed a little embarrassed by her words. "A friend set me up, so..." She shrugged. "I thought, why not."

"Oh," Rob said as the wind beneath his sails suddenly died. He couldn't quite believe that Matilda had moved on so quickly. He'd only seen her a few days ago, and there'd been no hint of this then. He felt lost and defeated and wasn't sure how to reply.

"Don't worry," she said, stepping closer and gripping his arm. "It's just a date. And besides, you did say you didn't want to get involved right now."

Rob took a breath as he made an effort to shove his feelings to one side. He couldn't afford to get upset right now. Plus, she was right. He'd rejected her advances several times, telling her that he simply wasn't in a position to get involved with anyone. Things might change in the future, but he couldn't expect her to wait for some unknown date when things would be different. She had a life to lead and couldn't just put everything on hold for months, or even years.

And yet, he couldn't help but feel somewhat betrayed. He'd hoped that maybe one day they might be able to work things out and come to an arrangement... Or was that just a pipe dream? Certainly, there was no end in sight to the threat his family posed. The Mason gang was as strong as ever and still very interested in him, which put anyone close to him in danger.

The murder of Scarlett's friend was just one example of the threat this family posed, and he had little doubt that there would be more to come in the future.

Putting Matilda in their crosshairs was simply not something he was prepared to do, but that came with inevitable consequences, such as this.

"I know," Rob replied to her. "You're right. I did say that."

"Have you changed your mind?"

"No. I'm sorry, I can't."

Matilda shrugged. "I wish you'd open up to me as to why, but I respect and trust that you have your reasons."

"I do. Thank you."

"No problem," she answered with a conciliatory smile. "Well, Mr Baron is ready for you, so..."

"Okay, thanks. I'll be with you in one moment. I'm just waiting for my partner."

"Sure thing," she answered and walked back to the interview room. He watched her go, feeling adrift, as if she'd somehow cut him loose and he was falling into a yawning abyss.

Time seemed to stand still as he felt her slipping away from him.

Was this it? Had he lost her?

"Everything okay?"

He turned to see Ellen standing beside him.

She'd returned from the bathroom, and he realised he'd been staring into space, lost in a sea of churning thoughts and regrets. "Sorry, yeah, I'm fine. Thanks. Right, let's go and see what Mr Baron has to say for himself. His solicitor said he's ready."

"Brilliant," Ellen said and gathered her things from the nearby chair before following Rob into the room.

When Ellen saw it was Matilda sitting beside Keegan, she gave Rob a brief look but said nothing.

"Good afternoon Mr Baron. Let's get on with this, shall we? I have no desire to drag this out." Rob then proceeded to introduce himself and Ellen for the benefit of the recording, followed by Matilda and Keegan stating their names.

"So, tell me, Keegan, why did you do it?"

"No comment."

The words were incredibly familiar and totally expected. Unflustered, Rob continued, "Why did you kill Ernie Newton?"

"No comment."

Rob gave him a look, which Keegan met with a calm reassurance that Rob found amusing but cold. He no doubt thought that by answering no comment to everything—something that was undoubtedly suggested to him by Matilda

304

because that's what all solicitors did—he'd somehow be mysteriously freed, but this couldn't be further from the truth. He glanced at Matilda, who gave him a brief smile and shrug before looking back to Keegan. "Alright, let's go over this, shall we. Your name is Keegan Baron, right?"

"No comment."

"Well, you just said it was, so let's take that as read, shall we?"

"No comment."

"That was a rhetorical question, Keg."

"No comment."

"Your friends call you Keg, don't they? That's your nickname, right?"

"No comment."

"So, it's not your nickname?" Rob asked, curious to see if he'd continue saying no comment. It was early on in the interview, but this was a chance for Keegan to poke a hole in their case against him, and Rob wanted to see if the young man was bright enough to see it coming or not.

"No comment," Keegan answered.

Nope. He wasn't that bright after all. No-comment interviews were the norm, but they also didn't really help people like Keegan if it ever got to trial, namely because of the Caution.

He had a right to silence, just like everyone else, something that the Caution set out quite clearly in its wording of, 'You do not have to say anything.'

But it was the next part that could trip people like Keegan up. The Police Caution goes on to say that while they do not need to say anything, it may harm their defence if they do not mention something when questioned that they later rely on in court.

Keegan's nickname, Keg, was one such thing. Providing the CPS charged Keegan with murder, and this made its way to court, Keegan would have months of waiting to look at the evidence and come up with a defence. So, one way he could defend himself was to say that his nickname wasn't Keg. This would mean that, when Ernie found out that someone called Keg was having an affair with Tess, Keegan wasn't that person. He wasn't Keg. But that chance had just passed him by because he had just answered no comment to Rob's questions about his nickname.

But now, if he says Keg wasn't his nickname in court, the fact that he answered no comment to Rob's questions would harm that defense.

Rob glanced at Matilda and smiled. She knew what he was doing and just barely shook her head at him. He answered that with a quick shrug of his shoulders, mimicking her earlier gesture.

Settling into the rhythm of the interview. Rob pressed on, getting the impression that this wouldn't take too long.

"Okay, Keegan. Well, on Wednesday the fourth, we discovered the body of Ernie Newton in his home on Maple Street, Nottingham…"

40

With everything cleared and snacks on the table, Rob stood back to admire his handiwork. Everything seemed to be in place and ready for the evening's fun and games, and he could finally take a breather while waiting for the first of his guests to arrive.

Interestingly, after days of dreading this evening, he was actually looking forward to it. It was an unexpected feeling but one that he quite liked, and for the first time, he'd started to wonder if this might become something he did regularly.

It would all depend on how this first gathering went, he surmised, because if it did not go to plan or there were some clashes of personalities, then he might need to rethink things.

But there was no need to worry about that right now or to assume this wouldn't go smoothly.

He turned and wandered over to the window with his hands in his pockets, gazing over the lazy River Trent to the Forest ground and the city's southern side. Off to his right, just a short distance away, was the Trent Bridge with its copper-green facade and a constant stream of traffic flowing across it. It didn't feel like three days since they'd driven Vivian to the far bank to discover the location of Malcom's disappearance. The Crime Scene investigation team had long since left, and people were using the footpath beneath the bridge once more.

That kidnapping and possible murder had kicked off a series of events that had so far led to the murder of Ernie Newton and the arrest of Keegan Baron, both of whom were linked to Malcom through his mother. And yet, they were still no closer to the truth about what happened to the boy, with no new leads or clues.

Even Keegan's arrest failed to reveal anything about Malcom's fate, with the interview being distinctly one-sided. This was to be expected these days, as every lawyer advised their clients to either stay silent or answer no comment to everything, even though it usually harmed their defence further down the line. They did this to ensure that the suspect didn't say anything that might incriminate them, which was fair enough given that not all cases actually went to court. And besides, most duty solicitors just wanted to get the interview over and done with and go home. But for the few that did end up in court, a 'no comment' plea, wasn't helpful.

And yet, on the Malcom aspect of the case, Rob was starting to believe that Keegan didn't actually know anything,

But, if he didn't, who did?

As for Keegan himself, things did not look good.

Rob had followed the standard interview technique of layering up the evidence, starting with the least damning and getting him to deny that with a no comment. Then he slowly built it up, adding layer after layer of increasingly damning evidence until there was nowhere for him to go.

By the end of the day, they'd remanded Keegan in custody and referred the case to the CPS. They would decide whether or not to charge him with murder and refer the case to the magistrate, who would have no choice but to keep Keegan where he was and push the case up to the Crown Court.

Everything from this point on was pretty much out of their hands, but their work on the case was far from over. Ahead of them lay endless hours of reading through the evidence to make sure there were no gaps that his defence could use. There would be meetings with the CPS and the prosecution barristers, who would undoubtedly request that certain lines of enquiry be followed up, while the disclosure of evidence was also arranged in preparation for the trial.

They were still working through these things with the Lee Garrett case and the Clipstone Prostitute murderer, which had yet to go to trial.

Someone knocked on his door.

Rob jumped and checked his watch. It was a little early, but not by much. Curious to discover who it was and be a good host, he strode across his apartment to the door and pulled it open.

Erika was standing on the other side, smiling and holding a stack of napkins. She handed them to him. "Will these do?"

He suddenly remembered texting her, asking if she had any spare. "Oh, yeah. That's great, thank you."

"You've got some friends coming over then?"

"Yeah." He turned the napkins over in his hand.

"I didn't know you had any friends." He looked back up, but she was smiling with glee.

"Cheeky!"

She grinned and started to back away. "Have fun."

"I will."

"If you need anything else... Well, tough, because I'm going for a run. So, you're on your own."

"You're so helpful," Rob muttered, rolling his eyes.

"I know," she answered. "I'm a delight."

"Aren't you just..." But she was already gone.

He returned to the kitchen, laid out the napkins, and after another check over the setup, heard the buzzer go down at the main door to the building. Rob rushed over and pressed the button on the intercom.

"Hello?"

"Hey, it's Ellen," she squawked over the speaker.

"Come up. I'm on the first floor," Rob said and pressed the button to unlock the main entrance. He walked to his apartment door, and after a few moments, Ellen stepped out of the stairwell with a bottle in one hand while holding hands with another woman behind her.

"Hi," Ellen said with a grin. "This is Christabel."

"Call me Chrissy."

"Hi, Ellen." Rob smiled and welcomed them in. "Lovely to meet you, Chrissy. I've heard plenty about you. Come in, come in."

"We're first," Chrissy said as they moved into the main room. She gave Ellen a look. "I told you we were early."

Ellen shrugged. "I just wanted to be prompt, that's all."

"We should be fashionably late, El."

"Well, I think your timing's perfect," Rob said as Ellen passed him a bottle of wine. "Thank you for coming."

"It's not as if we have anything else going on," Ellen snarked with a smile.

"Ellen!" Chrissy gasped.

Rob laughed. "If that's the best you've got for me, well, you're going to have to try harder."

"This is lovely," Chrissy said, changing the subject as she walked across his apartment to the windows overlooking the Trent. "Check out that view."

"Of a football stadium..." Ellen added, drolly.

"Don't be a Debby Downer, El. This is really nice, Rob."

"Thank you," Rob replied before turning to Ellen. "At least someone appreciates my choice of apartment."

Ellen smiled as she wrapped her arm around Chrissy's waist, and pulled her close. "I'm just pulling his leg, don't ruin my fun," she stage whispered.

Rob rolled his eyes.

"Oh, you have a cat?" Chrissy exclaimed and darted over to the sofa where Muffin had been sleeping. The furball meowed as Chrissy sat and started to stroke him.

"His name's Muffin," Rob offered.

"Oh, he's gorgeous," she replied, fussing over him.

"And he'll stay there all night if you keep that up," Rob said. "Drink? Red? White? Beer? Soft drink?"

"White for me," Ellen said.

"And me," Chrissy added.

He walked to the kitchenette and opened one of the bottles on the island as Ellen joined him. "Good job with Keegan today."

"It was hardly all down to me," she answered. "It was a team effort."

"That rugby tackle was all you." Rob gave her a meaningful look. "If you'd not been there, he might have got away."

"Nah, you'd have got him," she answered as the buzzer went again.

Moments later, Tucker walked in with a young woman Rob had never seen before.

"Evening," Tucker said, shaking Rob's hand and handing him a six-pack of Peroni bottles. "This is Ingrid."

"Thanks." He took the bottles off him and then smiled at Ingrid. "Nice to meet you Ingrid, I'm Rob."

"Pleasure," she said, shaking his hand limply. She seemed quite nervous.

"Hiya," Tucker said to Ellen as he walked over and hugged her.

"Who's this?" Ellen asked as she moved toward Ingrid.

"This is Ingrid. We met online a couple of weeks ago."

"A couple of weeks ago?" Ellen nearly choked on her drink. "And you brought her here?"

"Yeah. So what?"

"Jesus, Tucker. I'm so sorry Ingrid. Talk about in-at-the-deep-end."

"That's okay," Ingrid answered. "I don't mind."

"Good thing, really. Here, have a drink," she said, pouring another glass of wine. "Come with me."

Ellen took Ingrid's hand and led her across the apartment to Chrissy and Muffin.

"Bringing a date to a work do?" Rob remarked once the women were a few metres away. "That's either brave or stupid."

Tucker shrugged. "The Lord works in mysterious fucking ways, and so do I. Besides, she'll be fine. Anyway, you clever bastard, I hear congratulations are in order. You arrested Ernie's killer, right?"

"Keegan Baron, yeah," Rob answered. "I can't take credit, though. It was all down to a coordinated effort by the local residents. We just used their hard work and brought the law to bear."

"In-fucking-credible."

"Cheers. How about the Curt Gates case? Any movement since planting the bugs?"

"Diddly-bastard-squat," Tucker replied. "Monitoring those bugs is a full-time job by the way, and I've got disclosures to organise on the bloody Clipstone case." He shook his head. "It never ends."

"No, it doesn't," Rob answered as the buzzer sounded once more. He walked over to hear Scarlett on the other end of the line. He buzzed her through and moved to wait at the apartment door. Moments later, Scarlett appeared in a dark, fitted outfit with more make-up than she wore for work. She smiled as she walked out of the stairwell, brushing her blonde hair away from her face with one hand and holding a bag for

315

life in the other. Chris appeared behind her, gripping a bottle of wine by the neck.

"I have a surprise for you," Scarlett said.

"For me?" Rob glanced down at the bag.

She smiled. "Oh, and I don't mean this," she said, hiding it behind her back and taking it out again. "Well, I do. This *is* for you. But I have another surprise, too."

"Wow, really?"

"Yep," she said and turned back to the stairwell door. "Out you come."

Rob frowned. The door opened, and Matilda Greenwood stepped through, wearing a figure-hugging black dress and a smile.

In a somewhat awkward gesture, she threw her arms wide and waved her hands about. "Surprise."

Rob did a double take as he looked on in shock, not quite believing his eyes. "But, I thought you said you had a hot da... Oh. I see."

"Blame her," Matilda said, pointing at Scarlett.

Scarlett shrugged. "Someone's got to play matchmaker because you're bloody crap at this, Rob."

"That's true." He sighed and winked at Matilda, feeling unfeasibly happy. "Damn. I had no idea. You really had me going earlier when you said you were going on a date."

"Well, I am... With you."

"Thank you," he said and turned to Scarlett and pulled a face. "You, however, missy... You and I need to have words."

She visibly cringed and gritted her teeth. "Am I in trouble?"

Holding her gaze for a moment longer, Rob screwed his mouth up and narrowed his eyes in contemplation. "Let's see how the evening goes, shall we?"

"Right." Scarlett turned to Matilda and hissed, "Don't screw this up."

Matilda nodded. "Yes, ma'am."

Scarlett grinned wildly at Rob, before gesturing to the man standing with them. "Oh, and this is Chris."

"Nice to meet you, finally," Chris said. He stepped up and offered his hand. "I've heard a lot about you, sir."

Rob chuckled. "Well, thanks. No need for 'sir', though."

"No problem. Oh, and here." He offered Rob the bottle.

"Thanks." Rob held it up to check the label. "Oh, cheers."

"And here's a few nibbles we brought," Scarlett said, holding out the bag.

"Thank you," Rob said, taking it from her and peering inside. "A little bribery goes a long way... Oooh, nuts, Bombay mix, pringles and... pork scratchings?" He pulled out the bag. "Locally made Pork Scratchings. Mmmm."

"Courtesy of our neighbour," Scarlett remarked. "We've had some. They're very nice. Meaty."

"There's only so much you can eat, though," Chris added. "So we thought we'd share them about. Oh, and um, I had nothing to do with all that." He waved at Scarlett and Matilda.

"That's okay. Come in. We have drinks." Rob ushered them in. Scarlett grabbed Chris's hand and pulled him into the apartment, leaving him with Matilda in the short L-shaped corridor, out of view of the small but growing crowd in the main room.

Matilda's smile was genuine but concealed a flicker of doubt and vulnerability, "Sorry. I hope you don't mind."

Rob sighed, but he was brimming with joy at the sight of Matilda. "No, of course not."

"I hope Scarlett's not in any trouble."

He chuckled. "No. She's just trying to help. I'll give her a hard time about it but don't worry. I'm just pleased you're here and not on a date with someone else."

With her doubts eased, she leaned in and kissed him on the cheek. Rob felt a flush of heat wash over him as she pulled away and winked.

"Aaah…" he gasped.

She gave him a look. "Don't get any ideas."

"I wouldn't… I just—"

"How about a drink?" she interrupted. She seemed to be enjoying this.

318

"Um, yeah, sure," he stammered, still in shock. He wasn't sure what this meant or where this might go. She'd never been quite that forward with him before… but… he liked it.

Matilda wandered through into the main room of the apartment, and Rob followed. "Lovely place you have here."

"Thanks."

"Nice view, too."

Spotting Ellen nearby, he side-eyed her as he answered, "It's just a football stadium."

Ellen briefly shot daggers his way, before shaking her head and continuing her conversation with Scarlett.

"I think it's a little more than that. You've got the river and the bridges. It's quite breath-taking."

"Thank you. What would you like?" Rob asked, motioning to the display of drinks.

"A white wine, please," she replied, and Rob got to work pouring it for her.

"I don't want to chat about work too much," Matilda said. "But, well done today."

"Thanks. Is it weird representing killers like Keegan?"

She took a moment before answering. "I try to withhold judgement as much as possible. What they did or didn't do, is irrelevant to me at that early stage. I'm there to offer legal advice, make them aware of the law and how it will affect them. That's it. I'm not representing them at trial or anything,

319

and this is just part of the job. Everyone, guilty or innocent, has a right to good legal representation during a police interview."

"Fair enough," Rob answered before the buzzer sounded once more. "Oh, one moment."

"Sure," she replied as Rob darted for the intercom. It was Nailer. Rob buzzed him through and paused momentarily to look back into his apartment and take in the sight of his guests enjoying themselves.

Moving to his front door, he opened it to find Erika locking hers and wearing running gear. The door to the stairwell opened at the same instant, and Nailer walked into the hall as Erika turned to leave.

"Evening," Nailer said in passing and wandered over to Rob. Erika gave Nailer an inscrutable look as he walked away from her. Behind him, Nick and Guy followed, exiting the stairwell. They both turned and smiled at Erika, who waited for them to move out of the doorway.

"Hi," Nick said.

"Oh, hey," Guy added. "Let me get out of your way." He moved, and Erika thanked him before disappearing into the stairwell.

"Evening, Rob," Nailer said with a smile as he approached, holding up the bottle of red he'd brought. Rob shook his offered hand and noticed Guy give Nick a curious look before he disappeared after Erika.

"Evening," Rob replied, wondering what Guy was up to. "You're the last ones to arrive."

"Sorry," Nailer answered. "We had a drink at the pub before coming over. I hope we're not late."

"No, no. You're good," Rob reassured him. "Come in. There's drinks in the kitchen."

Nailer held up his wine bottle. "I've come prepared."

"Excellent," Rob said as Nailer passed him by. He turned to Nick. "Where's Guy gone?"

"I think he's chasing some tail," Nick answered with a wry smile before glancing back to the stairwell door. "I'm sure he'll be along soon. Anyway, I brought a bottle." He held up his gift. "How are you?"

"Thanks. Yeah, I'm good. Scarlett pulled a fast one on me and brought Matilda with her."

"Oh, really? Well, that's good, isn't it?"

Rob smiled at his friend. "Yeah, it is."

"Then don't give her a hard time about it," Nick warned. "She's done you a favour."

"Yeah, I know. But it's not that easy."

"It could be if you wanted," Nick replied as the door behind him opened, and Guy stepped back onto the landing.

"Aaah, Casanova returns. So, what was all that about then, hey?"

Guy held up his phone, the screen glowing in the dim light. "Read it and weep, Miller."

A closer look revealed it to be Erika's phone number, saved to Guy's phone.

"Damn it," Nick muttered.

"You snooze, you lose," Guy mocked, with a smile, before turning to Rob. "Sorry. Just having some fun."

"Sure thing," Rob replied. "You just treat her right, okay? I hear her neighbour can be a little protective."

Guy gave him a look. "Alright, Dad."

Rob let the mask fall, and grinned. "Come in."

"Thanks." Guy was all smiles again. "I think tonight's gonna be a good night."

Rob followed them in and got himself a drink, soon finding himself deep in conversation with several of the team and their partners, usually with Matilda by his side. Later, they ordered some pizzas, but they were in for a bit of a wait on a Saturday night.

Twenty minutes later, still with no sign of the food, Rob noticed Chris standing alone on the balcony. Wondering if he was okay, Rob excused himself and stepped outside.

"Mind if I join you."

"No, no. That's fine," Chris replied. "This is your home. Feel free."

"Thanks." Rob walked over to the railing and leaned on it. Night had fallen, and the city's lights were ablaze, creating pools of illumination in the darkness. On either side of them, the Trent Bridge and Lady Bey Bridge glowed in the gloom.

"Thanks for hosting this," Chris began. "It's been good to meet you all. I've heard a lot about you and the others through Scarlett. But it's been great to finally meet you all, for real, you know?"

"Of course. We've heard a lot about you too. Congratulations on your engagement, by the way. The wedding isn't far off now, right?"

"No, not far. It's this summer. It should be good."

The door to the balcony opened, and Guy popped his head out. "Do you mind if I use your bathroom?"

"No, no. Go ahead. It's back there. Turn left, and you can't miss it."

"Okay, thanks." Guy withdrew back into the apartment.

Rob watched Guy through the glass as he walked across the room and disappeared down the side corridor.

"Sorry," Rob said, turning back to Chris. "Yeah. The wedding will be good. I hope you enjoy it."

"I'm sure we will... Well, I hope so... What with all that's happened."

323

The mood shifted, taking on a more serious and dour tone. Rob knew exactly what Chris was referring to. "Ninette was going to be her Maid of Honour, right?"

"Yeah," Chris answered. "I honestly don't know how she'll handle her not being there."

"She's strong," Rob reassured him. "I'm sure she'll be fine."

"Oh, she's strong, alright. Stronger than I am, that's for sure. But this was her best friend from Uni, so I just don't know. I suggested delaying it and maybe doing the whole thing next year. There's no rush."

"She said no?"

"She did," Chris confirmed. "She was insistent that it go ahead as planned because that would be what Ninette would want. Which I get. I understand." Chris paused for a moment and took a long, deep breath. He gripped the rail with his hands, turning his knuckles white. "I didn't want her to go back to work. I thought it was too soon." He looked up. "How has she been? Is she okay?"

Rob smiled in sympathy. "She's been fine, actually. She's thrown herself into it with gusto, and apart from a desire to get some sort of revenge against the Masons, I've not noticed anything you should be worried about. She's dealing with things in her way."

"I see."

"I think you need to give her the benefit of the doubt. Give her a chance," Rob advised. "In all honesty, when she came back, I had the same doubts. I thought it was too soon and I nearly sent her home. But she's been fine. I don't think you have anything to worry about. Honestly."

"I hope so," Chris muttered, before looking up and smiling. "Thank you."

"My pleasure," Rob answered, allowing a smile to spread over his face. Chris loved Scarlett, it was written all over him, and he was clearly worried about her.

Rob could honestly sympathise, and while most of his doubts about Scarlett's return to work had faded, her desire for revenge was still a point of contention. Right now, Nick was focusing it onto something productive that helped them, but what would happen when they weren't actively taking on the Masons?

Time would tell, he reasoned.

"I hope you didn't mind Scarlett bringing Matilda with her."

Rob smiled to himself. "No. It was a nice surprise, but don't tell her that."

"I wouldn't dream of it."

***

Across the river, Madeleine sat in the car with her camera on a monopod, propping it up on the centre console. She adjusted her view and returned to looking at Rob and Chris talking on the balcony. But they seemed to have finished their conversation and were making their way back inside, utterly unaware of what had been going on around them.

41

Nick woke with a start. It was early. The room was still dark, with just a hint of the brewing dawn starting to filter through the curtains. He sat up with a jolt, feeling suddenly alert.

He'd been dreaming about some kind of shadowy person creeping up on him, and for one crazy moment, he thought someone was in the room with him, but it was just a dream, nothing to worry about. He took a breath and tried to calm down. He could barely see anything in the darkness of his bedroom.

After a moment, his adrenaline started to fade, and the beginnings of a headache began to claw at his mind while his stomach weighed heavy. It was possible he'd drunk and eaten too much last night. He grunted in annoyance and went to lie down again.

"Morning, soldier."

Nick sat bolt upright, his eyes wide. Now he was most certainly awake.

He looked over to see a figure sitting in a chair in the darkest corner of the room. For a moment, he was ready to jump out of bed and defend himself, which would have been a sight in his underwear.

But with his heart hammering and his body flooded with energy, he watched the figure lean forward. Their face moved into the dim light, and he could make out Calico Black sitting with her elbows on her knees and her fingers interlaced.

"Jesus," Nick gasped. "What time is it?"

"Early," she answered. "But you'll want to know about this. You're going to need time to plan."

"What? Why?"

"I've been monitoring the bugs overnight," she replied. "The deal happened just a few hours ago."

"Shit, really? The Masons have struck a deal with a cartel?"

"Via Emory Gates, and the first shipment's already on its way. There's a bunch of mules landing tonight at Nottingham East Midlands." She held up a USB flash drive. "It's all on here." She threw it to him, and Nick caught it.

"God damn it, they're working fast." He turned the small solid-state drive over in his hand. "Right, I'd better get up." He checked the time and groaned. Five AM. Far too early after a night out drinking.

"Okay, thank you. How will we know who the mules are?"

"I'm working with Reed on that. We'll have the info for you, don't worry. I'll be in touch." She got up.

"Thank you."

"That's okay. Oh, and one other thing. This might be unrelated, but you're being followed and watched."

Nick frowned. "By who? The Masons?"

"No. Someone else. I think they *might* be an undercover officer, but I can't be sure," Calico answered.

Nick furrowed his brow in thought. "Okay, thanks. I'll report it and see what comes back."

"No, don't. Hold off for now. It'll tip my hand, and I won't be able to keep an eye on them if they go to ground. I'll report back once I know more, okay?"

"Sure, thanks," Nick answered.

"See you later, sleepyhead." She walked out of the room, and, moments later, he heard the front door go. She was gone.

Nick held up the drive again. "Hi-ho, hi-ho, it's off to work we go…"

42

"Hi," Tom said as he approached the woman the receptionist had pointed out in the reception of Nottingham Central Police Station. "I'm PC Tom Reid. How can I help you?"

"I need to report my son as missing." The middle-aged tear-stained woman sniffed. "I can't find him anywhere."

"He's missing? Okay, well, how about you come with me, and we'll have a quick chat, okay?"

"Okay," she whimpered and followed Tom through to a backroom, where he settled her down and made her a cup of instant coffee from the machine. She seemed nice enough and was clearly upset.

"Right then, first off, what's your name?

"Pearl Douglas," she answered, looking terrified.

He'd never heard of her before, which was always a good thing. "Okay, Pearl, and what's your son's name?"

"Seth."

"Same surname?"

"Yes," she answered.

"And, how old is he?"

"He's twenty-four."

Tom narrowed his eyes and looked up. When she'd said her son had gone missing, he'd been expecting him to be a teenager, not a grown adult. "Twenty-four? And, when did he go missing?"

"Yesterday," she replied. "He lives at home with me and he went to the gym on Saturday morning, like always. But he didn't come back. I thought it was odd because he always comes home for a shower and a change of clothes, but he's in his twenties now, he doesn't need me fussing over him all the time, and he can do as he pleases. But I was getting worried by the evening, so I called him. The call didn't go through, though. Then, later that evening, one of Seth's friends turned up at the house, asking if he was in. Seth was supposed to meet him but didn't show up."

"And this is unusual behaviour, is it?"

"Very unusual. He always comes home and tells me where he's going. Also, he'd never let his friends down like that. It's so unlike him."

"And this was last night?"

"That's right." She nodded. "I was worried, but I didn't want to cause you any bother, so I thought I'd try and find him myself. I called the gym to see if he'd been there, and they said he had. But they also said they couldn't give me any more information."

331

"Alright, so Seth got to the gym as he'd planned but went missing sometime after that but before he got home to you," Tom summarised.

"Yes, that's right. Something's happened to him. I know it has. You have to help me. Can you call the gym? They might know more than they're telling me."

"Yes, of course," Tom agreed, jotting down the gym's name and number as the woman read it out. Leaving the mother in the side room, he nipped back upstairs.

Once at his desk, he made the call and soon got through to the receptionist.

"Hi, yes. This is Constable Thomas Reid from the Nottingham Central Police Station. I was wondering if I could check some details about one of your customers, please."

"Sure, of course. How can I help?"

"Can you tell me if Seth Douglas was in yesterday morning?"

"Seth?" the receptionist asked, apparently recognising the name. "Yes, he was in, as usual. We had a complaint about him, actually."

"Oh, I see. What kind of complaint?"

"One of our female members reported him leering at her. You know, the usual."

"Okay. Well, apart from that, did he do his usual workout? Did you notice anything unusual or strange?"

"No. Everything seemed normal, except he left his car in the car park. He needs to come and collect it."

Tom frowned. "His car's still in the car park?"

"Yeah. It was locked in overnight, and it's still there now. I can see it from where I'm standing."

A shiver rushed down his spine. He didn't like the sound of that at all. "Okay, thanks. Do you have CCTV there?"

43

"So, Mr Gates, we should talk business," the man on the recording said, his voice thick with a South American accent that coloured his words. Emory had referred to him as Sergio several times, but the name meant nothing to Rob.

Rob had been listening to the men on the recording for nearly twenty minutes as they talked about everything from the flight to the weather, while drinks were being poured and enjoyed.

"Finally," Rob muttered and glanced around Nailer's office at the others.

Nailer sat behind his desk, staring into space as he listened, while Nick, Tucker and Scarlett were either standing or sitting, listening in silence to the audio. During a gap in the talking, he heard Nick's stomach rumble. He looked a little green around the gills, no doubt from overindulging the night before.

And now, he was paying the price.

Unlike Nick, Rob had purposely taken it easy at the gathering and hadn't stuffed his face with pizza or drunk too much either. As a result, he felt perky and awake.

"Absolutely," Emory Gates answered on the audio. "Let's get down to brass tacks. We're keen to work with you and build up some kind of relationship going forward. We already have a network in place for distribution, so we could be a valuable partner for you."

"Excellent. In that case then, I see no reason to delay."

"Absolutely."

"We have a shipment coming in tomorrow evening, and I have been authorised to offer the whole thing to you. If you're ready, that is?" Sergio sounded smug, as if he was testing Emory's operation and how quickly it could accommodate them.

"Tomorrow night?" Emory asked, sounding surprised.

"That's right. It would be regrettable if you were not set up for such a quick turnaround, but I understand. We have other interested parties who could step in, you understand."

"No, no. We can take it," Emory answered, sounding only slightly flustered. "How much are we talking?"

"Fifteen kilos of product at fifty-five thousand US per kilo," Sergio answered as if it were nothing at all. The staggering amount of money being discussed was mind-blowing but in line with known wholesale prices for the drug. Rob glanced around the room to see the reactions of the others, with only Scarlett looking outwardly surprised.

"Fifteen kilos?" Emory asked.

"Of course, it's too much—" Sergio answered.

335

"No, it's not," Emory cut in. "But fifty-five K, US? This is a bulk buy, Sergio. You need to work with me here and look at this as an investment. If this goes well, there will be more where this comes from."

"We know the value of our product, Mr Gates."

"And *I* know that I can go to your Mexican competitors and negotiate a better deal, Sergio. But I don't want to go to them, I want to buy from you. But you need to work with me."

"Work with you? I think you need to be careful who you're talking to, Mr Gates. I'm not some idiot fucking street dealer. Our product is purer than the Mexican shit. You come direct to me, and you buy the best."

"I do not mean to insult you, Sergio. This is business, and it's not as if I'm asking you to front me the product. I can pay you today. But fifty-five is too steep."

"Then make me an offer, Mr Gates."

"Forty-five," Emory answered without hesitating.

Sergio started to laugh, long and loud. "Oh, Mr Gates. You are the funny one, yes. You begin with a joke offer. Very good. Now, please, we must get serious. What is your serious offer?"

"That was serious."

"Mr Gates. Do not mess me about. I have others who will happily pay me what I ask, you know this."

336

Emory sighed. "Forty-seven, then."

"Fifty-three," Sergio countered.

"Forty-nine, and you're really pushing me here."

"Mr Gates, you drive a hard bargain, but okay. Fifty-one, and that is much lower than what it's worth."

"Fifty, and an order for a second batch next month."

"Aaah, very good Mr Gates." Sergio seemed to think about it for a moment. "This is acceptable. Fifty thousand per kilo it is, then."

"You won't regret it," Emory replied.

Rob shook his head in bewilderment at the utterly alien nature of the negotiation that had just taken place and continued to listen as they discussed how the payment would be made. It involved large sums of cash, off-shore accounts and shell companies, and would be completed by third parties that Rob would look into later. After all, there was more than one way to bring down a criminal organisation.

Once that had been discussed, Emory and Sergio moved onto the logistics of picking up the fifteen mules who'd each stuffed around a kilo of cocaine in the form of wrapped pellets into their digestive tracts. They were all due to land at Nottingham East Midlands airport on a flight from Antwerp, Belgium, the following night. Each mule would have instructions to look for someone carrying a sign with a name on it once they were through customs. And those names would be given to Emory once the money had cleared.

Scarlett asked why the flights were coming in from Belgium rather than Columbia. So Rob explained that direct flights from certain countries were screened more thoroughly for mules, so the cartels had to be more innovative and use less direct routes, with one of their current favourites being to ship the drugs into Africa by container ship, then into Europe through ports like Antwerp, before they were then distributed across Europe and over to the UK.

Little else of interest was discussed, and the meeting drew to an end.

"We need those names," Rob said, turning to the group.

"My contact is on it," Nick replied. "She'll be in touch as soon as she knows something."

"Fifty thousand dollars per kilo?" Scarlett exclaimed. And there's fifteen kilos coming in? That's insane. That's seven hundred and fifty thousand dollars. That's crazy money."

"And on the street," Nailer answered, "it goes for around a hundred and fifty per gram. Can you do the math on that?"

"You mean, maths, sir," Scarlett grumbled. "But yeah. That's one hundred and fifty thousand per kilo. Christ."

"It'll be more than that, though," Rob added, "because they'll cut it, and it'll go from about ninety percent pure to maybe sixty percent pure, giving them more product to sell and making them more money."

"I should invest in cocaine," Scarlett muttered, sounding bewildered. "So, what's the plan? When do we arrest them."

"We could pick them up at the airport," Tucker suggested. "As soon as we know who they are, we can swoop in and grab them."

"But then we don't get Emory," Scarlett stated. "I'm not keen on that."

"That means allowing them to drive off into the country," Nailer said. "It's risky, and it'll mean a much bigger operation."

"Everything about this is risky," Nick replied. "But I think Scarlett's right. This could be a chance to really hurt the Masons. Not just by swiping their drug shipment, but if we can catch one or more of the Masons red-handed with the drugs, that's a much bigger win."

"Bigger risk, bigger reward," Scarlett added. Rob could see the fierce determination behind her eyes again. She wanted to hurt the Masons, and she wanted it bad.

"And if you get this wrong," Nailer countered, "then we've just let a massive shipment of drugs into the country."

"I can do this," Nick reassured them. "They won't get away."

Rob nodded. "I'm with Nick on this. I don't want to just hurt the Masons. I want to catch them in the act. I want to take them and everything they've built and burn it to the ground. I say we go for Emory."

"Seconded," Scarlett agreed.

"The chances of Emory having a direct hand in this are pretty slim," Nailer said as he sat back in his seat, and took a moment to think it through. "But I'm willing to go with the majority on this."

"Great, thank you," Rob said and turned to Nick. "You're going to need a team of cars in place to follow them from the airport and a mobile unit of officers ready to rush in as soon as we know where they are. Can I leave that up to you to organise?"

"Of course," Nick confirmed. "I'll sort it."

"Excellent. Right then, off you go. Let's get these bastards."

There was a knock at Nailer's office door.

"Come," Nailer called out.

Ellen leaned in and looked at Rob. "Sir, you know you asked me to keep an eye on new missing persons reports?"

"Yeah?" Rob asked, his curiosity piqued.

"Well, we've had one come in at Central which you might want to take a look at."

44

Tom followed the manager and receptionist into the back room behind the counter and found himself in a small staff office where a man sitting at a nearby table was eating while reading the paper. He looked up as they walked in and seemed a little surprised to see a police officer in full uniform interrupt his lunch.

"Everything OK, Stu?" the man asked.

Ahead, the manager nodded to his work colleague. "Yeah, don't worry," he replied and dropped into a cheap office chair facing a PC straight out of the stone age. He woke it up and turned to the receptionist that had walked in here with them. "Right then, Deb, when was Seth here?"

"Aaah, yesterday morning. It must have been around eight AM, maybe?"

Tom watched the interplay between the receptionist and her manager as the girl tried to work out when Seth had been in. They both wore gym clothing and looked like they were about to jump on a running machine at any moment. Just the thought of it made him feel out of breath.

"Eight-o-clock," Stewart muttered as he opened up the CCTV app and clicked back into the footage from the previous day. He scrubbed through and soon found the recordings from the previous morning. The pair leaned in towards the screen as the manager played it back.

"There he is," Debra said, pointing at the screen. "That's Seth."

The manager clicked on the camera angle, and it filled the screen, hiding the other feeds. But even blown up, Seth was still just a small collection of pixels doing some leg lifts.

Tom looked closer. He couldn't be certain, but it looked like the man on the screen matched the photo that Seth's mother had given him.

"Okay," Tom said. "Can you speed it up? I want to see him leave."

"Sure," the manager answered and set the footage to play back at four times the speed.

Seth's movements became jerky and comical as his legs swung back and forth. As Tom watched, Seth started talking to a woman who'd been working out on the nearby treadmill.

"Who's that?"

"Deb?" Stewart asked.

"Oh, um, she's new. I'd need to check. Briana or something, I think?" Deb answered. "She's only just joined."

"She's being quite friendly with Seth," Stewart commented.

Deb shrugged. "I think she left before him."

As Deb spoke, Briana suddenly walked out, leaving Seth to his workout. But he didn't last much longer, and in a very short amount of time, he gave up on his routine and walked into the changing rooms.

Stewart switched back to the screen that showed all the camera feeds and pointed to the reception camera. "He should come out, yeah, here. There he goes."

Tom watched Seth walk out of the building as the video played back in real-time again. Once through the doors, he started to make his way into the car park but stopped after just a couple of steps out and turned. Watching closely, Tom caught sight of the woman, Briana, partially hidden behind a pillar. She was talking to Seth, and moments later, the pair walked off into the car park and disappeared off the edge of the screen. Seconds later, a modern Mini Cooper drove by the reception doors.

"They're gone," Stewart announced.

"Looks like they went together in that Mini," Tom remarked. "Do you have a car park view?"

"Yeah." Stewart pointed to one of the boxes on the screen with no feed. "That's that one, but it's been smashed up. It's the local kids, I think, vandalizing the place. We need to get it fixed."

"Yes, you do. So, you said Seth's car is still here?"

"It's outside, but it's this way," Stewart said, pointing to the screen, in a different direction from where Seth and Briana walked. "He must have left in her car."

"Makes sense," Tom replied. He'd check out Seth's car shortly. "So, tell me about this, Briana. Who is she?"

"She's on the system," Deb said, looking over at Stewart, who clicked to a different screen and ran a search. He typed in the name Briana and got several hits. He sorted them by the date they joined the gym and clicked on the most recent.

"There," he said. "Briana Sullivan."

Tom leaned in again to get a good look at the photo the gym had taken when she'd joined. "Can you print that off for me?"

"Sure thing."

"And Seth's too?"

"Yep," the manager confirmed.

Tom stared at the screen for a moment longer before he turned to the receptionist. "You said you had a complaint about Seth."

"Yeah. Another of our regulars, Candy, said he was leering at her while she was working out."

"Has he shown that kind of behaviour before?"

"No. This is the first complaint against him. We'll issue him a warning, and if it happens again, he'll need to find a new gym."

"You said he's gone missing," the manager stated. "Do you think this Briana had anything to do with it?"

"I can't really speculate about that," Tom answered, refusing to be drawn into this conversation. "Sorry."

The manager nodded, pulled the pages from the printer, and handed them to Tom.

He took them and scanned down the profiles. There wasn't much there. Just basic details, name, age, address, along with a photo taken at the reception.

"Alright, you've been very helpful. Can you show me Seth's car now, please?"

"Are *you* alright to do that, Deb?" the manager asked.

"Sure," she answered and smiled up at Tom. "This way."

"Thank you," Tom said to the manager and followed the young woman from the staff room, through reception and out into the car park.

"It's over here." She led him a short distance into the car park and pointed out the black Ford Fiesta with a body kit. "It's this one."

"Thank you," Tom said and peered through the windows. It looked well-maintained. He wandered around the vehicle, but didn't touch it in case they needed to dust for prints.

As he navigated around the car, his phone rang. He didn't recognise the number and frowned at his phone before answering. "Hello?"

"PC Reid? This is DI Rob Loxley. You're on speaker with myself and Scarlett."

"Hi," Scarlett added.

"Oh, hello, sir. Scarlett, hi. What can I do for you?" Tom answered, remembering the inspector and constable from their previous encounters.

"I hear you're investigating a missing person. Is that right?"

"I am," he confirmed, wondering what Rob's interest in the case might be.

"Would you mind running me through the details? We're dealing with a missing persons case and wondered if it might be linked."

"Sure thing. Our missing person is Seth Douglas. He's a twenty-four-year-old man who went missing after visiting his local gym. He was reported to us by his mother, who he lives with, and is a little worried about him."

"Okay, thanks. Can you keep us updated on any developments?"

"Of course."

"Any leads?"

"Just the one, so far. It looks like he left the gym with a woman called Briana Sullivan and left his car here in the gym car park."

"Wait," Scarlett interjected. "Briana Sullivan? You're sure of the name?"

"I am," Tom replied, looking at the print-off from the gym. "Why?"

"She's the daughter of one of my neighbours," Scarlett explained.

"I have her address," Tom said, wondering where this was going. "You can meet me there if you like."

45

Rob spotted the police car on the side of the road in the Nottingham borough of Lenton and slowed down.

"If this really is Miriam's daughter, this is really weird," Scarlett remarked as Rob pulled in and parked up behind the marked car. She'd been saying variations of the same thing the whole way here and seemed a little freaked out. But given her recent history with the Masons and her friend, Rob wasn't too surprised and spent the trip offering reassurances that it was probably just a coincidence.

At least, he hoped it was.

"Well, we'll find out soon enough," Rob replied. "I doubt she's the only Briana Sullivan in the world."

"But, in Nottingham?"

Rob shrugged, feigning indifference, but deep down, he felt sure that this would be her neighbour's daughter. There was no way that it wasn't. "Who knows. There's a lot of people in this fair city of ours."

"How very poetic," Scarlett muttered. "Come on then, Keats, let's get this solved, shall we?"

"I'm a poet, and yes, I am aware of the fact," Rob replied, playing fast and loose with the old saying as he climbed out of the car to find Tom stepping out of his.

"Afternoon, sir," Tom said with a deferential nod. "Scarlett."

"Hey," Scarlett greeted him with a bright and breezy smile. "Good to see you."

"Afternoon," Rob added. "Have you been in?"

"No," Tom answered. "Figured I'd wait for you, so we can experience that joy together."

Rob looked up at the collection of terrace houses packed together on the small green opposite. The houses seemed a little run down in places, and he could see some washing flapping in the breeze. They were little two-up, two-down, boxy affairs made from beige brick that were starting to look a little dated.

"Where are we then? Which is Briana's."

"Over there," Tom said. "Follow me." He led them across the street and up a tarmac path boarded by grass on both sides, to an address he referred to on some sheets of paper.

"Is that her?" Scarlett asked, pointing to one of the print-offs.

"Yeah," Tom confirmed and handed her the sheet. "She was working out at the gym at the same time as Seth and seemed to hit it off with him. I watched him talk to her on the gym's CCTV and then meet up with her outside the main entrance. I think she was waiting for him. They talked briefly, and then he followed her to her car, leaving his in the gym car park."

"She chatted him up?" Scarlett asked.

Tom shrugged. "Dunno. I mean, yeah, maybe. It was her first day at the gym, too, apparently."

Scarlett furrowed her brow and glanced back at Rob. "She's a bit forward then, which seems odd."

"Why?" Rob asked, curious.

"I don't know. It just… We had a neighbours' meal at Miriam's the other night, and she spent half the night complaining about her daughter, who she painted as some kind of shut-in that doesn't talk to anyone, so…"

"So, her coming to a gym and hooking up with a guy right away seems a little strange," Rob added, expanding on Scarlett's point.

"It sounds out of character, based on what her mother said," Scarlett clarified.

"Wouldn't be the first time a parent is unaware of what their offspring is up to," Tom remarked. "Maybe she just doesn't know her daughter as well as she thinks she does."

"I guess…" Scarlett muttered.

When they reached the front door, Tom knocked and rang the bell. "What do you expect to find in here?" Tom asked.

"I have no idea," Rob replied, honestly unsure. "I thought this might be linked to our missing person's case, but I don't know. This seems odd to me."

"So it's different to your case?" Tom inquired.

"Ours was a young man, a teenager, who was apparently attacked and had his throat cut before being taken away. We found a lot of blood at the scene, but I don't know if this fits our kidnapper's style."

"Hmm," Tom grunted in reply. "Well, no one seems to be answering. What do you want to do?"

"We need to get in there," Rob answered. "Seth or Briana's lives might be in danger, so I say we get in."

"Sir." Tom nodded, and backed up.

Rob turned to the door and shouted. "Police, we're coming in."

Tom ran at the door and kicked. It took several tries to get it open, and by the time Tom kicked it through, a couple of neighbours had appeared.

Rob shooed them off with a wave of his badge as Tom stepped carefully inside.

"Briana," Tom called out as he crept in. "Seth? Anyone here?"

Scarlett waved him in ahead of her. "Go on. Age before beauty."

"Too kind," Rob muttered and followed Tom into the front hall. Tom moved a few paces in and stopped as he looked into a room on his left.

"Well, shit," Tom grunted.

"What?" Rob asked and moved up as Tom cautiously stepped into the room, being careful where he stepped.

Reaching the door, Rob looked in and felt his stomach flip. There was blood splattered all over the units and ceiling, although, curiously, not much on the floor. Just a couple of smears.

"What is it?" Scarlett asked.

"Blood, and a lot of it."

Scarlett reached the door and looked in. "Aww, Christ. Yeah. That's a lot."

"Tom, call it in," Rob said. "We need boffins down here."

"I'm gonna check the other room," Scarlett announced and moved off down the corridor, calling to Briana and Seth, but there was no answer.

As Tom stepped back towards the front door and made the call, Rob inched further into the kitchen, scanning the surfaces and units, hunting for anything that might offer some clue. The fridge was covered in bits of paper, photos and magnets, which drew his attention. As Rob neared it, he spotted several sticky notes urging the reader to 'Join the Gym.'

"You can cross that one off your list," Rob said to himself as he scanned over the faces in the photos.

"Rob." Scarlett appeared at the kitchen door, holding a photo frame in her latex gloved hand. "Have a look at this." She stepped nimbly around the room and held up the frame. Two women, one middle-aged, the other in her twenties, beamed out at him with happy smiles. Scarlett pointed to the older of the pair. "That's Miriam, Briana's mum, right?"

"I don't know, is it?" He'd never met her before.

"It is. I recognise her," Scarlett answered. "Which means this must be Briana."

"Yeah, makes sense," Rob agreed and pointed to the photos on the fridge. There were several selfies on there featuring the same dark-haired young woman either alone or with others, including her mum. "She's here, too."

"Right. But is it really Briana?"

"What? What do you mean?"

Scarlett held up the print off from the gym. Rob took a long look at the face labelled as Briana Sullivan and then at the face on the photos.

"What the...?"

46

Rob drove carefully through the streets of the exclusive Park Estate in the centre of Nottingham, following Scarlett's directions. Behind them, another unmarked police car followed. It carried DC Heather Knight, the Family Liaison Officer Rob had called in for Briana's parents after reporting what they'd found at Briana's house. They'd called in Forensics and waited until the house was secure before racing across town. From what they could discover, Mr and Mrs Sullivan had no idea what Briana had been up to, and probably didn't even know their daughter was missing.

But as they approached the Sullivan residence, Rob's gut told him that this disappearance was more than it seemed.

"Do you have any idea where this is going or what's going on?" Scarlett asked. "Because I'm not sure I do."

"Then break it down," Rob suggested. "What do we have so far?"

"Alright. Well, we have Malcom," Scarlett said, raising a finger to count off her points. "He disappeared in some kind of attack at Trent Bridge, and we have no idea where he is, apart from the phone call from the person we think might be the killer."

"Right," Rob agreed.

"Then we have all Malcom's crap," she added, raising another finger. "His druggy, cheating mother and her criminal bit on the side that killed Tess's long-term partner and caused Malcom to be walking the streets that night."

Rob nodded along as Scarlett laid it out.

She raised a third finger. "But now, we have Seth disappearing from the gym..."

"Who, as far as we know, is unrelated to Malcom in any way," Rob added.

Scarlett pointed at Rob to emphasize his point. "Right. But he disappears from the gym." She raised a fourth finger. "Then we have Briana also at the gym, apparently picking Seth up and taking him... somewhere. Probably home, but we can't be sure, and there's also evidence of some kind of attack at Briana's house... Oh, pull in here, it's that one." Scarlett motioned out the window to a house just a few up from her own. "Christ, this is weird," Scarlett remarked.

"To be so close to home, you mean?" Rob asked.

"Yeah. We were here just a few nights ago, having drinks and meeting some of the locals. It was lovely. But now..." She shook her head.

"I know," Rob sympathized. "Come on, let's go and chat to Mr and Mrs Sullivan and get to the bottom of this."

355

"Absolutely," Scarlett confirmed as Rob turned the engine off and got out. Behind them, Heather did the same and walked over to join them.

"Ready, ladies?" Rob asked and then turned to Heather. "You're all briefed and up to date on this?"

"I am," she confirmed. "I'll follow your lead."

"Right." He turned to Scarlett. "In here, is it?"

"Yeah, this way," Scarlett said, walking with Rob as he made his way up the driveway to the house. "Are you sure you want me with you on this house call?"

"Yeah. I'll take the lead, but they might want to see a friendly face to offer some reassurance, and that's where you come in."

"Alright," Scarlett confirmed with a smile. "Fair enough."

Rob nodded and pressed the doorbell. It was one of those fancy camera jobbies that were increasingly common these days, bringing surveillance into areas that previously had none. They were a massive boon to the police in their investigations, leading to footage of all kinds of crimes that might once have slipped through the cracks.

Moments later, the door opened, and a middle-aged woman appeared at the doorway. "Hello," she said.

"Miriam Sullivan?" Rob asked and held up his ID. "I'm a detective with the Nottinghamshire Police, and we were wondering if you might have a moment?"

"Aaah, yes, of course…" She looked over Rob's shoulder and seemed suddenly surprised. "Scarlett?"

"Hi, Miriam," she said.

"What's this about?"

"We'd very much like to come inside," Rob pressed. "Please."

She frowned. "Is this about Briana? What's happened? Oh God. What's happened to her?"

"Miriam?" sounded a voice from further into the house. A man walked around the corner. "Is everything okay? Scarlett, is that you?"

"It's the police." Miriam gasped and sobbed. "It's about Briana. I know it is."

"Can we come in?" Rob asked the man, who he presumed to be Charles, Miriam's husband.

"Yes, yes. Please," he urged, and grabbed Miriam, pulling her in for a hug and comforting her as Rob moved into the hall, followed by Scarlett and Heather.

"Where can we talk?" Rob asked.

"Through here," Charles suggested. He led them into the front room where they took their seats.

"Please, you must tell me, is this about Briana?" Miriam asked.

"It is," Rob confirmed, causing Miriam to sob.

"What's happened?" Charles asked. He was clearly the more stoic one.

"Right now, we're not sure," Rob replied. "But we need to talk through some recent events and show you some images because we would like your help with our investigations."

"Okay," Charles said.

"Is she okay? Where's Briana?"

"Right now, we don't know," Rob answered. "But we were hoping you might be able to help with that."

"I'm guessing she's not here," Scarlett asked.

"No," Miriam whimpered.

"What happened?" Charles asked.

"Alright, this is what we know. Yesterday morning, Briana was at a local gym. It was her first day there, and she got talking to a man called Seth Douglas. Have you heard that name before?"

"No," Miriam said, looking confused.

"Me neither," Charles added.

"Okay, well—" Rob began, before he was interrupted by Miriam.

"Wait," Miriam cut in. "She was at a gym? Are you sure?"

"We'll get to that," Rob continued. "We have CCTV of Briana talking to Seth inside and then meeting him outside the gym and driving off somewhere."

"I can't… I just can't… A gym? I know she wanted to join a gym, but she's been saying it for over a year at this point. She would have told me."

"Are you sure?" Scarlett asked.

"Absolutely."

"Okay, okay," Rob said. "Let's stick to the facts. We've visited Briana's house, and there are signs of a struggle, but Briana is nowhere to be found. We've called her number too, which the gym gave us, but there's no answer. Do you know where she might be?"

"I thought she was at home," Miriam sniffed. "Do you think she was attacked?"

"We don't know yet," Rob answered. "Do *you* know where she might be? Was she going anywhere?"

"No," Miriam confirmed. "She should be at home tonight. She's got work tomorrow. I'd know if she'd been away, she'd have told me."

"She never goes away," Charles added. "She's quiet and keeps to herself. Are you sure she went to a gym?"

"One other thing before we get to that," Rob added. "Do you know anyone she might have upset recently? Anyone that might want to hurt her? A former partner or someone?"

"No, no one," Miriam answered.

"Okay, alright. In that case, I've got some photos to show you. Firstly, do you recognise this woman?" Rob took out the print-off from the gym, showing Briana's headshot, and handed it to them.

Miriam furrowed her brow in confusion and shook her head. "No, who is this? Why does it have Briana's name and address on it?"

"Okay, so, how about *this*? Who's this?" Rob handed her a photo that had been removed from Briana's house.

"Yes, that's me and Briana," Miriam confirmed and then held up the printout. "But, I don't know who this is. What's going on?"

"Okay, we have a video showing this woman," Rob pointed to the printout, "at a local gym. She joined yesterday under the name of Briana Sullivan, giving your daughter's name and address, and then while she was there, she got talking to a man called Seth Douglas. After their workouts, Seth got into this woman's car and left the gym, leaving his own vehicle in the gym's car park, and he's not been heard from since. In fact, just have a quick look at this…" Rob pulled his phone out. While they had been coordinating the arrival of the forensic team at Briana's earlier this afternoon, Tom had been back in touch with the gym and requested that they send the video of Seth to him, which they had. Rob now had it on his phone too. After opening the video, he shuffled through to the very end, where the Mini Cooper car drove past the reception window, and played it for Miriam and Charles.

"Do you recognise that car?" Rob asked.

"That's Briana's car," Miriam said.

"Yeah, it certainly looks like it," Charles confirmed.

"Great, thank you," Rob replied. They would have found that out eventually by going through Briana's documents, but it was good to get it confirmed by her parents, early doors.

"In fact, I have a photo of it here," Miriam said and whipped her phone out. Moments later, she handed it to him. On it, a beaming Briana was standing in front of a gleaming red Mini Cooper. Rob could also make out the number plate. "We took that photo when she got the car."

"And that's her correct numberplate," Rob asked.

"Yeah, she's not changed it or anything."

Rob made a note and asked Miriam to forward the image to them.

"So, who is this woman, and why is she impersonating my daughter?"

Rob bit his lip. "Right now, we don't know. We're still trying to work that out. But rest assured, you will be the first to know if we find out what happened to your daughter. You've been most helpful, thank you. I'm going to leave Constable Heather Knight with you and she can answer more of your questions, talk you through what will happen next and keep you updated on the case, okay?"

"Yes, thank you," Miriam replied, as her bottom lip started to quiver, and more tears fell.

"Much appreciated," Charles added as he hugged his wife.

Rob and Scarlett made their way back outside and into their car.

"So, what the hell is going on?" Scarlett asked. "Is this the same case? I thought Vivian said a *man* attacked Malcom, not a *woman*."

"That's what she said she saw, but she didn't see their face, and it was dark, so who knows? Also, there's nothing to say that this isn't actually more than one person. Could it be two people?"

"A man and a woman?"

Rob shrugged. "It could be. Look at the two crime scenes. Both were soaked in blood. We know that Malcom was removed from the scene at Trent Bridge in a van. Now look at the house. It looks to me like someone was attacked in the kitchen, right?"

"Right," Scarlett agreed. "And the Scene of Crime officers found smears of blood leading through to the garage that leads out to the back road. So, one or more people were attacked, possibly killed, and removed from the scene."

"Seth and Briana."

"Which, if true, means someone killed Briana and then used her home and identity to lure in Seth and kill him too."

"That's what I'm thinking," Rob answered. "But, what I don't get is their choice of victim. They're very different. Malcom was a teenager that the attacker found beneath a bridge with two homeless people."

"Well, if we assume that caller who left the message was the killer, he admitted that he thought Malcom was homeless."

"Exactly," Rob agreed. "He also said he was upping his game, and I think 'game' is the operative word here. He's looking for a challenge, right?"

"So he started small, with homeless people," Scarlett said, expanding on Rob's theory.

"Vivian said there'd been unreported attacks before Malcom," Rob added with a knowing look at Scarlett.

"She did."

"So after Malcom, a scrawny kid, the killer goes for a woman, Briana, and then wants to go bigger and better, and chooses Seth by impersonating Briana and luring him in."

Scarlett nodded and then paused in thought. "But why? Why are they doing this? What's the point, and what are they doing with the bodies?"

"Right now, I dread to think," Rob answered.

47

Scarlett stared across at the huge building, waiting for something to happen. They'd been here for nearly an hour now, patiently waiting for the flight to land, so their operation could begin.

About twenty minutes ago, Nick got a message from the officers in the terminal. The flight from Belgium had arrived. But since then, the officers watching for the arriving mules had seen nothing.

They had eyes on three guys waiting in arrivals holding cards with handwritten names on them; names that the mules would be looking for.

Nick's Army friends had come through for them on that front. So now it was just a case of remaining hidden, and waiting. But the waiting was the worst part, and Scarlett was itching for something to happen. Unable to get comfortable, she kept shifting her position and fiddling with her hair, her eyes locked on the terminal doors.

"What's taking so long?" Scarlett muttered, desperate to finally strike a blow against the Masons and do them some damage.

"They'll be here," Nick reassured her. "Just give them a chance."

"You're confident that this will all work out, then?"

"Absolutely, I have complete confidence in the team I've assembled."

"I'm glad you do," Scarlett grunted, feeling annoyed. She felt impotent sitting here. She wanted to be out there, tracking down the mules and following them through the terminal.

"I heard you made progress on the kidnapper case," Nick said, changing the subject.

Scarlett smiled at his attempt to distract her. She shook her head and decided to play along with it. Why not? It wasn't as if they were doing anything else.

"We think we have two more victims to go alongside Malcom," she replied, describing the sequence of events, from Seth's mother reporting her son's disappearance to their meeting with the Sullivans about Briana. Nick listened patiently while staring at the East Midlands terminal building.

They'd parked in the short-stay car park, where arriving passengers would be picked up, and there was a steady stream of people coming and going and plenty of vehicles all around them.

To the north, Scarlett could see the occasional blinking lights of jets in the evening sky as they came in to land, or took off to destinations unknown, and wondered if she and Chris should think about booking some kind of holiday.

365

Maybe she needed a break to get away from all this and focus on Chris... Or maybe not...

These constant late nights were starting to take their toll.

"So you think there could be two of them? Two killers?"

Scarlett shook her head and shrugged. "I honestly have no idea. I guess Vivian may have seen the back of a woman when she witnessed Malcom's kidnapping."

"So what's your plan going forward?"

"That's simple. We need to find them," Scarlett answered as she thought back to the actions she and Rob had enacted after their interview with the Sullivans. They'd tasked the ANPR cameras to look for Briana's number plate, passed out details to all patrols, and tried everything possible to find some hint of where the victims might be. They'd also passed the car's description onto the media in the hope that the public might spot the vehicle.

But that last one was risky, as it would alert the killers that they were onto them and looking for Briana's car, which could go either way. Either they'd make a mistake and expose themselves, or they'd hide the car and remain hidden for longer.

It was a risk, but right now, they just needed to find the three missing people and give their families some peace.

"Heads up, the mules have arrived and are on their way out," a voice on the radio called out.

"Copy that," Nick confirmed while Scarlett watched the terminal. Seconds later, three small groups of six people exited the building opposite. The three thugs that had met them were all in black and looked very different to the drug mules. The other fifteen looked bedraggled, tired, and not very happy.

"They're all out," the voice on the radio said. It was Calico Black. She was here, somewhere, but she'd not seen her. "One of the mules in the last group looks unwell."

Scarlett could see the group being referred to and watched as two of them helped a third. The man was sweating badly and doubled up—with his face contorted by the pain—twice on his way to the two waiting vans.

"They're loading up," Nick said into the radio. "Be ready, people. Is everyone in place?"

One at a time, the officers in the operation sounded off, confirming their readiness.

Nick started their car and waited as the mules were loaded into the backs of the two vans. Once they'd set off, he pulled out and took his place in the rolling tail they'd set in place. They had a good idea of where the group was heading, and as they drove north, they planned to cycle through the five cars that were part of the operation. Each vehicle in the group would take a turn to be the one behind the vans before eventually turning off and letting another take its place. They

367

coordinated the operation via radio, making sure the next car was in place when the point car was ready to turn off.

It was a complex operation, and Scarlett had to concentrate and keep the lines of communication open the whole time.

"Where do you think they're going?" Scarlett asked as they left Nottingham behind and pressed north in the growing darkness of the night.

"At a guess," Nick replied, "I'd say Retford. It's where the gang is based, and they're bound to have garages and lockups they can use there. I know if I was the leader of the Mason gang, I'd want to keep the drugs close."

"Makes sense," Scarlett agreed with a nod as they continued to push north, driving through the countryside. Following along using the map on her phone, they travelled up the A614, Blyth Road, passing Clumber Park on their left.

They'd taken point behind the two vans a mile or so back when Nick spoke up, "They're speeding up."

"What? Are you sure?" She'd been so busy coordinating the group she'd not been paying attention.

"One hundred percent."

Scarlett checked the speedometer, and sure enough, they were picking up speed. "Have they spotted us?"

"I don't know. I think we need to hand off."

"On it." Scarlett checked the map. They were approaching the junction with the A1. It was perfect. The roundabouts on either side would give them plenty of opportunity to juggle the positions of the cars. She took a moment to work out what to do before issuing orders across the radio. "This is Charlie One. We're handing off. They're likely to cross the A1 and drive towards Retford, so we'll circle the roundabout and follow at a distance. Charlie Three? Move up, you're on point."

"Moving up." Nick's other Army friend, Barton Reed, was in number three, and so far, he'd been great.

Moments later, the van hit the roundabout at speed. But instead of turning right towards Retford, they banked left, taking the A57 towards Worksop.

"What the hell?" Nick exclaimed as he watched the two vans take the unexpected turn. "Where the hell are they going?"

"Three?" Scarlett called out. "Are you on them, three?"

"I'm on them," Barton answered. "What happened to them turning right?"

"No idea. Keep on them. We're coming back around," Scarlett answered as Nick made a complete circle of the roundabout.

"I'm behind three," Calico in Charlie five said over the radio.

369

"Copy that," Scarlett confirmed as Nick turned off the roundabout. "Charlie Two and Four, where are you?"

"This is Charlie Two. I'm on the A57, just behind Charlie Three."

"Charlie Four here. I'm behind you, two cars back."

"Copy that."

"They've driving like crazy," Barton said over the radio. "They've completely disregarded the speed limit."

"Keep on them," Scarlett said. "Don't lose them, but keep your distance. They cannot know we're following them."

"They won't lose me," Barton answered as Nick gunned the engine and pushed them to catch up.

"Do you think they're going to Emory's?" Scarlet asked, curious.

"Yeah, maybe," Nick said. "This could be perfect, just what we need."

Scarlett nodded in agreement as the vans careened around the A57, arcing around Worksop, and then struck out north.

"They're going to Emory's house," Nick commented.

"You might be right," Scarlett agreed, as visions of them catching Emory Gates red-handed flashed in her mind's eye.

"They've turned off," Barton called out over the comms. "They're on a private road... No, it's a track between fields, leading to a big house with some outbuildings."

"That's Emory Gates's house," Nick replied, recognising it. He frowned over at Scarlett. "Why have they gone there?"

"They can't have known we were following them," Scarlett said. "Can they?"

"I wouldn't put anything past them," Nick replied. "Either they know we're onto them, or something's happened."

"So, what do we do?"

"We regroup and move in. If they didn't know we were onto them, this is our chance. We can catch them red-handed."

Scarlett nodded and lifted the radio. "Park up just north of the property. We'll move in on foot."

"Roger that," Barton answered as Scarlett prepared to jump out. She was keen to make this work and didn't want to waste a single second. Within moments they'd pulled up behind three other cars just north of the turn-off to Emory's house, and as Scarlett jumped out, the fifth and final car pulled in behind them.

Already wearing an armoured vest, Scarlett felt a little under-equipped with her baton and stun gun. Nick and the four other police officers were all armed with pistols, leaving only Calico and Barton without a firearm. Instead, both carried a light backpack, and Scarlett noticed Calico playing with a roll of carpet tape. And yet somehow, they gave off a

371

reassured confidence that gave her the impression they wouldn't have too much trouble dealing with this situation.

As Scarlett checked her equipment, Nick called in their position and requested backup. If this went wrong, they'd need more people here, fast.

While waiting, Scarlett noticed a clear difference between the police officers and the former Army personnel. Calico and Barton just seemed so much more relaxed about the whole thing and were swapping in-jokes while they waited.

"Alright, bring it in," Nick said and beckoned to the group. Scarlett stepped closer, but it didn't go unnoticed that Calico and Barton kept their distance.

"I don't want to sit here waiting for backup," Nick began. "If we wait here too long, they'll notice and cover their tracks. We need to get in there and catch them neck-deep in the stuff."

As Scarlett listened, she noticed Calico whisper something to Barton, who nodded. Two seconds later, the pair jumped through a gap in the nearby hedgerow and disappeared.

"What the…" Scarlett remarked.

"Let them go," Nick said. "They'll do things their way. We'll do things ours."

"And Nailer's okay about this?"

"He is, and Landon is too. Don't worry."

"Fair enough," Scarlett agreed, and thirty seconds later, they were hustling up the side road, approaching an open gate. She could hear voices up ahead. Yelling, shouting, and some cries of what sounded like someone in pain. What the hell were they walking into? She spotted the abandoned vans as they drew closer to the grounds surrounding the house. Both of them had been left idling with their doors wide open.

As they neared the gate, Scarlett frowned. "Where are the security guards?"

Without turning, Nick pointed to a shadow behind the gate. "There."

Scarlett paused momentarily and peered into the darkness. After a second of confusion, she realised she was looking at an unconscious man lying in the dirt, his hands zip-tied behind his back.

"What the…"

"I told you my friends were good," Nick remarked.

"Holy crap," Scarlett muttered, and within moments, she spotted another taken out in the same way. Beyond the vans, the dark edifice of the house loomed before them, its windows glowing in the night. Scarlett spotted two more bodies lying prone on the ground, their mouths taped up to keep them quiet.

"Christ, they could do this on their own, they don't need us."

"Never a truer word…" Nick muttered.

Following the voices, they rounded a hedgerow and saw a large outbuilding less than a hundred meters away from the main house. Outside it, Calico and Barton silently took down two more guards with violent choke holds. The judicious and practiced use of zip-ties and carpet tape quickly secured them, before Calico and Barton grabbed the guards' guns and checked them over.

Unable to quite believe what she was seeing, Scarlett could only gape in awe at the skill and violence on show. These two knew exactly what they were doing. Seeing them take these men out buoyed her spirits and boosted her confidence. She puffed her chest out and pushed on with renewed vigour.

The main barn doors to the outbuilding were ajar, and there were lights on inside. As they approached, Nick nodded to the weapons Calico and Barton had picked up. "What are you doing?" he whispered.

"If we're going in there, we're going in armed," Calico answered under her breath, almost challenging him to say no. Then she smiled and stuffed the pistol in the back of her trousers. "But it's a last resort. Life or death only."

Nick nodded. "Give it up when you're done?"

Calico raised an eyebrow. "Absolutely. I've got no use for their shitty guns. Right then, are we going in?"

"We're going in."

Scarlett sneered. "Excellent," she growled to herself as they crept swiftly forward and took flanking positions on the doors. She could hear voices inside.

"Are we fucking done yet?" Someone cried out in the barn. "You need to get this shit out of here. Fucking hell. You're just fucking morons, the lot of you. What on earth were you thinking?"

Scarlett found herself on the opposite side of the door to Nick and came in behind Calico, who was behind the armed officers.

Calico turned to Scarlett and then gestured for her to take her place. "This is your op."

"No, it's Nick's," Scarlett answered, rejecting the offer. "You go ahead. You're much better at this stuff than me."

Calico smiled. "Maybe I'll teach you a thing or two."

Scarlett stared at her for a moment, stunned, but before she could say anything, Calico retook her position by the door as Nick and the others readied themselves on the other side. Using his fingers, he counted down and then gave the go sign.

Scarlett rushed in behind the others, yelling "Armed police" at the top of her lungs.

The scene that greeted them was straight out of a horror movie.

Straight ahead, the unlucky drug mule that had been in obvious pain when he'd walked from the terminal building was laid on his back, his shirt pulled up, and his belly sliced open. His guts had been ripped out and cut up, spilling ruptured packets of blood-soaked cocaine on the barn floor. One man was crouched down beside the dead mule, covered in gore and holding a bloody knife. Another was washing undamaged pellets of cocaine in a bucket. And standing over them both was Emory Gates, holding a couple of cocaine pellets in his hands. He'd been yelling at the three thugs that had driven the mules here, one of which was sporting a split lip and black eye.

To their left, three armed men brandished guns and intimidated most of the other men and women who'd been recruited to be drug mules. The mules whimpered and cried at the scene before them, clearly terrified. Against the far wall, two mules wore their trousers and underwear around their ankles while defecating into buckets. They did not look like they were having fun.

Every person in here turned and stared at Scarlett and the others in shock as they charged in. A second later, one of the guards by the mules raised their gun. He snapped it up and fired. Scarlet ducked and ran for cover as chaos erupted. Two of the officers fired back, and the thug fell with a spray of blood. Scarlett ran around behind some shelves and came face to face with another thug, who levelled his gun at her.

"Don't move."

"Eh…" Scarlett gasped, freezing to the spot as another couple of gunshots rang out. There were shouts behind her. "You don't have to do this."

There was fear and panic in the man's eyes as he glanced between Scarlett and whatever was going on behind her. He seemed desperate. "Fuck it," the man hissed, apparently making his choice.

He tensed as he focused his aim.

She clamped her eyes shut as a loud bang rattled through Scarlett's head.

But there was no pain.

A second or two later, she realised she was still alive and unhurt, apart from the ringing in her ears. She opened her eyes to see the thug on the floor, a single gunshot wound to his head.

She turned to see Calico rush in with calm, measured movements. She came up beside the man and gave him a kick before checking on Scarlett.

"You okay?"

"Yeah, fine, thanks to you. I think you just saved my life."

Calico shrugged and turned back to the scene in the central open area of the barn. Calm had descended once more, and two of the other thugs lay on the floor, either dead or injured. Luckily, no one on Scarlett's team seemed hurt. Nearby, with his gun held ready, Nick stood over Emory Gates.

Nick inclined his head, inviting her over.

For a moment, she thought he might be inviting her to kill him or take some kind of revenge, but that would be crazy. Scarlett stalked over and raised a questioning eyebrow. "You got him."

"We did. Red-handed. Care to do the honours?" He nodded to Emory.

Scarlett smiled and removed the cuffs from her belt. "With pleasure." She scowled at Emory. "It's been a bad day for you, Mr Gates. A very bad day."

Emory sneered and spat at her feet.

"Emory Gates, I am arresting you…"

48

Leaning against Scarlett's desk with his arms crossed, Rob nodded along as Scarlett explained how they'd arrested Emory Gates the night before. They'd caught him red-handed after one of the mules had the misfortune of a cocaine pellet rupturing in his gut.

Each pellet contained several times the amount needed for a lethal dose, and he'd died in agony in the back of one of the vans.

It seemed, as much as they could tell from the scene and the interviews so far, that the van driver had panicked and decided that his best course of action was to rush to his boss's house. Unfortunately, that had led to Nick, Scarlett and their team scoring a massive win for the EMSOU.

"Naturally, most of them are pleading ignorance," Scarlett explained. "It's 'no comment' across the board. Emory is talking more than the others and denying what we think we saw, so this will no doubt drag on. Plus, he's got some of the best legal representation in town."

"Of course he has," Rob said. "He'll try to wriggle out of it."

"I know. I tell you what, though, it felt good reading him his rights and slapping those cuffs on him."

379

"Good. I think you needed that."

"I did," she admitted brightly before her tone darkened again. "I'm far from done, though. I won't rest until they're all behind bars or pushing up daisies."

"I know, and I'll be right there with you."

"Thanks. And thank you for bringing me in on this. I really appreciate it."

"You should thank Nick for that. It was his call, not mine."

"But you could have vetoed it if you'd wanted to."

"Yeah, I could. But what would be the point of that? You needed this. Right? You needed to get out there and hurt the Masons. I get it."

"Thanks."

"A note of warning though, if you'll indulge me?"

She held his gaze for a moment, before nodding in agreement.

Rob smiled. "It's simple, really. Don't let revenge control. It will if you let it, but there's much more to life than that, and I don't think Ninette would want to see you consumed by it. You wouldn't want to turn into Bill, now, would you?"

"Err, no. Certainly not," she agreed with a smile. "I'll be okay. Don't worry about me."

"Okay, good. So, Nick's down at the custody suite with Tucker, is he?"

"Yeah, they're doing the interviews. They sent me back to help you with the kidnapping case."

"Excellent," Rob muttered. "Hell of a thing to do on a Sunday night."

"Sounds like you had a fun night," Guy said. He was sitting at his desk, listening to the tale with interest. "Shame I missed out on it."

"It was all kept on a need-to-know basis, and I have no idea why I needed to know," Scarlett remarked. "I'm sure there were other people better suited to this than me, but…" She shrugged.

"Yeah…" Guy muttered. "But, you got your man. That's the main thing."

"We did."

Rob's phone rang. He pulled his work mobile from his pocket and answered. "DI Loxley."

"Inspector Loxley, this is control. We've just been informed that one of our cars has spotted a vehicle of interest to you. It's a red Mini Cooper?" The woman went on to give further details, including the number plate and the location of the car at an industrial estate in the city.

"Thank you," Rob replied. "We'll be right there." He hung up.

"What's up?" Scarlett asked.

"We might have found Briana's car," Rob announced. "Grab your coat. We're going to check it out."

Rob rushed to his desk and picked up what he needed, including his coat, and within moments, the pair of them were in a pool car and racing across town towards the industrial estate in question.

"They were just doing a routine sweep after someone said they spotted some kids hanging around. They spotted the car, ran the plate, and called it in," Rob explained. "I just hope it's not been dumped here at random."

"Hopefully not," Scarlett agreed and smiled to herself. "You know, when you got that call, I thought it might be Matilda or something."

"Oh?"

"You get on so well."

"Still holding out hope for us, are you?" Rob grumbled.

"I kept watching you at the party. You're so cute together. You should ask her out, you know. I know she'd say yes."

"I don't know." His natural reaction was to resist, but he could feel his defences crumbling.

"You know I'll just set you both up again, right?"

"So this is blackmail, is it?"

Scarlett grinned. "If it works."

"I'll think about it," he muttered with a sigh.

They pulled into the estate a short time later and soon discovered the marked police car waiting for them. Rob pulled up behind them and frowned at the locked gates beside them. It was Monday morning, and there were people working and going about their day all around. Everywhere, that is, apart from here in the unit right beside them. Completely fenced in, the property was silent and in a very poor state of repair.

"What's wrong with this picture?" Rob asked.

"It's quiet."

"Too quiet," Rob added and smiled back at her.

"You're just a walking cliché," Scarlett remarked. "Come on." She nodded to where the uniformed officers were climbing out of their car.

Rob got out and wandered over. He held up his ID. "DI Loxley. You have a car for us?"

"In there, sir," one of the constables said and pointed beyond the fence. Rob moved in closer and spotted the red Mini Cooper parked towards the unit's rear. A dirty sheet had been draped over it, but the number plate was visible.

"We noticed it as we drove around and ran the plate," the officer said.

"Shit, yeah. That's her car," Rob said as he glanced over the eerily quiet unit. "Crap."

"If that's her car, then it's logical that she might be inside it?" Scarlett suggested.

"This is a missing person's case?" the constable asked.

"Kidnapping and maybe worse," Rob clarified. "Scarlett's right. We need to get in there."

"Shouldn't be a problem," the constable said and moved to the boot of his car. He fished around inside after opening it and pulled out a pair of bolt cutters and some other tools. "Think this might do the job for yeh."

"Aye, it might," Rob agreed. "Off you go, then. Open sesame."

Rob watched as the officer cut through the padlock and, moments later, opened the gate. Striding over to the abandoned car, Rob pulled the sheet off, revealing the otherwise pristine red Mini. He double-checked the number plate and peered through the windows, but there was nothing incriminating inside.

"Unless she's in the boot, there's nothing here," Rob said and turned to look at the nearby building. Scarlett and Officer Bolt Cutter were with them while the other one was taking a closer look at the building.

"I can get this open," Bolt Cutter said, brandishing a crowbar he'd carried in. He set to work on the boot, making the metal creak and pop as he forced it until there was a sudden, loud bang as something broke, and the boot yawned open.

There was little of interest inside.

"Shit," Rob cursed.

"Sir?" It was the other officer near the building. She'd been nosing around the loading entrance and had her eyes locked on something as she waved them over.

Sensing the urgency in her voice, Rob marched over with Scarlett hot on his heels.

"Here we go," Scarlett muttered, putting voice to his thoughts about how this was going.

Reaching the constable, Rob leaned into where she was looking.

"Does that look like blood to you?" she asked, and pointed to a smear and a couple of red drips.

"It does," Rob confirmed, as a grim feeling settled around his stomach. He took a step back to look the property over. There was a door to the left of the roll-up loading dock.

"You know," Scarlett said. "With Briana missing, blood found at her house, her car dumped over there, and what looks like blood on the loading door, I think we have grounds for entry. She could be alive in there and in very real danger."

"Agreed," Rob confirmed. He turned to the constable who'd opened the gate and the car. "What's your name, son?"

"PC Wolf Sutton, sir," he answered.

Rob took a moment to process that.

The female PC had a wry smile on her face. "Not the name you were expecting, was it?"

"No, not really," Rob confirmed. "But I like it. Well, Wolf, it looks like we have another door that needs your tender caress." He pointed to the one beside the loading dock.

"On it," he said and strode over with purpose.

Rob turned to the female PC. "Can you head over to the gate and make sure no one else leaves or enters the property, please?"

"Sir," she agreed and jogged back to the main gates.

It took Wolf several kicks, but he soon had it open, leaving a gaping dark hole where the door had once been. Wolf waited for Rob and Scarlett to join him at the door.

"Wait here," Rob said. "No one else in or out, okay?"

"Sir," Wolf answered with a nod.

Satisfied, Rob stepped through the door and fished a small LED torch from his pocket. He flicked it on and peered around the loading area on the other side of the roll-up. He didn't need to go far.

"More blood," Rob said, and pointed to the floor so Scarlett could take a look.

"Damn," she muttered. And then called out. "Briana? Are you in here?"

"It's the police," Rob added at the top of his voice. "If there's anyone in here, please make yourselves known."

But there was no answer.

Moving deeper, Rob saw a couple of doors leading to more rooms, as well as flat-packed boxes and packing material. Towards the centre of the room, a couple of chairs were set up beside a small makeshift table made of piled-up bricks and a square of wooden board.

Recently used coffee mugs had been left here. Rob pointed to them. "We need Forensics here."

"Aye," Scarlett answered as Rob swept his torch around the room. He spotted more blood smears around one of the doors, including a gory handprint on the wall.

"Let's see what's through door number one," Rob remarked as he noticed the first hints of a rancid smell. Peering at the blood stains as he passed them, he walked into the smaller, darker room. A large metal table dominated the space, with smaller tables around it. A sweep of his torch revealed what looked like surgical or butcher's tools laid out on one of the smaller tables. They seemed clean, but there were also many more blood stains on the floor. That was probably where the smell was coming from.

"What on earth is this?" Scarlett asked as she moved closer to the table and the tools. "What's he doing to them? Cutting them up?"

Rob peered at the cruel-looking meat cleaver in disgust. "I think that's a given. Although, I'm not sure why." He looked up and let his torch rove over the walls, spotting two more doors. One was a standard, open door, and the other a metal door with a handle, like you'd find on a walk-in freezer.

Rob walked over to the open door first and shone his torch inside. The room was simple but dressed up nicely, complete with a patio table, chairs, and a well-used candle as decoration. It would be almost romantic if not for the surrounding rooms. A nearby sink had plates and cutlery on the drainer.

"They eat here," Rob said as Scarlett looked in.

"Weird," Scarlett remarked.

With a deepening furrow to his brow, Rob turned, walked over to the metal door, and tried the handle. It opened easily, and a blast of cold air washed over him. As the door opened, a light flickered on, revealing a gory scene.

Rob counted at least three human bodies inside at first glance, or what was left of them. He recognized Briana right away. She'd been hung naked from a meat hook, she had a badly cut throat and an entire leg was missing. Nearby, he thought he could see the remains of Malcom too, but there was even less of him left. He could make out a very nasty and deep cut across the throat, though.

"Vivian was right," he muttered to himself. As he walked further into the freezing cold room, he spotted more remains. He saw a couple more severed heads and other body parts on tables and in boxes.

"Oh, shit," Scarlett exclaimed.

Rob turned to her. "I have a horrible feeling…"

"Is that Briana?"

"I think so. And I think that's Malcom. I don't know the others, though, and I can't see Seth."

"Well, I think you'd better come and see this," she said and beckoned him back into the room with the metal table. Rob followed her out and shut the door behind him, shivering as he adjusted to the warmer temperature.

"What have you got?"

"This." Scarlett pointed to an open book on a side table. It was some kind of ledger with handwritten entries. Rob leaned in. He saw columns and a list of names on the left. At the tops of the columns, meat products were listed. Steak, ribs, breast, and even scratchings. Above that, the title of the page read, SSL Orders. What was SSL?

Taking another look at the names in the far left column, he recognized several of them. They were shops. Scarlett pointed to one of them.

"That's the Deli one of my neighbours recommended. It's where the pork scratchings came from."

Rob took a step back. He looked at the freezer, the metal table, and the small packing boxes with SSL printed on them. The sinking feeling that had already taken hold deep inside him suddenly gripped and twisted that much harder. He felt sick.

"Let's get out of here. Call the factory. We need the circus here."

"On it," Scarlett said, pulling out her phone.

A thought occurred to him. "You said you recognized a Deli on that ledger?"

"Yeah," Scarlett said, looking back.

"Do you know where it is?"

49

Following his satellite navigation system, Rob raced across town, using the unmarked pool car's hidden lights and siren when needed to punch through the traffic and get to the Deli listed in the ledger. They'd waited at the commercial property long enough for it to be secured and briefed the Crime Scene Manager about what they'd found before jumping into the car and leaving them to it.

"You said this Deli was recommended to you?"

"Yeah, by a neighbour at the dinner party, I went to. I've even visited the damn place myself and picked up a few things." She'd gone a little green and was holding her stomach. "I just… I don't want to think about what… Oh God. I feel sick."

"Hold it together, Scarlett," Rob urged as he pressed on through the Monday traffic. He couldn't really say why he'd chosen to go to the Deli out of all the shops listed, apart from the link to Scarlett. Naturally, they'd need to visit them all, but this seemed like a good starting point for this next step in their investigation.

Whoever was killing these people had some kind of relationship with these shops, which meant they might be a key part of the puzzle. Finally, after days of getting nowhere, they seemed to be making some progress.

Scarlett wasn't the only one feeling nauseous over all this, he thought as the knot in Rob's stomach tightened. He'd eaten the scratchings Scarlett had brought to their party, and the thought that what he'd eaten wasn't pork was frankly grotesque.

But it all seemed to fit.

He thought back to the phone call they'd had from the killer, and the almost manifesto-like speech he'd given about changing society and breaking taboos. He'd said he wanted to introduce the world to new experiences and that he'd already begun.

Was this what he'd been talking about? Was this his great and 'delicious' mission?

Moments later, they pulled to the side of the street and rushed into the Deli, demanding to see someone in charge. The girl behind the counter did as they asked and rushed into the back of the shop. While they waited, Scarlett pointed out some products behind the glass, labelled as SSL meat, from a local producer.

A woman appeared and approached. "Can I help you?" She glanced at their IDs.

"Hi, yes. We were wondering if you can help us with our investigations. Are you the owner?"

"Yes. I'm Jill Parker. I'll do my best to help," she answered happily. "Is there something I should be concerned about?"

"Possibly," Rob answered and then pointed to the large steak labelled SSL. "We'd very much like to know where that came from and who sold it to you."

"What? The steak?"

"The one labelled SSL," Rob clarified.

"That's from SteinStar Limited," the woman answered. "He's a local producer, I believe. Nice man, actually."

"I'm sure. What can you tell me about him?"

"About Gordon?" She shrugged. He's been coming in for weeks, selling us stuff. It's very cheap, but good cuts of meat. They sell quite well, and they're very profitable."

"You said, Gordon?" Scarlett asked. There was an undertone of worry to her voice.

"That's right. Gordon Stein. It's his company."

As Rob watched, Scarlett closed her eyes and seemed to deflate as she hung her head. "Crap, crap, crap," she muttered as she pulled out her phone and hunted through her recent photos. She enlarged one that was a group pic taken at a diner table and zoomed in to one of the faces.

"What's this all about?" the shop owner asked.

Scarlett held up her phone and showed it to the woman. "Is that Gordon?"

She removed her glasses and peered at the photo. "Yeah, that's him. That's Gordon."

Scarlett turned her phone around and zoomed back out as she showed it to Rob. He clearly saw Scarlett and Chris sitting with Gordon and several others at the table. This must be the neighbors' meal they'd been to. Then he noticed the beef casserole sitting in the middle of the table and swallowed and sudden surge of nausea that caused his stomach to clench.

He took a steadying breath to settle his nerves before he looked up at the woman again. "I'm afraid I need you to remove all SSL products from sale, right now. I don't think you've been selling beef or pork."

The woman frowned. "What? Why? What have I been selling?"

"Just do it," Rob ordered. Beside him, Scarlett was looking decidedly ill, and raised a finger.

"I need a minute," she squeaked and rushed outside.

"What's going on?" the woman asked. "Have I been selling horse or dog or something?"

"I can't say anything further right now, but you must not sell any more SSL products. They need to be removed from sale and boxed up. In fact, I'd recommend closing for the day and chucking anything that could be contaminated by the SSL meat. We'll be sending someone to collect the products very soon. Do you understand?"

She looked suitably panicked. "Yes, of course. I'll get right on it."

"Thank you," Rob said and rushed outside, looking for Scarlett. She'd rushed to one side of the shop and was standing in a corner, bent at the hips with a hand on the wall. Rob checked the floor at her feet but saw nothing.

"Are you okay?"

"Yeah, I'm fine," she said, straightening up. "I just, it got a little too much for me. Just the thought that I'd eaten… that…"

"Human flesh," Rob finished for her. "Yeah, I feel about ready to puke myself."

"Have they…?"

"She's removing the products now," Rob said and glanced through the window to confirm that she was doing as they'd asked. She was, and one of her employees was shooing their customers out and locking the door. He turned back to Scarlett. "So, you know him, this Gordon Stein?"

"Apparently." She turned and put her back to the wall and her hands on her hips. "Christ, this case…"

"I know," he sympathized as a thought occurred to him. "Can I see that photo again?"

"Yeah, sure," Scarlett agreed and grabbed her phone again. Once she had it on the screen, Rob took it and zoomed in.

"That's him, right? Gordon?" he asked.

"Yeah, that's him."

Rob peered at the smiling face and couldn't help but think that he was in some way familiar. "I know that face," he remarked. "I can't place it, but I've seen him before."

"Oh, really? He's a businessman, I think. Well, that's what he told us."

"Mmmm. It'll come to me," Rob said and returned her phone. "Let's end it, shall we?"

She nodded.

50

It wasn't far to Gordon's house, but by the time Rob drove into the exclusive Park Estate with its restricted entry and expensive homes, Scarlett had made a couple of phone calls.

"All sorted?" Rob asked, curious.

"Yep. Nailer's been informed, Ellen and Guy are coordinating the operation to recall the meat, and we have a unit meeting us at the Stein's residence."

"Excellent," Rob stated as he drove around the arcing roads. They pulled up several properties away from the Sullivan's home, outside another large, Victorian-style home with a couple of gleaming cars parked out front. The owner was clearly doing well for himself. Seconds later, a marked police car swung in and helped them block the house's driveway, just in case Gordon somehow got by and tried to escape.

"I am wondering, though, if the killer is Gordon, who was the woman that seduced Seth?" Scarlett asked. "His wife?"

"Maybe." Rob agreed. "I've not yet figured that out yet, or where I know him from. Come on, let's get this done." He climbed out of the car and met the waiting uniformed officers.

"Morning," Rob said. "You might want to bring your Big Red Key for this. We have reason to suspect that the people inside might be harbouring a kidnapping victim whose life is in danger."

"Understood, sir," one of the constables answered, before he strode to the car's boot and opened it.

"We need to get in there as quickly as possible to stop them from running or destroying evidence," Rob continued.

"Are they dangerous?" the second PC asked.

"Yes, but we have no reason to suspect firearms would be present on the premises."

"Ready, sir," the first PC stated as he hauled the crimson battering ram from the car's boot. "Lead the way."

Scarlett appeared and handed him a stab vest. Rob slipped it on before marching up the slabbed driveway, past the parked vehicles and towards the front door. After a quick look at the door for anything untoward, he stepped to one side and waved the constable with the ram through. The PC indulged in a short run-up and slammed the ram into the door, right where the latch would catch into the frame.

The constable was a big lad, and opened the door in a single hit.

It swung wide.

Rob rushed in. "Police, hands on your heads, where I can see them," he yelled, running into the hallway. At the end, through a door, a woman leaned into view wearing a shocked expression. She wore an apron and held a carving knife in her hand. Rob barreled down the hallway, brandishing his baton.

"Police. Drop it," he shouted. "Drop the knife."

She did as he asked, dropping the knife onto the table as Rob got a better look at her. She was the same young, pretty woman from the gym photo, and on the table before her was a partially dissected human leg that had been cut off at the hip.

"I'm sorry, I'm sorry," she gasped as Rob cautiously crept into the kitchen, checking his corners as he went.

"Are you alone?"

"Um…"

A ragged roar erupted from Rob's left as a man wearing an apron covered in blood charged out of a side door holding a meat cleaver aloft. He swung it down in a wide arc as Rob raised his baton to fend the man off.

Cleaver and baton met with a clang. Rob whipped the blade wide.

"Arrgh," the man yelled as the cleaver flew across the room and hit the wall close to Scarlett. The attacker's face was contorted with rage, but he recognized Gordon right away, although he couldn't place him yet. Where did he know him from?

Gordon swung for him with a clenched fist.

Rob caught the man's arm and twisted. "No, you don't."

He fell.

"Aah, no," Gordon bellowed. "You can't. You can't stop this. Nell. Nell, help me."

Rob looked up to see the woman pick up her knife again. She sucked in a long breath through her nose, roared, and ran around the table with the knife held high.

Behind him, Scarlett charged and slammed her baton into the woman's arm. Rob heard the crack from where he was crouched. The woman screamed in pain as she stumbled back.

"Arrgh, my arm!" she yelled. "You broke my arm."

"Arresting me now, changes nothing," Gordon cried out. "I've already done so much. People love this food. They love it, and all thanks to me. I've changed things, you know. Changed them for the better…"

Rob ignored him as he secured the man's wrists and handed him over to one of the uniforms. By the time he got up, Scarlett had already done the same.

"That looks like a male leg to me," Scarlett commented, pointing to the remains on the table.

"Mmm. But where's the rest of him?"

"Through there?" Scarlett suggested, pointing to the door Gordon had come charging out of.

"Aye, probably." Rob waved to the doorway. "Ladies first."

Scarlett gave him an incredulous look but took the lead anyway and walked through the door. Rob followed and found a set of stairs leading down to a basement. Rob followed as she stepped out into a room.

"Aaah, yeah. He's here," Scarlett said as Rob followed to find the rest of Seth laid out on a wooden table in the middle of the room. The smell was particularly ripe down here.

"Well, that's all of them," Rob remarked and sighed.

Scarlett walked over and took a closer look. "His throat's been cut. Really deep too."

"That matches what Vivian saw and the wounds on Briana and Malcom's bodies," Rob said, feeling a little vindicated for believing her. Not everyone would, but she'd not let them down before and hadn't this time, either.

He shook his head at the senseless killing and the madness of the two people upstairs, but he took solace in the knowledge that they had finally found the killers and stopped them.

51

"Gordon Stein. I knew I recognized the name, but I couldn't place you until after we arrested you. But it's so obvious now," Rob said, sitting across from the killer in the interview suite. Scarlett sat beside him, and opposite next to Gordon was his lawyer. His expensive lawyer, who was observing proceedings and making notes.

Gordon sat calmly, with his hands clasped on the table before him, staring across at Rob with barely a flinch.

It had been several hours since Gordon's arrest, and they'd used that time to delve deep into his history while bringing together various aspects of the case, ready to use in the interview.

It didn't take long for Rob to realise why he recognised him.

"I remember the news reports from a couple of years ago and the tabloid stories that were floating around about what had happened. It was all speculation back then, of course. Speculation that you denied, but now... Now I'm not so sure." Rob leaned forward, placing his arms on the table. "You ate people on that island, didn't you, Gordon. That's what happened, right? You resorted to cannibalism."

"You have no idea, what it was like," Gordon answered. "No idea at all. We were starving. Literally starving, so it was eat what we had or die. That was it. Do you have any idea what that did to us all? I'm fairly sure, looking back now, that I lost my mind. I went mad. We all did."

"So, this is your ill-fated trip to…" Scarlett said, checking her notes. "Inaccessible Island? Is that an actual place?"

"It's a real place," Gordon confirmed. "It's part of the Tristan Da Cunha Island Chain in the South Atlantic. Basically, halfway between South America and Africa, and one of the most inaccessible places on earth, hence the name."

"Can you run me through what happened?" Scarlett asked.

"We were wrecked. I charted a private boat ride. It took seven days to get there, and as we arrived, we were hit by a storm and wrecked on the island in the middle of the night. Several were killed outright, several were badly injured, and we were on an island in the middle of nowhere, where no one lived, with minimal survival skills. No one knew we were out there, and…"

"You'd cut corners, Gordon," Rob added. "Nell told us that you didn't follow proper procedure and didn't tell people what you were doing. You thought the rules didn't apply to you."

"I'm a thrill seeker, detective, always have been. It's one of the great luxuries that my wealth has afforded me. I have the means and the time to do amazing things. So few people have that luxury these days. I understand that. But I've also worked hard for my money and built my business up, which allowed me to reap the rewards, such as visiting one of the most remote places on Earth."

"Why?" Scarlett asked.

"Because why not? Because it's there. Do I need any other reason?"

"So what happened? You were wrecked on that island, and then what?"

Gordon took a moment to focus himself. "We burnt through our supplies pretty quickly, and none of us was great at hunting... Not that there's much out there. Some birds and stuff, maybe some fish if you can catch them. Not much else. We were starving, and before long, our dead friends started to look pretty appealing."

"How...?" Scarlett muttered.

"You won't know. You won't ever know. It was eat or die. It was that simple. I won't deny that it affected us. I know I've never been the same since then." He sighed. "We ended up fighting between ourselves, between those who chose cannibalism and those who didn't. Things got violent. People were killed. You get the idea. We were desperate. But eventually, someone found us, and we were rescued."

"So the rumours were true?" Scarlett asked.

"Some were."

"So what happened?" Rob asked. "Why did you kill Malcom, Briana, Seth, and the others?"

"Honestly, I don't know. We just started to crave it more and more. I don't even understand it myself. I don't know why I did it, but we just had to have it again, and I had to share it with all of you. I needed you to experience it. It's life-changing. I have to have it again. "

***

"His lawyer's going for a partial defense of diminished responsibility," Scarlett said, relaying their findings to Nailer who was sitting on the edge of a nearby desk and listening. "And honestly, he might get it. I can see his sentence being reduced to manslaughter based on what Gordon and Nell went through. It sounds insane, but seeing how he gets when he starts talking about it, I think it's fairly clear that he's not in his right mind. Neither of them are."

"Agreed," Rob said, sitting at his desk in the EMSOU office. "Nell kept referring to Gordon as her saviour, for Christ's sake. That can't be healthy."

"Nell is Gordon's wife, right?" Nailer asked.

"Yep," Rob confirmed. "They went through hell on that island, and their psychological evaluations following that event confirm that they went a little crazy out there, with a high probability of issues further down the line."

"I think something triggered them to relapse," Scarlett added. "I have no idea what, and we might never know, but that's what I think might have happened. Something sent their heads right back to that island, and things spiralled from there."

"So they started off by hunting homeless people?" Nailer asked.

"Anyone who wouldn't be missed," Rob confirmed. They successfully kidnapped several people who'd slipped through society's cracks before they messed up with Malcom. They thought he was homeless, but he wasn't, and after that, it's as if they thought, fuck it, who cares. That's when they went after Briana, who they learned of at the meal Scarlett attended, and then Seth. They wanted better meat, basically."

"It's gross," Scarlett muttered, almost gagging. "I can't believe we ate… Ugh. I don't like to think about it."

"Alright, keep me updated," Nailer said, standing up. "Good work."

"Thanks," they both answered him before he walked back to his office.

"I think I'm going to need like, five showers tonight," Scarlett said.

"And no steak for lunch, right?"

"No way."

Having heard his phone ping earlier, Rob picked it up and checked his messages. He saw one from Matilda and smiled.

"What's that smile for?" Scarlett asked.

Rob smirked. "I took your advice from earlier today and messaged Matilda."

"What? You asked her out?"

"Well, I asked if she'd like to come over for a drink."

"That's great, Rob."

"I still don't know if this is the right thing to do but... I don't know. I enjoy her company, so..."

"Brilliant," Scarlett said with a smile. "Good on yeh."

"Thanks."

52

Adjusting the cap she wore, Madeleine took a deep breath and strode as confidently as she could up to the café's front door and walked in. She scanned the room in a heartbeat, noting the locations of the handful of people inside.

There was the businessman on his phone, talking animatedly about some client as he waited to be served. The overweight man sitting further in, eating a full English breakfast even though it was Tuesday evening. A scruffy blonde woman on her right sitting with her back against the wall while reading the paper, and a gruff, stocky man who'd just been served a bacon bap, turned to the room and hunted for a place to sit.

She glanced at the two mums sitting with pushchairs, drinking coffee, and the two labourers in their overalls that had just finished their meal.

But none of these people were of great interest. The only person of significance to her, and the one reason why she'd even consider coming in here, was sitting at the front of the shop on her left, no more than a couple of metres away.

The target glanced up at her, but only for a moment, and she ignored him as she approached the counter and waited her turn.

The businessman ordered a takeaway coffee and darted out the shop the moment he got it. Madeleine watched him go, using the chance to glance at her target and make sure he was still there.

He was still staring out the window, ignoring the rest of the room, unaware that he was being watched.

After ordering a coffee and brownie, she took her purchases to a table halfway to the door, close to the wall, and sat with her back to the man she was most interested in.

She placed her bag on the table, making sure one end was pointed towards the man, and took her seat. She pulled out her mobile and popped in her earbuds, which quickly linked to her phone. She tapped the screen to open an app. Seconds later, the phone linked to the shotgun mic concealed in her bag. With everything connected, she could hear her target's movements quite clearly.

She'd been following the EMSOU team for days, focusing on different members depending on how accessible they were. But this person had taken on a special significance since the gathering at Loxley's apartment.

Overhearing him arranging this meeting yesterday had been a stroke of luck, but being so close to him was risky.

She'd been following him for days, so there was a chance he'd recognise her from somewhere else, but he'd shown no sign of that so far.

It was worth the risk.

Arranging a meeting at a random greasy spoon in the city was surely something that would be of interest to her.

Picking up her brownie as she pretended to listen to music, she took a small bite and opened up a paper left on the table. She could be here a while.

People came and went, ordered food, sat down, or finished and left, while Madeleine watched and listened.

Fifteen minutes later, she heard the door open again. She made sure to check who it was each time, doing her best to keep track of who was in here with her.

She glanced up at the new arrival and froze.

It was a good second or two before she realised she was staring and turned away, cursing herself in the process.

Isaac Mason and a bodyguard had just walked in. She'd recognise the kingpin of organized crime anywhere. She'd even been in the same room as him on a couple of occasions as part of her undercover role within the Masons. She doubted he'd recognise her as they'd never actually spoken, but she thought it best to keep her face turned away, just in case.

What the hell was the godfather of the Mason gang doing here, of all places?

Was he here to meet with…? No! He couldn't…

But out of the corner of her eye, she watched Isaac shuffle over to the table of her target and place his hand on the man's shoulder.

"Guy," Isaac said with a smile. "It's good to see you, son."

What. The. Actual. Hell!

On the inside, her mind was a riot of shocked thoughts and emotions roiling around in a storm of chaotic thoughts. But outside, she had no other option than to remain calm and collected, despite her thundering heart and spiking adrenaline.

"And you, sir," Guy Gibson replied. "Please, sit. Would you like anything to drink?"

"From here?" Isaac asked, dryly. "No fucking way. I plan to live well into my old age, son."

"No problem," Guy muttered.

"Why the hell did you choose this place?" Isaac asked, his voice coming through Madeleine's earbud loud and clear. "Of all the places we could meet, you choose the scummiest dive in town? I don't come to Nottingham much, son, but when I do, I like to enjoy myself. Especially after the right royal fuck up you made."

Guy grunted. "You mean... with the shipment, and Emory?"

"What do you think? Why the hell did you not know about that, Guy? What use are you to me if you don't know about a major operation like that? I've lost hundreds of thousands, maybe millions, and the trust of the fucking Columbians," Isaac hissed. "What the hell happened?"

"It was out of my control. They cut me out, had me on another case, and their op was on a need-to-know basis." Madeleine imagined Guy making quotation marks with his fingers.

"Do they suspect you? Have you been made?"

"No. They don't know."

"Are you sure?" Isaac rumbled, his voice low but deeply threatening. "Because if you're no more use to me..." Isaac let the threat hang in the air.

"No, I'm good."

"Good." Isaac sighed. "I'll admit, you've been useful. I only know about Rob's appointment to the EMSOU because of your hard work."

"Exactly," Guy agreed. He sounded keen to prove himself. "And don't forget about that kid they turned into an informant the other week."

"Aaah, yes. Ambrose. That was a messy operation."

"Yeah. I didn't see Scarlett rejecting us like that."

412

"You underestimated her," Isaac remarked.

"If I underestimated her, then you turned her friend into a martyr." There was a moment of silence as Madeleine imagined Isaac giving Guy an evil look. But Guy jumped in before things descended further. "Look, you need me. You know you do. In fact, I have something going on right now that... Well, I don't want to say too much, but if my plan works, your wayward son might have nowhere else to turn."

Isaac paused for a moment before answering. "You mean Rob?"

"He's going to have a little trouble, shall we say."

"What kind of trouble?"

Come on, Madeleine thought, silently urging Guy to spill the beans about whatever his plan was. Was it something to do with what she saw at his apartment?

As she listened, Guy finally opened up and shared the details of his plan, laying out what he'd prepared and how it was about to go down. He sounded so smug about it, to the point of making her skin crawl.

She needed to get out of here and let Rob know, but not yet.

"That's ambitious," Isaac remarked after listening to Guy's plan. "But if it works, you will have done something no one else has been able to achieve."

"Thank you."

413

"You might not be my flesh and blood, but you're more of a son to me than Rob has ever been. You know that, right? I'm only hard on you because I know what you're capable of and what you've proved to me time and again. I hope your plan works, but if it doesn't, it's no great loss. Rob is no son of mine."

"Thanks, sir."

"Now, if that's all, I'd quite like to get out of here before a layer of grease builds up on me. I'll see you around, son."

"You will."

"Oh, and that other issue? Best deal with it quickly, okay?"

Madeleine frowned. What other issue?

"You can count on me," Guy confirmed.

The pair said their goodbyes, and as Isaac left, it was as if the pressure in the building suddenly dropped. It was probably all in her head, but the tension was very real.

Then a minute later, Guy left, too, walking in the opposite direction to Isaac.

Utterly shocked by what she'd heard, Madeleine finished her cake and drink and planned her next move. First off, she needed to get out of here and then somehow get this recording to Rob or someone else in the EMSOU.

Gathering her things, she got up and turned to the exit but found herself rooted to the spot. The idea of leaving by the front door filled her with a deep and numbing fear. She felt suddenly vulnerable, and wondered if she'd been made. Had they noticed her sitting three tables away, listening to them?

Scanning the room, she noted a small side corridor leading to the customer toilets, and above that door was a fire exit sign.

Perfect.

Madeleine strode across the café, up the corridor and walked straight out through the fire door into a side alleyway. Glancing back to the street, she experienced that same fear and turned away. If she could get behind the shops and somehow cut back through, maybe everything would be okay? Pushing through the paralysing fear, she walked away from the street, round the corner, and straight into Guy Gibson.

He grabbed her and thrust his hand into her gut. A blade lanced into her, cutting deep.

"We knew we had a mole inside the organisation," he said, his face close to her, his breath hot and smelling of cheap coffee. "And now we know who it was."

He dragged her around the corner, behind a storage container, where he withdrew the blade. "Sorry, it has to end like this. But we can't have you fucking up our plans, Madeleine." As she dropped to her knees, he stabbed her twice more in the chest before she collapsed in agony. Pulling her bag from her shoulder, he tipped its contents onto the tarmac. Guy then grabbed her phone and the memory card from her camera and smashed the remaining bits with a brick he picked up.

She rolled to look up at him, but he was just a blur to her now. "Coward."

Guy laughed. "Fucking pigs." He turned and disappeared from her view.

The pain was intense, and there was blood everywhere. She tried to pick herself up, but her strength was gone. There was nothing she could do. This was the end for her. There was no escaping this. She was done for.

As the world around her faded, she heard movement and voices. Suddenly a shadow appeared and came in close.

"No," she cried. "Get away."

"Hey, I won't hurt you," said a softer, kinder voice. "Hold on. Don't you die on me. Don't you dare die!"

Madeleine reached out and grabbed onto something as she tried to speak but was overcome by a wracking cough that brought up blood.

The darkness was calling to her, pulling her down.

This was the end.

53

"You know, when you invited me over, I thought I was hearing things," Matilda said as she finished pouring herself a gin and tonic. She handed it to Rob. "Right, try that."

"I'm not sure I've had gin before." Rob took the fat-looking glass and peered at the pink liquid inside. "But I'll give it a try."

"If you don't like that, I have an alternative," she said and smiled at him.

"Alright." Rob took a sip and immediately cringed. "Oooh, no. No, I'm not a fan of that. Urgh."

"Of the gin or the tonic?"

"Um, I don't know, actually," Rob admitted, unsure. "If I had to guess, I'd say it was the tonic, though."

"I figured as much." She smiled. "You remind me of a former boyfriend who liked gin but not tonic. He preferred this."

Rob watched her reach into the bag she'd brought and fish out a third bottle. But this time, it was a bottle of lemonade.

"I'm guessing you like lemonade, right?"

"I do," Rob confirmed, as she proceeded to pour another measure of gin and add lemonade to it.

417

"There, you heathen," she said, handing him the drink. "Try that."

Feeling more confident about this one, Rob took a more generous sip. The sensation couldn't be more different. "Ooh, yes. Now that is nice. I like that."

Matilda shook her head but smiled. "You're such a child."

"Growing up's overrated," Rob answered, enjoying a second sip. "My body might be ageing, but I will remain stubbornly young at heart until the day I die."

"Good plan," Matilda agreed with a smile, raising her glass to him.

Rob returned the gesture and found himself getting a little lost in her eyes. He might have invited her over, but he really wasn't sure what his plan was. He still wasn't sure it was the best thing to do for either of them. The only thing he did know was that he enjoyed her company, and she seemed to enjoy his, and surely that was the only reason he needed to spend some time with her.

This didn't need to be anything profound or life-changing. Nothing needed to happen. They were just sharing a drink and enjoying each other's company.

"I wasn't sure what to think when you said you'd brought the drinks," Rob admitted. "But, if you're going to bring stuff like this, then you can come again."

"I feel honoured," she answered, with an amused expression.

There was a sudden flurry of knocks on Rob's door that verged on panicked banging. He turned towards the short corridor that led to his front door. "What the hell."

The bangs continued.

"My God," Matilda exclaimed.

"Hold your horses," Rob shouted and placed his drink down before rushing to the door. His first thought was that it might be Erika, although he wasn't sure why she'd be trying to bang down his door on a Tuesday night.

"He was about to open it without checking when he suddenly thought better of it and decided to peer through the peephole."

He saw a scruffy-looking blonde on the other side that he didn't know.

"Who is it?" Rob shouted.

"A friend of Nick's," the woman answered, looking at the spy hole. "Open up."

"Nick?" Rob asked, wanting a little more info before he did as she asked.

"Miller. Nick Miller. I'm a friend of his from the Army. We need to talk."

"How did you get through the main door?" he asked, realizing he hadn't buzzed her in.

She raised an eyebrow and gave him a condescending look.

"Never mind. Why now? Can't it wait?" Rob asked, wondering why one of Nick's Army mates would want to speak to him.

"Open the damn door, or I'll break it down, Rob." She took a step back and stared at the door with clenched fists. She meant business, and her stocky, powerful frame left him in no doubt that if she wanted to get in, there was no stopping her.

"Everything okay?" Matilda whispered from the corner just behind him. "I'd suggest calling the police, but…" She waved at him. "Well, you are the police."

Rob raised an eyebrow at her before he turned back to the door. He wasn't sure there was a good reason why he shouldn't talk to this woman, and everything seemed to check out, so… "Okay, one moment." He unlocked the door and opened it.

The woman grabbed it and strode in. She went to barge past him.

"Oi." Rob resisted, pushing her back. "Hold on there."

There was a flurry of movement, and he suddenly found himself imobilised in an arm lock without understanding how she did it.

"Stay out of my way. It's for your own good," the woman said before looking up at Matilda.

Matilda raised her hands in surrender and then yelped as the woman shoved Rob into the wall and let go.

"Jesus," Rob gasped as he looked up to see the woman stride past Matilda and out of sight into his apartment. "Hey, where do you think you're going?"

Straightening up, Rob rushed after her. He rounded the corner to find her marching up the corridor to the bedrooms and bathroom, Nearby, on the sofa, Muffin raised his head at the commotion and then went back to sleep.

"No, don't get up," Rob muttered to his pet before rushing after the crazy woman. She turned left into his bedroom. "Hey. No. Hold on." He jogged after her and found the woman in his en suite, having lifted the lid off the toilet cistern and plunging her hand in the water. "What the hell?"

Rob grabbed her arm and pulled it out. Her hand emerged, holding a tightly wrapped bundle about the size of a small house brick.

He stared at the dripping package in confusion. "What the hell is that? Who are you? What is going on?"

"Well, let's get out of the toilet, and we can talk."

"Oh thank God, I thought this was some kind of house invasion or something," Matilda said.

Rob pulled a face to himself, not daring to admit that this kind of thing seemed to be a regular occurrence, as they wandered back into the kitchen.

"What is in there," Rob asked, and then added, "or do I not want to know?"

Calico lobbed the package to him. "Open it up if you like. I'll get rid of it for you, though."

Grabbing a pair of scissors from the drawer, he started to pick at the tightly wrapped package. "How about this explanation, then."

"As I said, I'm a friend of Nick's from back when he was in the military. We ran some missions together, and I've been helping him on the sting operation against Emory Gates."

"Oh, I see. He mentioned you," Rob replied, as he started to carefully remove the watertight plastic wrap.

"While on the job, I've been keeping an eye on Nick, and I noticed someone tailing him. I dug a little deeper, and it turns out she was an undercover police officer, who I saw watching you, Tucker, Scarlett and Nick. She might have been investigating the rest of your team, but I'm afraid I don't know them. I just know what I saw. But then it all went wrong today. I followed her into a greasy spoon café in town. I'm not sure why she was there, as it seemed a little out of character for her. Anyway, she had a drink and a cake and then left, but went out the back. She looked scared. I followed as soon as I could, but she'd been attacked by the time I found her. Before she died from her wounds, she told me to get that." Calico pointed to the package that Rob finally peeled open.

His insides tightened as he stared at the great wad of cash.

"Wow," Matilda said under her breath. "That's a lot of moola."

"Someone planted that in there. Do you have any idea who might want to frame you? Or who's had access to your apartment?"

His first thought was the team party they'd had recently, but it wasn't as simple as that. Just a few weeks prior, his dad and brothers had broken in and surprised him. Even Erika had a key.

"Um, the list is quite long, and growing," Rob said.

"Really?" Matilda asked. "Like who?"

Rob grimaced as he looked over at Matilda. Maybe it was time that she knew the truth, after all.

"Okay," he said and turned to Matilda. "I planned to tell you this at some point, as you deserve to know, but I wanted to protect you from it for as long as I could. I guess after this, though, you need to know."

"Know what?"

"My dad is Isaac Mason," Rob admitted. "The current leader of the Mason crime family."

"What?" Matilda sounded shocked. "You mean, that's you? I'd heard rumours of something like that, about someone with links to the Masons but... I didn't think it was you."

"There's your answer," Calico muttered.

"I lived and grew up within the Mason family until I was seventeen, protected from the worst of it by my mother, who'd grown to hate what my father and older brothers stood for. Then when I was seventeen, she disappeared. In the months after, my father tried to get me more involved in the gang until I went on a job with Owen, the youngest of my three brothers. He locked me in at a crime scene, leaving me to be discovered by the police and sealing my fate as a criminal. Luckily, I was found by DCI John Nailer, who saved me from that life. I left my family behind, and I've never looked back since. That was twenty-one years ago. I've barely had any contact with them since then, until recently. They seem to have taken more of an interest in me now that I'm an Inspector within the East Midlands Special Operations Unit, and just a few weeks ago, I returned home to find Isaac and my brothers in here, waiting for me. They tried to recruit me, but I want nothing to do with them." Rob looked up and met Matilda's shocked eyes. "And that's why I've not wanted to get involved or too close to anyone, because I come with a lot of baggage, and just getting close to me might put your life in danger."

"Shit..." Matilda squeaked.

"Well, it looks like you two have a lot to discuss," Calico remarked. "So, I'll just take this and get out of your hair."

"What are you going to do with that?" Rob asked, nodding to the package.

Calico glanced at the wedge of notes. "I'll think of something."

54

In the gloom of the early evening, street lamps splashed pools of light onto the roads and pavements, lighting the way for pedestrians and drivers as they went about their business. But away from the yellow and white bloom of the street lights and glow from the windows of occupied houses, darkness and shadows reigned supreme, hiding those that grew, worked and thrived in the night.

Guy drove west along Derby Terrace on the north edge of the Park Estate and pulled in when he spotted a parking space. Annoyed at his sudden manoeuvre, the car behind him honked in aggravation.

Guy ignored the horn, turned off his car, and looked out at the row of smart, three-story terrace houses on his left. He'd parked almost right outside Nailer's home, and judging from the lights that were on downstairs, someone was in.

Good, at least that was one less hurdle for him to jump.

As he slumped back into the front seat, Guy couldn't help but feel conflicted. This plan was risky, and there was always the potential for blowback.

Tomorrow, Bill would raid Loxleys house and discover the package he'd planted in the en suite cistern, incriminating Rob and hopefully sealing his fate. Naturally, Nailer would investigate. He'd want to know how this happened, how the package got there and if Rob was truly guilty. Rob was his friend, so it was only natural that he'd want to help him.

But this was where the photos of Owen's visit would come in.

They were circumstantial at best, especially as they did not show Rob taking the bribe, but maybe they'd help.

What other choice did they have?

Guy sighed as he massaged his forehead in an attempt to soothe the looming headache that was taking root. It was this looming flashpoint and its potential for blowback that led Guy here tonight.

This was an exercise in damage limitation and an effort to mitigate anything that found its way back to him.

All day, he'd wondered if there was anything that might point to him, and he'd been weighing up the ways he could deflect the blame. He'd run through a number of options, and the one thing he kept coming back to, was the idea of giving Nailer some kind of cryptic warning. Something along the lines of his contacts telling him that the PSU has something on Rob, so he wanted to warn Nailer, just in case.

But this could be overkill, though. He could be worrying over nothing, and maybe it would be better if he left well enough alone? The major weak point, as far as Guy was concerned, was Bill, and he was starting to wonder if this obsessed anti-corruption officer might be the death of him.

He might need to take measures into his own hands if things went bad.

He didn't know. The only thing he wanted to be sure of was that Nailer and Rob didn't suspect him. He needed to seem like he was on their side.

So, should he warn Nailer, or not?

Frustrated and unsure of what to do, Guy slouched down into his seat and rubbed his forehead in annoyance.

Movement at Nailer's door drew his attention.

Nailer's front door was being opened. Guy pulled his hood up and sank lower into his seat, hiding in the shadowed interior. He frowned in confusion as Erika stepped out of Nailer's house.

What the hell was Erika doing here? They barely acknowledged each other when they ran into her outside Rob's apartment. Eager to know more, Guy tapped the button to lower the offside window, dropping it just enough to hear them. They were only a few metres away.

"Thanks for having me, Dad," Erika said and hugged Nailer, kissing him on the cheek.

What the hell? She called him Dad. This can't be right.

"Hey, careful." There was a note of warning in Nailer's voice as he gently pushed her away. "You don't know who's around."

"No one's around, Dad. No one's watching. You worry too much. I'll see you soon, yeah?"

"Yeah, you will. Look after yourself."

"I will. Say hi to Mum, for me."

"I will, bye."

"Bye."

Staring in shock at the scene that had just played out before him, Guy watched as Erika walked away from Nailer's front door and set off up the street. Nailer also watched her for a moment before returning to the safety of his home and closing his front door.

This was all very odd. What on earth did this mean? He'd seen Nailer walk right by Erika and all but ignore her, and she him. But there was more to it than that. Rob had been quite clear that he believed Nailer to be an eternal bachelor who was living alone, but this suggested he was seeing someone who was also Erika's mother, and no one knew about it, including Rob.

Was this somehow significant, perhaps?

He thought about it for a moment more, and then pulled out his phone and composed a text.

'Hey Erika. Good to see you the other night. We should grab that drink sometime if you're game? What do you say? From Guy.'

He read the text back a couple of times and then hit send. He turned in his seat and looked back to where Erika was walking away. Moments later, she fished her phone from her pocket and read something.

On Guy's phone, the message updated to let Guy know that she'd seen it. She typed something, and then continued on her way.

A minute later, a singe world appeared on Guy's phone.

'Sure.'

He smiled. Glancing up at Nailer's house, he dismissed the idea of warning his DCI and started his engine. He'd wait to see what tomorrow would bring.

55

Standing in his kitchen with a mug of fresh tea in one hand, he stroked and scratched Muffin with the other. Apparently, the black cat had sensed his troubled mind, leapt onto the island counter, and demanded some fuss with several loud meows.

Rob was only too happy to oblige and found himself staring out the far windows of his apartment at the River Trent while thinking through recent events.

The discovery of the package in his apartment had been troubling and only served to remind Rob about how desperate and ruthless his family could be. It seemed they wanted him either discredited, jailed, or on their payroll, and nothing else would do. Luckily for him, Nick's friend was on the case, and the Masons would need to try again. The idea of further attempts to infiltrate the unit or hurt him personally did not sit well at all. Scarlett had already lost a friend to the machinations of the Mason gang, and had things turned out differently, Rob could have ended up in much deeper trouble.

But this attempt to ruin him was not without its casualties. The body of the undercover officer had been discovered and dealt with overnight, and an investigation was already underway to discover who'd killed her. She'd given her life in the line of duty, and it served as another reminder of the violence that Masons were capable of... as if he needed it.

He knew full well how dangerous they were, and yesterday's sudden interruption of his evening had caused another, much smaller and less serious concern. But even though this latest worry wasn't life or death, it consumed his mind more so than anything else, leading to a sleepless night and a loss of appetite that showed little sign of abating.

Following the discovery by Calico, Rob had been forced to reveal the truth about his family to Matilda. It had clearly shocked her, and it wasn't long after Calico's departure that Matilda chose to leave too. She'd refused to talk about it, saying she needed time to think about things, and Rob saw no reason to doubt her. He'd just dropped a massive bombshell on her that had changed everything. He was probably not the man she thought he was, and by getting involved with him, she'd be walking into a potentially dangerous situation.

He couldn't blame her for wanting to think things through. It was only natural, given the nature of the revelations and the implications that getting involved with him would have for her. This wasn't a small issue by any stretch of the imagination, and no matter what Matilda chose, Rob couldn't say for certain that he'd agree to a closer relationship anyway, even if she did want it. They'd both be taking a massive risk, fraught with dangers, and he kept thinking, could he really live with himself if something happened to her because of him?

It seemed they both had a lot of issues to work through, and he accepted that.

Rob sipped his tea again, still ruminating about what all this would mean for him when there was a loud banging at his front door.

Surprised, Rob left Muffin on the counter and walked to his front door, much to the annoyance of his cat, who meowed for him.

He opened the door to find Bill standing on the landing with a small group of uniformed officers and a clipboard. He smiled smugly at Rob.

"I have a warrant to search these premises, Mr Loxley," Bill announced, whipping the printed sheet of paper from the board.

Aaah, so this was how it was going to happen. He'd been wondering how the Masons might use the planted package, and it seemed they'd tipped off the Professional Standards Unit. Rob smiled back calmly, despite his spiking heart rate, and waved Bill inside. "Please, come in. Be my guest."

A brief frown of concern flashed across Bill's face, but then it was gone. "Detain him," Bill called out, and marched past. Four officers followed Bill in, sending him furtive glances as they walked by until the last pair walked in.

"Sorry, sir," one of them said.

"Can I at least stay inside?" Rob asked. "I'll sit or stand wherever you want."

The officers glanced at one another, nodded, and then led Rob around to one of the sofas in the lounge. Its cushions had already been flung off, so Rob grabbed one and replaced it before sitting. It wasn't long before Muffin joined him after Bill had roughly shoved the cat aside while rummaging through the apartment.

Rob watched carefully, trying to ascertain if Bill already knew about the package's whereabouts. It was tough to be sure, but he did get the feeling that Bill was going through the motions a little until he finally headed for the bedroom.

Rob heard the ceramic cistern lids clang in both the en suite and the main bathroom, followed by the frustrated noises of Bill, who'd found nothing.

Minutes later, Bill reappeared in a raging fury and stormed into the main apartment.

"Where is it?" Bill bellowed, furious.

Rob raised his eyebrows. "Where's what?"

"You know what?"

"I'm quite sure I don't," Rob lied, knowing full well what Bill was looking for. "What are you after? A bag of sugar? Do you want a drink? I make a good cup of tea."

"Don't play games with me," Bill raged. He stepped closer and grabbed Rob by the scruff of his neck, almost lifting him from the seat. Muffin hissed at Bill. "It's in here. I know it."

"Sir," one of the officers guarding Rob said, a note of warning in his voice as he looked aghast at Bill's actions. "What are you doing?"

The apartment's buzzer sounded, and Bill froze. "What's that?"

"There's someone at the door," Rob said flatly, as if it was the most obvious thing in the world.

Bill frowned and pointed to one of the guarding officers. "You, answer it. Tell them to get lost."

They both watched the officer walk to the intercom, only for Bill to shake him by the front of his shirt again. "Don't play games with me, you little shit. You know what I'm talking about. You know what's missing from this picture. Where the fuck is it?"

"Sir!" It was the officer who'd answered the intercom.

"Fuckin…" Bill hissed under his breath. "What?!"

"Um, it's… Well." She pointed to the screen and the video feed from the front door. "You need to see this."

"Bloody idiots," he muttered as he walked over. But the instant he saw the screen, he froze. "Oh…"

"What do I do?" the officer asked.

Bill jabbed the speak button. "Um, hello, sir. Ma'am. Please, erm, come up, I suppose." He pressed the door release and turned to the overturned room. All the colour had drained from his face. They'd made a mess by throwing seat cushions around and pulling things out of cupboards in the kitchen, but it was as if Bill was seeing it for the first time, judging by his expression.

With a visible gulp, Bill walked towards the front door, where Rob couldn't see. After a few moments, there was a knock. Rob heard the familiar sound of his door opening.

"Sir, Ma'am, Ma'am. I err, I wasn't expecting…"

"Luckily, we were expecting," Rob heard Nailer answer with a note of smugness. Rob smiled to himself. "Are you going to let us in?"

"Well, I'm… I, err… I think this could be a crime scene, maybe… So, um…"

"Get out the way, Inspector," Nailer rumbled.

"Yes, of course."

One second later, Rob watched DCI John Nailer, DCI Page Clements and DS Burton White from the PSU, and Superintendent Evelyn Landon, appear and walk into Rob's apartment. Rob got up to greet them, much to the annoyance of Muffin, who ran and hid behind the sofa.

"Bill, you stay right there," Paige ordered. "Everyone else, out! Right now."

"But, Ma'am," Bill protested as the uniformed officers filed out.

Paige turned to him and got right in his face, wagging her finger at him. "You've gone too far, Bill. Too far. This is it for you. You're done."

"But, I have evidence," Bill countered. "He's been on the take. I know he has."

"Rob?" Burton asked. "On the take?"

"Yes. He's been meeting his brothers and taking bribes. I have proof."

Burton frowned and glanced at Rob. "What proof?"

"Just over here, if I..." Bill moved to the island in the kitchen and grabbed the clipboard he'd placed there. He flicked over a few pages and showed it to Burton. "See?"

Paige snatched it out of Bill's hands and showed it to Rob. It was a photo of his brother, Owen, standing in his apartment, offering a package to Rob. "Can you explain this?"

"He can," Nailer interrupted. "And so can I. Ever since Rob joined the EMSOU, his family have taken a renewed interest in him and paid him several visits, with this being the latest. Rob has never hidden these visits from me, telling me about

437

each one as they happen, and in fact, before this latest one, he installed a camera inside his apartment to record any more visits." Nailer pulled out his phone and turned the screen to Paige and Burton, who watched the video file Rob had sent to Nailer yesterday, following Calico's visit. It showed the visit by Owen and Rob's refusal to take the package. It even had sound, allowing them to hear the conversation.

Paige nodded and then looked to Landon. "Are you aware of this too, Ma'am?"

She nodded. "I am. I've been kept in the loop from the beginning. In fact, we anticipated this happening and believe Rob's links to the Masons might be useful to us."

This came as a surprise to Rob, and he didn't hide his shocked expression. "Really?"

"Absolutely," Landon answered. "Nailer and I discussed this well before we invited you to the EMSOU."

"Oh... That's... good then."

"But!" Bill pleaded. "No. This can't... He's corrupt. I know he is."

"Bill!" Paige snapped. "Drop it. It's over. I warned you about this dangerous obsession, but you pursued it anyway against my direct orders. There will be consequences." She turned to Rob. "I'm sorry for the mess. Let me know if anything's broken, and I'll make sure you're reimbursed."

438

"Thank you."

Paige nodded and then turned to Bill. "Out, now!" She then marched him out of Rob's apartment.

Burton followed, but not before smiling and nodding to Rob. "Good job," he said, before turning and walking out.

Rob smiled back at Nailer. "Thanks for showing up."

"No problem," Nailer replied. "Your suspicions were dead on. It seems like Nick's friend is quite useful."

"She was," Rob agreed. "Thank you for coming down here. And you, Ma'am. I didn't expect it at all."

"It's the least I could do," Landon answered. "We felt it necessary to show a united front from the top down, to leave Bill in no doubt about our position on this."

"And I'm very grateful to you for it."

"Well, hopefully, he'll be no more trouble for you from now on."

"One can hope," Rob replied. "What will happen to him?"

"That's for DCI Clements to decide, but I don't think things look good for him."

"Agreed," Nailer said, and turned to Rob. "And thank you for keeping us up to date on the Masons visits. Keep that up, okay?"

"Will do, sir."

"Excellent. Well, we'll get out of your hair, Rob. It looks like you have a lot of cleaning up to do."

439

Rob sighed as he stared at the mess the investigating officers had created. "Yeah, no shit."

THE END

Loxley will return in book 5
Blood Red Ford

Available here;
www.amazon.co.uk/dp/B0C6DYQYSL

Author Note

Thank you for reading book 4 of the Detective Loxley series. I really appreciate everyone who reads my crazy stories.

I hope you enjoyed it.

Now, before you read any further, I'm assuming you've read the book and not just jumped to the back to read this note, (and if you did, why on earth would you do that?) because I'm about to talk spoilers.

After three books of Bill at the PSU, causing trouble for Rob, I thought it was about time we moved things on a little, and I'm looking forward to showing you where that particular storyline will go.

This is not the last you'll see of Bill "The Sheriff" Rainault.

Also, the reveal about Guy Gibson was a lot of fun to write. I've been planning that since book 1.

The killer in this book was fun to come up with, especially the part of looking for a place remote enough for him to be stranded.

And yes, Inaccessible Island is indeed a real place. So please google it and check that out. I loved the name of it and knew I had to use it when it popped up in my searches.

Now I need to work out the plot of the next book. I have an idea, and I'm looking forward to exploring it and seeing what I can come up with.

So, I'll see you in book 5.

Thank you.

Andrew

Come and join in the discussion about my books in my Facebook Group:
www.facebook.com/groups/alfraine.readers

Book List

www.alfraineauthor.co.uk/books